Death on the GO

Keith Peirson

First published in Great Britain by:
Deira Books, 42 Moor Lane, Newby, Scarborough YO12 5SH

© Keith Peirson 2004

Keith Peirson asserts the moral right to be identified as the author of this book.

All characters in this publication are fictitious and any resemblance to real persons, living or dead, is purely coincidental.

A CIP record for this book is available from the British Library.

ISBN 0 9548540 1 2

Typeset, printed and bound in Great Britain by:
York Publishing Services Ltd., 64 Hallfield Road,
Layerthorpe, York YO31 7ZQ
Tel: 01904 431213; Website: www.yps-publishing.co.uk

All rights reserved. No part of this publication may be reproduced, stored in a retrieval system, or transmitted, in any form or by any means, electronic, mechanical, photocopying, recording or otherwise, without the prior consent of the publisher, nor be otherwise circulated in any form of binding or cover other than that in which it is published and without a similar condition being imposed on the subsequent purchaser.

CHAPTER ONE

The call came late Thursday afternoon after a rough day on a divorce case which was moving slowly and pushing expenses through the ceiling as it went.

As Mungo Slat picked up his battered briefcase and prepared to leave the office for the train to his Port Credit home the phone rang shrilly three times then stopped just as he was reaching for it. He still has his hand on the receiver when it rang again. This time he decided he would ignore it, expecting it to stop after another three rings. No such luck.

Whoever was calling was persistent to the point of offensiveness. Slat let it ring fifteen times before picking it up.

"I knew you were there all the time," said the voice before he could identify himself.

"What can I do for you?" the investigator snapped.

"How would you like to make a great deal of money in a very short time?" the impeccable English accent countered.

"Naturally, as long as it's legal," Slat snapped again.

"Right ho, old chap. Just present yourself here at noon tomorrow and we'll start the proceedings right away."

"Where the hell is here?" snarled an impatient Slat. This mysterious and over-confident voice giving him orders was beginning to get on his nerves.

"Why, Mr Slat, 1547 Ashwarren, of course."

The owner of the plummy voice seemed astonished that Slat might think there could be any other address in the world worth considering.

Ashwarren was in the ritzy section of Toronto and Slat smelled big money and prestige. He adopted a jollier attitude.

"Right ho, old chap, and for whom should one inquire?" he asked in a mock upper crust accent matching that of his caller.

"We'll be expecting you sharp at noon then," the voice said sharply and the line went dead.

Slat hung up the receiver and threw himself into a chair, puzzled. He scratched his head and dragged furiously on a cigarette even though he had promised himself to quit the habit.

In the five years he had shared this shabby office with an insurance broker and his bulldog he had never had a call like this one.

He was intrigued and at the same time miffed at being controlled by someone he didn't know and who only sounded interesting for financial reasons.

With a start he looked at his watch, realizing that by now his turkey pie would be reducing itself to a pile of goop and ashes from which no self-respecting phoenix could be expected to rise no matter how urgent the crisis.

He reached for the phone again to call his landlady and ask her to pop downstairs, shut the oven off and dispose of its burnt offerings.

Marge McCracken was a widow, in her seventies, Slat guessed, fond of a "wee nip" as she called it, but never before 5 p.m. on some sort of quasi-religious principle. After five the bottle was reverently opened and she started to drink like ten men until she was pie-eyed as an owl and twice as ornery.

She listened to Slat's request, nodding in agreement, promised to toss out the immolated meal, then launched into a description of her Christmas preparations. He account was long and boring. As she nattered he became hungrier and hungrier, knowing this was the price for asking the favour.

He was groping for a way to politely end the conversation when something she said suddenly caught his ear.

"I was lying on the couch looking at the Christmas tree when I realized it must be a male tree because all it had on it was balls," she said in her already slurred voice, bursting into peals of laughter at her own ribald humour.

"Then the phone rang and a man asked me to ask you if you know what a Krick Halt, Kirk House, no, make that Creek Half, is."

Somehow that rang a bell with Slat. But what kind of bell? He struggled with the words trying to conjure up their meaning but unwilling to question her further in her condition.

"The man hung up without leaving a name or number," Marge said. "He sounded British, sort of hoity-toity."

That definitely rang a bell.

Slat finally managed to fob her off with a hastily-invented story about a German detective with that strange name and was able to escape after reminding her about his dinner. She promised to totter downstairs and salvage the remains and finally ended the call.

By now Slat was too perplexed and hungry to start a new meal from scratch. He decided to walk to the Eaton Centre for a burger and fries at one of the swanky eateries catering to the bankers and head office staffers who prided themselves on their high incomes, well-coiffed, manicured appearances and the absence of offspring to clutter up their acquisitive lives.

He hoisted his five foot eight inch frame, all two hundred and fifty pounds of it, out of the reinforced swivel chair, grabbed the briefcase from the floor where he had tossed it earlier, and threw on the navy-blue trench coat, veteran of many nights of surveillance in dark alleys and streets and still wearing the stains of mustards and relishes from hot dogs and from coffee gulped from paper cups.

After a hurried meal among the glittering minions whose bank and office towers dominated the Toronto skyline he hauled himself off to a cheap movie theatre to relax and think.

Mungo Slat loved movies and the junkier the movies, the better he liked them.

In the darkness of the cinema he would sit in a corner, glance occasionally at the flickering images on the screen, absent-mindedly fill his face with hot buttered popcorn, and chew over his problems. Next to sitting on the toilet, puzzling among his own fumes, the theatre was his favourite place of cogitation.

He had clung to his habit through all his years on the Metro Toronto police force where he has risen to the rank of detective sergeant, retiring after his wife, Clare, had been killed by a drunk driver on the Queen Elizabeth Way near Grimsby while coming home from a visit to Niagara Falls one winter night five years earlier.

He sat for a long time while a skinny man with an orang-utan for a partner beat the hell out of a posse of inept bikers. As he watched a tiny memory began to crystallize in the recesses of his mind.

In the stillness of the mind two words began to surface. They danced in tantalizing motion before his mind's eye. Round and round like whirling dervishes they danced until finally they slowed and began to resolve themselves into a name.

Cornelius Krieghoff.

That was it. He had it. But what exactly did he have, he wondered.

Dashing the unfinished popcorn to the floor he grabbed the briefcase and charged up the aisle towards the exit, fumbling in his pockets for change.

He found a payphone in the lobby and dialed the number from memory.

"Tribune newsroom," said a curt and perfunctory voice on the other end.

"Regis Yakabuski, please."

There was a short silence, a click on the line and a familiar voice.

"Yakabuski. May I help you? "

"Regis, listen, this is Slat. Have you ever heard the name Cornelius Krieghoff? If you have, who the hell is he?"

There was a long pause. When the reporter spoke there was a note of uncertainty in his voice.

"I believe he was a Canadian painter from about a century ago. I'll tell you what. Leave me a number where I can reach you in a couple of hours and I'll have the librarian here check for you. Our art files must have some information about this guy somewhere."

Slat gave his home number and the conversation ended.

His interest piqued, his stomach satisfied and his feet feeling like lead balloons on the ends of his short, stout legs, Slat trudged to the nearest subway station for the ride to Union Station.

After a short wait in the frigid November air in the bowels of a station built more for the glory of engineers than for passenger comfort he heard the clanging bell on the double-decked green and white train as it droned into the station and the commuters surged forwards to its doors.

Named GO for the Government of Ontario, the trains were the brainchild of a provincial premier desperate to reduce traffic and pollution in the burgeoning city of three million souls. As Toronto became the nation's corporate capital it spawned suburbs of commuters who brought congestion and chaos to highways once capable of handling the flow but now, in 1984, hopelessly inadequate.

The train was uncrowded at this late hour and Slat found a seat upstairs where he planned to nap while the voice of the conductor over the tinny tannoy intoned the names of the stations in a boring litany.

"This train is westbound to Oakville making all regular station stops. Westbound to Oakville. Next stop is Mimico. Mimico. Stand clear the doors please."

Glad the train was almost empty he planked his briefcase on an empty seat beside him, thumped his leg onto the metal cowling of a heater and shrugged his head into his shoulders seeking repose.

A glance through slitted eyelids showed the city lights receding as the train slid out of the station past Roy Thomson Hall and the Globe and Mail offices towards the shore of Lake Ontario.

The train accelerated past what was billed as the world's largest Kentucky Fried Chicken bucket, in reality a painted water tower, and set out for the Canadian National Exhibition grounds and out past the St. Joseph Health Centre near the Humber River.

Slat couldn't afford to fall asleep lest he miss his station. After Mimico came Long Branch and then Port Credit. The trip would take about twenty minutes.

Even while dozing he knew where he was at every minute. His sense of time and place, shared by thousands of commuters, was born from years of daily travel on the same line, hearing the same sounds from the wheels, exposed to the same asinine proclamations of conductors announcing station stops rather than just stations or stops.

Tonight was no exception and he was soon standing waiting for the doors to slide noiselessly open to release him onto the Port Credit platform.

As he started to step down two youths in hockey jackets rushed into the train, cannonaded into him without apology and rushed inside, elbowing aside passengers before running up the stairs at the far end of the carriage.

Slat, watching their rudeness with anger and disbelief, was jerked back into reality by the sharp elbow of the man behind, eager to get home to his family.

"Cheeky young buggers," the man said as he passed Slat on the platform. "They need a swift kick in the rear end to teach them some manners." He set off into the tunnel and disappeared from sight.

Slat stepped to the rear of the platform and scanned the carriage he had just vacated. He saw two men where he had been sitting. They were engrossed in conversation, unaware that he was watching them. He made a mental note of their appearance. One was tall with shoulder-length blond hair. The other was shorter with swarthy complexion and greasy black hair. Both wore open-necked shirts under maroon and white hockey jackets.

The short one noticed Slat looking at them and they moved out of his view as the train glided out of the station.

Pulling his coat collar around his ears as protection from the biting wind blowing off the lake two blocks to the south, Slat set out for home.

Pulling into the driveway he noticed Marge McCracken's main floor apartment was in darkness. It was 9:10 p.m., unusually early for her to be in bed.

"Silly old bugger probably drank herself to sleep again," he muttered, smiling to himself, as he locked the car and fumbled for the key to his downstairs apartment door.

He found it, cursing the darkness, stumbled downstairs and found the inner door by groping along the wall. Another four steps led down to the laundry room and bathroom outside his front door.

As he struggled with the lock his phone rang, seeming louder than usual in the blackness.

Frustrated, he threw a hefty body check at the wooden plug and it burst open, catapulting him into the room. He hurled the briefcase in the general direction of the sofa which doubled as his bed, reaching in the inky blackness for the phone on the kitchen counter.

It was Regis Yakabuski with information gleaned from the Tribune library about Cornelius Krieghoff.

Slat stood in the darkness, listening intently, as he read out the fruits of his research.

"Cornelius Krieghoff (1815-1872) had an alert mind, fine intelligence, and was educated in languages and science. He was a botanist, sometimes earning money collecting Canadian specimens for German universities. He spoke several languages fluently, was a capable musician and a competent painter. Born in Dusseldorf, son of a wallpaper manufacturer, he spent most of his youth studying music at Mainburg Castle in Schweinfurth. He later moved to Rotterdam and applied himself to painting, modern languages and sciences. Soon he sailed for America where he joined a United States force assigned to quell the Seminole Indians in Florida. There are references to his visiting a brother in Toronto before settling in Longueil, Quebec where he married a French-Canadian girl and they moved to Montreal. In Quebec Krieghoff produced his finest work. He entered the social whirl of the city but also enjoyed the life of the habitants, the Canadian winters with sleighing, tobogganing and parties at Lorette and Jolifeu. He loved hunting and fishing, the Indians and the autumnal glory of the wooded Laurentian Hills. These he depicted on canvas with a Victorian love of detail. He omitted nothing of significance and left a valuable record of a people and an age. Cornelius Kreighoff owes much to Quebec, for it provided him with a virgin field of material and a ready market for his paintings."

Yakabuski told Slat the largest extant collection of Krieghoff's works was owned by Clement Vanderhoof, owner of Corey Newspapers, a newspaper chain founded by his late father.

Corey holdings, he said, included shares in several international department store chains, North Sea oil exploration, forestry and pulp mill operations in northern and western Canada and outright ownership of the Goldsun Corey resort hotel in Aruba. The company's wealth was enormous and its major stockholders were all Vanderhoof family members.

Some company executives held shares as part of their profit-sharing package but nothing was allowed to lessen the family's eighty five per cent control.

The Kreighoff collection was not part of the company holdings but was owned solely by, and for, the exclusive enjoyment of, Clement Vanderhoof. Its estimated value was $10 million and it was housed in a personal, climate-controlled art gallery adjacent to the billionaire's suite of offices atop a downtown skyscraper.

As he listened to the recitation of the Vanderhoofs' wealth Slat felt his gorge rising.

A socialist all his life he despised the rich who played and frolicked around the world as their capital made more capital for them while he toiled and moiled for his daily crust.

"Where does this rich bastard hang his hat?" he asked.

"Oh, up in mortgage heights, "Yakabuski said cheerfully. "Here it is ... 1547 Ashwarren Grove."

"Thanks, Regis," Slat said slowly and thoughtfully. "I may have a story for you yet. The usual conditions will apply, of course. You get an exclusive in return for waiting for the right time and for my usual anonymity. Agreed?"

The agreement made, the conversation ended.

Slat hung up the phone and, still in pitch darkness, groped for the light switch.

White light flooded the room, momentarily blinding him.

When he opened his eyes he found himself staring straight into the dead eyes of Marge McCracken.

She was slumped in a kitchen chair, shot cleanly in the head.

CHAPTER TWO

Shaken, Slat reached for a chair and fumbled for a Camel filter. With trembling fingers he lit it and inhaled deeply then picked up the phone and dialed 911, asking for the Peel Regional Police. As calmly as he could he outlined the situation and the officer promised to send a squad car immediately.

Standing on wobbly legs he made a quick tour of the premises looking for signs of damage or a struggle. There were none.

Whoever killed Marge Mc Cracken had been let into the apartment.

It must have been someone she knew, he figured, since there had been no struggle and there were no pry marks on either door jamb or the small below-ground window sill.

The search over he took a closer look at his former landlady. She slumped there, mouth half open, wispy white hair covering part of her face.

Out of respect, out of disgust and anger and partly to hide the gruesome reminder of what had happened, he whipped the beige tablecloth from the arborite table top and placed it respectfully over her face and head. That done, he sat down to think and to steady his still wobbly legs.

This death, unlike many he had seen in his years as a police officer, was the first to come close to home since Clare's sudden, unfair, wrenching removal from his life and it shook him to the core.

Still, he couldn't just sit there. He had to do something until the police arrived.

He rose and tottered to the cooker, lit the gas jet and filled the kettle for a cup of coffee.

His mind was reeling with the images of Clare and Marge McCracken, two people he had never thought of before in the same context. He suspected his mind was revisiting the night he heard the news of Clare's death and felt he was somehow comparing those feelings with what he was undergoing now.

The kettle began its thin, piping whistle. As he shut off the gas he heard heavy footsteps on the stairs and a sharp rap on the door which hung loosely in its frame where he had smacked it what seemed like hours ago.

Two officers from the Peel Regional Police walked in, quickly conducted a silent tour of the apartment, then addressed themselves to the still shattered Slat.

They asked their questions, noted his answers, called the forensic investigators, the coroners and the ambulance and accepted coffee, saying they would stay with Marge's body until it left for the morgue.

Slat knew the procedure but was grateful for their consideration and kindness.

His police record had been checked and his credentials verified. He sensed their respect, comradeship and embarrassment at what they probably saw as a shabby end to a career, life in a bed-sit with few home comforts or redeeming features.

They couldn't know, and he wouldn't tell them, that he lived there by choice, not from necessity.

He had always believed that possessions divert attention from what life is really all about and when Clare died had decided to embark on a life of poverty, sharing his possessions with their friends, giving his only daughter money to attend art school in New York City. He had sold the house, found Marge's bed-sit in the ads in The Tribune, the two had hit it off from the outset and he had moved in five years ago.

Once the officers had left he donned his trench coat and set out to clear the cobwebs from his fuzzy brain. Thoughts of staying in the apartment were repugnant even after he had scrubbed it until all traces of the crime had been obliterated.

It was after midnight and the streets were almost empty. Only a few punks and their sluttish girlfriends were shattering the peace with their ghetto blasters and shouted obscenities.

Slat strolled down to Lakeshore Road and headed west across the Credit River bridge to an all-night doughnut emporium he frequented when he needed a place to ruminate.

He ordered black coffee and a plain doughnut and picked a corner table where he could watch the customers come and go. It was a habit from his police days, one he had not bothered to change.

As he chewed the doughnut he pondered his relationship with Marge McCracken.

He was seldom in the apartment. His work took him all over the country as cases demanded and he would often be absent for weeks on end, leaving his home in Marge's custody. She would collect his mail and keep an eye open for unwanted visitors.

The few times their paths crossed were usually late at night when he wheeled into the driveway dog tired, ready for his bed. She would tap on her window, coffee mug in hand and he would force a smile and join her at her kitchen table for coffee, small talk and his mail.

Over the years she had learned little about him. She knew he was widowed and sensed he was still mourning his lost love.

She had been widowed three times, the latest a year earlier. Despite that she was unable to fathom the deep well of sorrow and loneliness that was his daily companion.

He would tell her where he had been as she listened, all agog at his descriptions of the Rocky Mountains or the prairies, wishing she could see them but knowing she never would.

There was never a word or gesture of impropriety between them, just social intercourse over coffee cups in the unpainted kitchen of the old pelter of a house permanently for sale. Yet there was a kinship between them, an unspoken understanding, warmth and comfort in their occasional meetings.

Somehow he had taken it for granted that she would always be there, like the building itself.

Once a month he would invite her down for a reciprocal cup of coffee and slice of cheesecake. They would chat about their lives and she would complain about the other tenants before setting off back upstairs to her solitude and the gin bottle.

She was paid to supervise the apartment house by her son and his wife. She took the job seriously but found the responsibility tiresome. She had wanted to live out her days in a senior citizens' complex with all its amenities but lacked the funds and was obliged to stay in the house, feeling needed by her children as their agent.

She had to walk to the shops for her groceries and a bad leg made the going difficult, especially in winter when the streets were slick with ice and hard snow.

For all that she was a cheerful soul with a sly, if somewhat ribald, sense of humour. She missed little that went on in or around the house on Troy Street.

She had developed a soft spot for Mungo Slat, He always paid his rent in advance and kept the place neat and clean. He was a quiet tenant, away a lot, and observed the rules about which day he could use the communal laundry facilities. Of all her tenants he was the most polite and the only one willing to spend a little of his time with a lonely old woman.

Slat's thoughts drifted as he ordered a refill of his coffee and began to focus on who would want to kill Marge McCracken and why they would choose to do it in his apartment.

It became obvious that she was not the intended target.

It became equally obvious that he was.

The killer must have been waiting for him when she innocently stumbled downstairs to salvage his culinary holocaust.

But how did they get in and, more importantly, why was he their target?

He quickly reviewed his recent cases seeking the answer to that tantalizing question. Each check came up blank. There seemed to be no logical explanation.

He had only one case at the moment and even that seemed nebulous until he visited that ritzy address in Toronto. The divorce case could wait. He doubted it would ever amount to anything or that he would ever be paid for his work in any case.

So did the voice with the plummy English accent have anything to do with the murder of Marge McCracken? How could it?

He decided that his best course of action was to return to the apartment, grab a few hours of sleep if he could, then show up for that mysterious noon appointment at 1547 Ashwarren Grove and see what ensued.

As he rose he glanced at the coffee shop's clock. It was two in the morning.

Pulling the trench coat collar up to his ears he set out into the night.

A light snow was falling, dusting the streets with powder as it whirled and eddied in the biting wind.

The noisy youths had vanished and he was alone with the snow and his thoughts.

CHAPTER THREE

The commuters huddled on the platform of the Port Credit GO station, collars turned up, faces averted from the cold wind and from one another.

Mungo Slat stood at the rear of the platform observing the people emerging from the concrete tunnel connecting the platform to the parking lot.

It was his morning hobby, partly bred from years of police work, partly to satisfy his innate curiosity and to stimulate his fertile imagination.

Some passengers, mostly younger, gathered in clusters to chat as they waited for the huge locomotive with its trailing green and white liveried carriages to rush into the station, bell clanging, bringing with it a blast of frigid air and snow that drove the jostling hordes back from the platform edge.

The older ones usually buried their heads in newspapers, peering disdainfully at the younger element who had the temerity to laugh and joke at this time of the morning.

This senior majority tended to be loners, assiduously reading the morning news as if the thought of eye contact, let alone conversation, with anyone at this time of day was strictly anathema.

They created a caste of travellers seeking to look unobtrusive while forming the bulk of a crowd of two to three hundred people, looking on their fellows as if they were some species of vile toad.

These modern Pharisees were dressed alike, Slat noticed, in pin-stripe suits, pastel shirts with button-down collars, drab ties, expensive Gucci loafers or leather Oxfords.

Once in a while a pretty woman caused a silent commotion as she emerged from the tunnel. Bright colours, a swinging skirt or bold-brimmed hat drew unusual interest from the dowdy males but for the most part they were silent, the platform a grey mass of people cocooned in thought.

It reminded Slat of scenes from Stalinist Russia where thousands of serfs huddled together waiting for the cattle trains to haul them away to years of slavery and degradation in the Siberian gulags.

In his old trench coat, briefcase tucked between scuffed brown loafers beneath frayed brown trouser cuffs, Slat leaned against the wall, inconspicuous and glad to be so.

As he enjoyed the last puffs of his cigarette he saw two youths wearing maroon and white hockey jackets emerge further down the platform. They were carrying sports bags.

Slat strained to see them, cursing his lack of height when he most needed it.

One man was about six feet tall with shoulder-length blond hair. The second man, shorter, appeared brown skinned with greasy black hair.

He began to sidle down the platform for a closer look. He was sure they were the pair who had bumped into him the previous evening but wanted a closer look before deciding on his next move.

The two seemed to sense his presence through the throng. They glanced nervously from right to left and once the taller man turned quickly to look behind, seeming to stare straight at Slat, who ducked behind a tall businessman reading a newspaper.

He set out again, working his way from one knot of travellers to the next, trying not to attract attention from suspicious commuters who would see this as an attempt to gain a head start in the rush for seats when the train arrived.

Slat inched closer to the men who were now leaning out over the platform edge in search of the bright light on the front of the oncoming locomotive.

To avoid the crush, Slat headed to the rear of the platform, satisfied these were the two men he had seen in the train entrance the previous night.

For him everything was relative when it came to commuting. You either found a seat or you stood and that was that.

The petty battles fought out in the carriages by people dressed to kill, using rolled newspapers as deterrents, struck him as some form of modern jousting with knight pitted against knight for the right to make the loser stand all the way to Union Station.

The carriages filled and he looked at the pasty, baleful faces of the victors staring in posed ennui from their hard-won seats. If his eye happened to catch theirs they averted their glances as if from an evil omen and buried their faces in their newspapers.

As the conductor called "All aboard, please," he swung onto the train and stood pressed against the now closed door as the locomotive gathered speed, trailing its string of twelve carriages behind it.

He was still amazed at the ease with which modern diesel locomotives accelerated. He had vivid memories of the laborious puffing and panting of the steam locomotives of his youth with columns of black smoke belching from the stack and the steam hissing around the wheels as they slowly rolled forward.

This train gathered speed effortlessly, almost angrily, as if the limits set by the railway were impediments it would like nothing better than to ignore, speeding to deposit its breathless cargo mere seconds after they had embarked.

After a few moments of being squashed by a burly chap who refused to remove his rucksack, looking challengingly around as if defying anyone to ask him to do so, Slat ducked away towards the rear of the carriage where he thought the two young men had gone.

He stepped into the second from last carriage and miraculously found a seat just vacated by a passenger departing at Long Branch. Across from him sat a bearded man in a turban, engrossed in the world of his newspaper.

With time on his hands Slat decided to play what he privately called his newspaper game.

The man was holding the newspaper upright and Slat could see the back page of the sports section.

He started the game by staring intently at that page's headlines, moving his head slowly from side to side as if to improve his angle of vision.

He was soon conscious of a pair of brown eyes glowering at him over the top of the broadsheet.

The newspaper was snapped into a half-page fold and its angle was lowered as its owner tried to ensure he could read its contents but Slat couldn't.

The challenge was accepted.

Smiling to himself, Slat wriggled slightly downward in his seat and, head cocked at an angle, pretended to concentrate hard on what he could see of the folded sheet.

Once again the brown eyes regarded him peevishly and once again the newspaper was folded, this time into quarter folds.

Slat rose to the new challenge. He slumped even lower in his seat, sitting almost on his shoulder blades, and pretended to be bent and bound on reading those headline no matter what their owner thought or did.

It worked. Still in silence the brown eyes flashed and a scowl crossed the reader's forehead. He folded the newspaper yet again, this time into eighths, and Slat had the satisfaction of watching a man peering at a newspaper too folded to read because he was too mean to allow a fellow traveller to scan the back page of a newspaper he hadn't paid for.

Slat's body shook with mirth. The man scowled at him again and went to stand by the doorway, reading his still-folded commodity, suspicious of new neighbours who also might want to sneak a peek.

Such games, adolescent as they were, relieved Slat's tedium as the train hurtled towards the city.

Above his head the two young men in hockey jackets passed from the rear car into the second carriage.

Once inside they parted company, the taller man staying aloft, his companion heading downstairs.

Tony Royce and Abdel Salam were on a manhunt.

They were under orders to kill anyone who posed a threat to their mission and that was all the incentive they needed.

They had botched their attempt the previous night and knew they would be in serious trouble if they failed to produce one very dead Mungo Slat.

It had been easy to tell the old woman in the apartment house they were a nephew from England and a university friend travelling across Canada who decided to look up an old relative living in

Toronto. The half-drunk Marge McCracken didn't doubt them for a moment and let them into Slat's apartment, heading upstairs after promising not to spoil the surprise when he came home.

They had waited in the kitchen, planning a swift execution with a bullet between the eyes the moment he opened the door. They would remove all traces of their presence and lock the door behind them as they left.

Then Slat had called Marge about his burning turkey pie and she set off downstairs to turn off the oven. Her heavy tread on the stairs sounded like the feet of a tired man coming home from work.

Forgetting the two visitors she turned the key in the lock, opened the door and was instantly shot between the eyes cruelly and accurately.

As she toppled in death she was grabbed around the waist by Salam who dragged her to a chair at the kitchen table and carefully positioned her still supple limbs to support her weight.

Tony Royce stood quietly, the silenced gun in his right hand, unable to believe he had shot the old woman instead of their intended victim.

He told himself they would have had to shoot her anyway once Slat was dead since she might be able to identify them later.

Now they had to get out of the house in a hurry. They couldn't afford to wait for the real victim to come home. There would have to be another time and place for his removal.

Swiftly and quietly they cleaned any trace of their presence, glanced at the dead woman, positioned to look as if she had fallen asleep at the table, slid the door open, locked it with her key, climbed the stairs and ran across the back yard, vaulting the fence onto the railway tracks behind.

Now they were tracking Slat, determined to kill him, finish their mission and contact their employers who would have them spirited out of the country within hours.

Running directly into Slat within minutes of killing Marge McCracken had been a second stroke of bad luck. Instead of killing him where he stood they had bolted inside the train and rushed from the upper deck when they saw him staring at them from the platform. They knew he would recognize them again and that added to the impetus to kill him this morning.

They had been at the Port Credit station early, waiting for Slat to drive in and park. Unable to carry out their assignment in the parking lot because of the volume of passengers rushing for the trains they had decided to board the train themselves and kill him en route.

They planned to make the hit as the train slowed for a station, escaping amid the throng of disembarking commuters and getting away during the resulting confusion once the body was discovered.

In the sports bag they carried were submachine guns and clips of ammunition in case the small pistol used on Marge McCracken was not enough to complete the task.

After searching eleven of the twelve carriages they still had seen no sign of their quarry.

That meant he must now be in the front carriage, right behind the locomotive whose throbbing engine would mask the sound of gunfire and cover any noise they made in jumping off the train at the right moment.

They opened the sliding door between carriages and stepped quietly into the front carriage.

The entrance was in the middle level at the rear of the carriage where there was a toilet, water fountain and a few seats in random configuration providing a perch for seventeen passengers.

Royce scanned the passengers and then those on the lower level three steps down.

At the far end, facing forward, sat a rounded, hunched figure in a navy-blue trench coat, reading a newspaper.

He nudged Salam with an elbow, indicating the victim with a nod of the head.

It seemed to Royce they had two choices. They could go upstairs to cut off any escape for the victim if he saw them or they could rush him where he sat and kill him quickly.

He wavered for a moment then decided on taking both courses of action simultaneously, motioning to Salam to take the upper route while he set off down the three steps towards his target.

As Salam climbed the stairs he started firing indiscriminately into the serried ranks of passengers on the middle level.

Royce vaulted down the steps, running full tilt towards the figure in the trench coat, firing as he approached. The sitting figure slumped forward, gouts of blood springing from a large hole where the back of his skull had been seconds before.

Royce whirled and began firing the submachine gun into the rows of passengers, watching with detached interest and without remorse as they twitched, screamed in agony and fear as they fell in heaps of writhing flesh on the blood-spattered seats and floor.

Upstairs he could hear the chattering of Salam's submachine gun and smiled grimly.

Backing up until his shoulders were braced against the bulkhead of the carriage, he kept firing into the bodies if he saw as much as a single twitch. The car was filling with acrid smoke from the gun and the stench of blood, vomit and excrement as the commuters fell to the slaughter.

In less than two minutes, which seemed like hours to the gunmen, it was all over.

Silence returned as the engine, pulling a carriage with shattered windows, bullet-torn upholstery and its cargo of death and gore, thundered on towards its final stop at Union Station.

Back in the third carriage Mungo Slat stepped out of the toilet and started reading a newspaper he found left under a seat, unaware of the carnage two carriages ahead.

In the fourth carriage Marvin Dilts, conductor, realized something was wrong when he tried to contact the engineer on the intercom system. A flashing red light showed a malfunction in the system whose wiring had been severed by a flying bullet.

He groaned inwardly, shrugged at some of the regular passengers, already remarking on the usual standard of government machinery, and set off towards the front.

Opening the door to the front carriage he stepped into a scene reminiscent of an abattoir and reeled back in horror, raising the speaker of his two-way radio to call for help. He was felled by a blast of gunfire, his throat ripped apart and his head filled with bullet holes, any one of which would have killed him.

In the locomotive, now entering the Mimico rail yards, the engineer saw the radio light wink on and just as quickly wink off again. He wondered why.

As the locomotive thundered eastwards, blowing up clouds of powdered snow from beside the track, he called the conductor on his radio but found the line was dead.

Realising something must be amiss he called ahead to Union Station to inform his bosses of the mechanical malfunction and started slowing the train, asking for clearance on the track so signal operators would delay other trains converging on the station at the same time. Then he cut the speed again, slowing the locomotive to a crawl.

This was exactly the moment Royce and Salam had been waiting for.

At the same time, not knowing how far the train was from the next station, they worried that they had already been discovered and would be surrounded by armed police and soldiers with orders to shoot them on sight.

Royce, always the cooler of the pair, found the manual control which operated the sliding door and yanked hard on it. The door hissed open, admitting gusts of freezing air and clouds of billowing snow kicked up by the wheels.

Covering his face with his forearm he peered into the mini-blizzard and saw they were passing rows of parked railway cars on a parallel track. They were in darkness, out of service. Some wore the green and white livery of the GO service, others the dark blue and yellow pinstripe colours of the federal VIA Rail, waiting to be dragooned into service.

As their slowing train squealed and lurched on the frozen tracks he nodded to Salam then pushed him bodily out of the door into the snow beside the tracks, leaping after him and rolling over and over on the frozen blue stones of the track bed.

Their departure was unobserved by the engineer, his vision already obscured by the billowing clouds of snow behind the engine. Neither did he see the red light indicating that a carriage door was open, so intent was he on getting his train into the station so the problem he spotted could be resolved.

As soon as Royce recovered his wits from the hard, bruising landing, he rolled under one of the stationary carriages on the next track, seeing his partner doing the same thing three carriages back.

Rolling underneath the carriage to the side away from the main line, he waited for Salam to join him and they started running down the alley between parked trains, staying well out of sight of the death train which was starting the approach the middle of the massive rail siding.

Ducking under other rows of carriages they worked their way northward across the yard, arriving at a high chain-link fence with an open gate through which they slipped into the bushes bordering a road.

They dropped their balaclavas and gloves into the bushes and set off down the road, trying to look like two joggers on their early morning run.

By the time they reached the corner of the street they could hear sirens wailing on the south side of the railway yards where police cruisers were racing along Lakeshore Road, heading for the train.

Sucking in deep breaths they ran harder, pelting down an alley between some warehouses and offices. At the end they paused for breath and to get their bearings.

Royce sucked in cold air while Salam leaned over a low wall panting hard.

Then it hit Royce like a frozen fist.

"Jesus Christ, Abdel! We left the bloody bags on the sodding train."

With a look of disgust he set off at a brisk jog, looking for a bus stop where he might catch a bus to the airport from where he would be flying to New York while his partner made his way to France on his way to Libya.

The train's sudden grinding halt left the passengers in the eleven cars behind the slaughterhouse carriage more than a little curious and, in some cases, angry at yet another interruption to their tight morning schedules.

Any delay, and the GO system was not without its fair share, left them out of synch, frustrated and grumpy for the rest of the morning.

This slowdown appeared to be yet another in a recent series of delays and for some it was the last straw.

Muttering and grumbling started, necks were craned in search of a conductor to berate, or at least snidely inquire if their mini-vacation on the rails was being funded by the railway company and would fresh towels and hot drinks soon be available.

No company official seemed to be in sight and the tannoy system appeared to have gone conveniently dead.

After a few minutes, during which strangers actually spoke to strangers they had ridden beside in silence for years, newspapers were rehoisted, card games and crossword puzzle solving resumed and life reverted to its former state of silence.

Mungo Slat looked out of the window into the rail yards reading the company names on standing lines of freight cars from the Chesapeake and Ohio Railway, Santa Fe Line, Burlington Northern Vermont, Canadian National and Canadian Pacific railways.

There was a sudden jolt and those in carriages closer to the front heard banging and clanging as the locomotive and first car were uncoupled. Squinting through the windows they saw the engine and carriage leave and realized there was a problem, deciding it was probably mechanical.

Complaints started afresh but cooler heads prevailed.

"After all, they can't leave us here all day in the cold," said a small man in a brown suit.

"Especially not on a bloody payday," growled a grandmotherly woman, looking up from her knitting and receiving a smile of empathy from her neighbours.

Back in the fifth carriage Ted Reynaldson, a tall bespectacled accountant, was furious. This was his first trip along the Lakeshore route in years. He was taking this route after spending the night with a leggy redhead from the public relations department of a major telephone supplier whose offices were close to his own.

After work they had travelled to her Oakville apartment where she poured him a Scotch before vanishing into the bedroom, to emerge minutes later in a blue satin gown with spaghetti straps which showed off her alabaster skin and the lines of her firm young figure.

He needed little persuasion to follow her undulating curves into the bedroom where a round waterbed beckoned under a ceiling mirror with tiny starlights twinkling on its surface.

Married for ten years, he was used to his chunky wife shuffling into their bedroom in fuzzy slippers, green flannelette nightshirt and a terrycloth robe which she laid across her feet as she sat in her glasses, hair in curlers, reading the sordid pages of a confession magazine for the lovelorn.

This young, beautiful, career-oriented woman snuggling beside him and whispering in his ear was a vision from heaven.

He hadn't been actively seeking this affair. The two had met which returning their lunch dishes to the kitchen conveyor belt in the cafeteria. A spark was struck and they agreed to meet after work for a drink. That led to the trip to Oakville.

Reynaldson's wife was in Jamaica with her parents and their three children. He had been going with them but at the last minute the crusty little martinet he worked for withdrew his holidays because of an impending computer conversion programme at the central office. It was the firm's first update of facilities in thirty years.

It left Reynaldson despondent and lonely and hence the redhead.

The night passed far too quickly for both of them and they were soon preparing for the return journey to their desks.

Because they would both have acquaintances on the train they separated at Oakville station, she entering the first carriage, he choosing the last one where some of his office colleagues rode.

Now, on the day of an important meeting which could enhance his career prospects if he played his cards right, the damned train had stopped in what looked the middle of the frozen tundra.

Suddenly a woman called out that she could see a line of police cars and ambulances rushing along the service road beside the tracks, heading for the front of the train.

Another woman said she could see a helicopter hovering above the train.

"Maybe the engineer had a heart attack or somebody died in the front carriage," a stout passenger remarked.

The doors suddenly hissed open and two Metro Toronto police officers climbed into the carriage, bringing with them a blast of arctic air.

"Good morning ladies and gentlemen," the older, taller officer said. "You may not know this but there has been a situation in the front carriage of this train and we have had to remove that carriage to a siding. Another engine will arrive shortly to pull you the rest of the way to Union Station. Before that happens I need to ask you to write down your names, addresses, home and work phone numbers on the cards my partner will be handing around. We may need to contact you further. I'm afraid I can't tell you any more at this point so please refrain from asking questions. Your cooperation in filling out and returning the cards will be appreciated."

As the cards were issued and passengers filled them in, the two officers climbed to the upper deck where they could be heard repeating the same information and requests.

The officers counted the passengers, counted the number of returned cards and when the numbers matched placed them in a plastic bag with the carriage number on it and sealed it with masking tape.

They then walked into the next carriage and were seen repeating the process there, leaving in their wake a hum of speculation and bewilderment.

Some people stared nervously out of the windows, more than a little disturbed by the terse announcement and the request for personal information.

Mungo Slat was subjected to the same procedure in his turn. After completing the details requested he wrote on the back of the card: "I am former police officer No.15647RCID, now a private investigator. If I can help, please call."

He made no mention of the two youths he had seen on the Port Credit station.

Further down the rail yards the death carriage was being shunted inside an unfinished hangar being built to accommodate equipment being moved from closer to the city where a new stadium for the Toronto Blue Jays of the American Baseball League was being erected on former railway land.

Two heavily-armed officers from the police tactical unit rode with the grim-faced engineer, directing him towards a phalanx of red, blue and green flashing lights signalling the presence of police and emergency services whose members were ready to assume the grisly task of identifying and cataloguing the shattered contents of the first carriage.

Once the engine halted the engineer was escorted past the carriage where the sight of shattered windows, bullet-pocked walls and roof staggered him.

He was ushered into a tiny cubicle inside the building, handed a mug of strong coffee, paper and a pen and asked to write down every detail of the journey that he could remember, leaving out nothing, no matter how insignificant he might think it was.

Outside a squad of tactical officers surrounded the carriage, weapons at the ready, while a second squad gingerly set about entering the vehicle, signalling to one another to proceed one step at a time.

After the platoon leader appeared at the far end of the carriage, reported briefly on the carnage and said all was quiet inside, Chief Inspector Andrew J. Hocking, in charge of the investigation, stepped inside for a first-hand look.

What he saw made him gag.

In all his years of police work he had never had to face a massacre like this. The sight of those anguished, terrified faces, frozen in grimaces of horror, was harrowing.

The carriage walls were awash in blood, brains and fragments of the skulls of passengers blown to bits at close range as they sat in their seats.

As he struggled to keep his breakfast down, stay calm and appear to be in command, one of the tactical officers reported finding two sports bags containing guns and ammunition.

"Get them to the forensics people immediately for identification and prints," Hocking ordered brusquely. "And get them to check for hair and other materials we can use for DNA cross checking."

As he walked the length of the carriage he thought about the oncoming onslaught of reporters, cameramen, railway officials and city politicians wanting answers to the motive for this carnage, the worst atrocity ever committed in the city long named Toronto the Good.

He and his men would be under maximum scrutiny and stress in the next few days. All leaves and sick days would be cancelled, overtime costs would soar and any thought of a home life in the short term would have to remain just that, a thought only.

Already there was a groundswell of opinions held by politicians and newspaper columnists about the inability of the police to solve crimes, their opinions fanned by the recent shootings of two black men. The department was under fire for being inherently racist and adopting a "shoot first ask questions later" policy.

He knew the new police chief would take a personal interest in this horrific situation, as would Hocking's friend Mayor Barney Sloan.

Hocking and Sloan had both been altar boys at St. Michael's Cathedral in their youth and both studied at the University of Toronto, from where Hocking had branched into a career with the police while Sloan parlayed a law degree into a political career on city council and now was its mayor.

Squaring his shoulders, Hocking walked slowly and confidently to the end of the carriage and stepped onto the platform, issuing a spate of commands to the assembled officers waiting for him.

He wanted pictures of each body, every detail of the carriage inside and out, top to bottom. He wanted a minute search of everything, fingerprinting each victim and every surface of the carriage before he would even consider releasing the bodies to the morgues for autopsies.

That done, police officers were to sit down with the list of victims' names and contact police forces in their home communities who would send officers to notify their next of kin.

Another team was to gather and collate all the recipe cards collected from surviving passengers then fan out to contact them in their offices, homes, shops and factories, seeking any details which might give some clue as the reason for this apparently senseless shooting spree.

"Most of all, I want any information, no matter how small or vague, that will lead us the people who perpetrated this massacre. When we identify them I want them taken into custody alive so they can face the full force of the law of this country," he said as he stepped down from the platform.

"Once the bodies are removed, I want this coach wrapped in tarpaulin, covered completely and kept inside this hangar with armed guards watching it around the clock until I say otherwise. I do not want to see pictures of this mess on the evening television news and on tomorrow's front pages until all the relatives have been properly notified. It's the least we can do for them after what has taken place in here today."

He stalked off to the toilets, fortunately deserted, and threw up his breakfast.

Blanched and teary-eyed, he surveyed his image in the mirror.

"You're getting too old for this racket, my son," he told his reflection. "You should have retired like old Slat five years ago. This bloody mess is going to take a hell of a lot of sorting out, that's for sure."

He scrubbed his face, dried it, tried in vain to get the stink of death out of his nostrils, straightened his tie and headed out to call his chief. He knew the advantage of accurate information as early as possible in an investigation before the trail went cold and wanted his boss fully briefed before he spoke to the mayor and the media.

As it was, it took less than an hour for news of the massacre to reach the media.

An eagle-eyed traffic helicopter pilot spotted the flashing lights around the rail shed and called his radio station with a news tip.

The station newsroom alerted Broadcast News something major was afoot. From there the feed spread to Canadian Press and through its wire service to the city's newspapers, including The Tribune.

Soon, based on information provided by Mayor Sloan, information drafted so no perpetrator could use it to advantage, radio stations were interrupting programmes to tell listeners that 128 people had been massacred on a morning GO train and police appeared to have no clues about the motives or whereabouts of the killer or killers.

In the streets speculation ran rife.

Some irresponsible commentators wondered aloud on air if Libyan terrorists had staged this event as a warning to the United States that they within a hundred miles of its border and capable of committing any imaginable type of heinous crime in retaliation for the recent United States bombings in Tripoli.

The mayor and the cardinal archbishop of Toronto took to the airwaves to express their shock and revulsion at the killings and to offer condolences and support to the bereaved families.

As Sloan left the microphones he was quietly approached by an envoy from Premier Bob Doyle asking for a detailed report for the legislature whose members would be shocked and horrified and would demand action while at the same time worrying about the public cost of potential compensation claims from survivors, families and other commuters on the same train

Sloan gave what sketchy details he could and promised to meet the premier over dinner and present a plan of action based on his meetings with the police chief investigator later that afternoon.

Switchboards at Union Station, city hall, police headquarters and the radio and television stations were jammed all morning as anxious travellers called to check the status of their trains and their own safety.

Names of the victims were not being released pending notification of next of kin. A tight skin of security was cast over the whole operation in its first critical hours, a move designed to allow police time to find clues while they were still hot and to allow possible time for the perpetrators to claim responsibility, a sickening development of modern terrorism.

With Toronto home to people from all around the globe the possibility of some ancient grudge being played out in the city was always real and the authorities had to consider this in their inquiries.

Once the remainder of the ill-fated train had been hauled into Union Station its passengers were divided into small groups and shepherded out of sight of journalists to back doors from where they could catch connections to their destinations in the city.

In his office Mungo Slat placed a short phone call, leaving a message with a secretary.

"Tell Inspector Hocking that Mungo Slat called and offered his assistance on the train case. Tell him Slat was on that train."

He left his home and office numbers and rang off.

Reaching for a cigarette he flicked on a small radio and heard a CBC announcer telling listeners that police had no ideas about who may have carried out this apparently random attack. Airports, bus, rail and ferry terminals were all closed by government order and all highways into the city were being blocked as police started a massive search. Further information will interrupt regular programming as it becomes available, the announcer said.

Slat poured a cup of strong coffee and sat back with his feet on the edge of the gun-metal grey desk, the events of the past eighteen hours crowding into his mind.

For once he was thinking in his office instead of in a movie theatre.

The image of the two men in hockey jackets stuck in his mind and he couldn't budge it, try as he might. Even though he had no reason to tie them to the murder of Marge McCracken he felt himself needing to connect them to the deaths of the commuters.

He knew Andy Hocking would call if the police inquiry bogged down early. The mayor would be squeezing him for answers and with all leaves cancelled and extra shifts added the force would be in high gear for the most important investigation in its history.

Over the years he and Hocking had come up with some pretty amazing solutions in impossible cases and he knew Hocking would think of him in that respect even after five years of retirement.

When two police officers arrived, inching their way past the large English Bulldog who lay in the hall and refused to move, Slat recognized the older of the pair from his days with the force.

He gave them coffee and chatted about the impact the incident would have on police officers and the public alike.

He did not tell them about Marge's murder, Vanderhoof's call, his contact with the Tribune reporter or the two men he had seen twice on the Port Credit rail platform.

He needed to think that through to find out what fit, what made sense and what didn't before disclosing the information to anyone. Once he had it sorted in his mind he would share it with just one person. That man was Andy Hocking, his old partner, now leading the investigation.

He promised the two constables he wouldn't leave town and would call with anything he remembered about his morning commute. He also said he had called Inspector Hocking and offered his assistance. That elicited a wintry smile from the unfriendly younger constable who had never heard of Mungo Slat, having joined the force after his retirement.

As they sidled out past the bulldog Slat reached for another cigarette and resumed his cogitations.

He remembered seeing the two young men boarding the train in Port Credit but could not remember seeing them getting off in Toronto. That meant they could have been among the victims or they could have been herded away in another group of passengers.

Somehow he doubted either was the case.

So where had they gone?

He decided he would definitely ride home on the GO train that evening and would keep his eyes peeled for a third encounter with the pair.

After rooting fruitlessly in his mind for more ideas he decided to go for walk, grab some lunch and head out for mortgage heights and his appointment with the plummy Vanderhoof.

CHAPTER FOUR

As he pressed the doorbell of the Ashwarren Grove mansion Slat could hear a grandfather clock booming on the other side of the ornately carved oak door.

After what seemed an eternity he heard a door slam and the sound of shuffling feet. A tiny speaker beside the door crackled to life and a plummy voice asked his name and business.

Standing in the pouring rain, cranky and in no mood for useless formalities he snarled into the machine, "Slat. Investigator. Open the bloody door, it's pissing rain out here."

He yanked the coat collar around his neck and grimaced as a dollop of cold water from a gargoyle above the door landed in the middle of his nose.

He stared glumly down the long winding driveway, its surface spattered with yellow and brown leaves from the massive oak and chestnut trees lining it. A sharp curve in the middle afforded privacy from passers-by, not that there were many in this enclave of the rich and powerful.

To his right was a series of outbuildings, former stables now used as garages, through whose open doors he could see the gleaming metal of a grey Jaguar and the hulking outline of a large limousine.

The front door finally swung open and he turned to face a spacious foyer with granite flooring, lots of plants in huge pots and a bust of Julius Caesar glaring at him from a marble plinth at the foot of a winding rosewood staircase with marble steps. Five rosewood doors, all closed, led off the entrance hall.

The butler, middle aged and silver haired in pinstriped trousers and black waistcoat, asked for his coat and seemed miffed when his request was denied.

"Mr Vanderhoof is expecting you, sir," he said insipidly in clipped tones.

Slat, who instinctively disliked the man, contemplated giving him a swift kick in the shins to enliven his morning, thought better of it and followed the black waistcoat across the foyer and through the far rosewood door, catching a whiff of polish, leather and cigar smoke as he entered.

The room was a library, dominated by a massive marble fireplace whose flaming logs crackled cheerfully, casting reflections in the book-lined walls, their symmetry broken at intervals by tiny grottoes containing oil paintings, each illuminated by an individual electric light to highlight its details.

Beside a small reading table and chair, the furniture consisted of a leather couch and a deep armchair with an ottoman, each red to match the bookcases and the door. A thick white rug lay in front of the fireplace. Standing on it, hands clasped behind his back, stood the owner of the house.

"Ah, Mr Slat, so good of you to come," said the voice Slat had heard on his phone the previous evening.

He decided to play it cool and aloof.

"Well, my dear old thing, one can scarcely refuse such an invitation as yours, can one?"

Vanderhoof smiled thinly.

"Why don't you take a seat and we'll get straight down to business. I'm sure there are other places you'd rather be than here with me today."

"Right in one, you old bugger," Slat thought maliciously.

He plopped himself into the armchair, wet coat and all, and faced Vanderhoof.

"I have a couple of interesting cases on the go at the moment but your call was so deliberately lacking in information that my curiosity got the better of me and I decided to come along and see how the other half lives," he said with a smile.

"Look here, Slat. I didn't invite you here for comic relief or to be insulted in my own home. I can get all the insults I want at my club and from wits much sharper than yours," Vanderhoof snarled, watching the water dripping from the less than spotless trench coat onto his leather chair, forming a small puddle at the edge of his white carpet.

He knew Slat by reputation and was aware that underneath the shabby exterior ticked an active, educated mind and a keen intelligence.

He also knew he was being baited and needed to regain the upper hand regardless of his distaste.

"Tell me, Mr Slat, do you know what a Krieghoff is?"

Slat smiled, knew he was being tested, and launched into a detailed summary of the life and times of Cornelius Krieghoff, drawn from the information supplied by Regis Yakabuski.

Vanderhoof's admiration for Slat's intellect grew visibly during the recitation and Slat, noticing it, played it to the hilt, becoming increasingly more animated, hands flashing, head cocked at an angle as he pretended to be a connoisseur of Canadian art, especially that of Cornelius Krieghoff.

As the narrative ended Vanderhoof looked positively friendly, beaming and nodding his head at the recital of facts about the subject nearest and dearest to his heart.

Slat sat back and crossed his legs, not an easy feat for a man with a twenty-six inch inseam and stout shanks. Sucking in his gut he tried to appear cheeky and self-assured.

"Excellent, Mr Slat. You certainly seem to know your art. Now let's get down to brass tacks."

Slat's ears perked up. This was why he had been invited here. This was where he hoped to find the first clue into the mystery of Marge McCracken's murder.

Vanderhoof reached for a box of rapier cigars which he proffered to Slat who dipped inside and selected one.

"As you are doubtless aware, I own the largest collection of Krieghoffs in the world. The artist was almost forgotten for a century until I took up the cause of promoting his works. As a result, anyone owning one of the few works not in my collection is pushing prices through the ceiling as they seek to sell me the works I need to complete my collection. I started gathering these works as a hobby and it has developed into a very lucrative one. Unfortunately is has also become an obsession for me and I have declined all offers to sell the set. This has served to drive up the value of the paintings, those I own and those I don't yet have."

He absentmindedly offered Slat another cigar which he tucked into his inside jacket pocket.

"At the moment there are three extant Krieghoffs outside my collection. I have tried to buy them at reasonable prices but without success. Some day they will be mine and will take their rightful place in my gallery beside their fellows. You must visit my gallery, Mr Slat. You will assuredly find it of the utmost interest."

He paused and leaned forward, lowering his voice.

"I have been alerted that an international consortium of art thieves is targeting my collection with a view to relieving me of these works of art. I want to hire you to prevent that from happening. Are you interested?"

The suddenness of the question almost caught Slat off guard.

After a brief silence he cleared his throat noisily, to the discomfort of his host.

"Well, I could be if I knew where to start, who wants the paintings and how much you plan to pay for my services. In my work I usually enter the scene after a crime has been committed, not before. This isn't my line of country, working as a security guard at an art gallery. Isn't there some security firm, you could hire to do that?"

He smiled blandly at Vanderhoof, watching the veins in his neck start to pulsate as they always did when he was denied his own way, and marvelled at the accuracy of the minutiae he had gleaned about the millionaire from the Tribune reporter.

"Mr Slat," Vanderhoof said disdainfully, pacing the white rug in front of the fire, "There is practically no limit to what I am prepared to pay you to protect my paintings from theft. However, I will caution you, since I am not a charitable institution or a government bureaucracy, I will not brook overcharging or gouging. I know what your usual fees are and am prepared to negotiate from that base. I am offering ten times your usual fee plus expenses so long as you provide receipts for them. There is just one stipulation. You must not breathe one word of this agreement to a living soul and especially not to Regis Yakabuski of The Tribune. Are we in agreement?"

Slat stiffened at the mention of the reporter's name. The depth and thoroughness of Vanderhoof's research into his fees and contacts was impressive.

"Well, Mr Slat. Do we have a deal?"

"Sure, that's fine with me," Slat said, wondering why the obsession with secrecy, especially on the part of a press baron who editors and readers would die for this story.

"How can you guarantee me the story, if there is one, won't be leaked from here to one of your editors and the leak pinned on me so you don't have to pay me for my services?" he asked quietly.

"Good point, Mr Slat. I have no direct communications with my newspapers other than through their publishers. I am much too busy to be bothered with the picayune details of their daily operations. That is why you have a sound proposition here. I would be contradicting my own submission to the Royal Commission on the Status of Newspapers if I ever gave a news tip to one of my newspapers and God forbid I should ever give one to a competitor. That is partly why I am insisting on secrecy as a condition of our agreement. I must inform you now that, if ever asked, I will categorically deny any knowledge of your existence or that you ever met me or accepted this challenge."

That final piece of perverse intrigue and the possibility of taking a great sum of money from an eccentric old art connoisseur proved too much for Slat to resist.

He nodded, lit the rapier and blew a cloud of blue smoke across the room. Then he got up and walked to the window where he stood with his back to the room, wreathed in smoke.

Turning, he faced Vanderhoof.

"I believe we can do business but as a token of your good faith I need to see some money up front. Fine sentiments and statements are well and good but in the end I, like you, work on money in the bank. Shall we say a cheque for $50,000, written by you before I leave, would be sufficient to get the ball rolling?"

He saw a flicker of surprise in Vanderhoof's eyes and thought "That shocked the socks off you, didn't it, you greedy swine?"

"You certainly don't come cheap, Mr Slat. I had heard your interest in matters financial had become minimal since you took up residence in that house in Port Credit. Such a degree of venality surprises me."

"Look, Vanderhoof, you get what you pay for and in this case you want much more than your money's worth. You want your paintings guarded and at the same time want me to find out who is planning to steal them. That could place my health or life in jeopardy, in case you hadn't thought of that detail. Then you want the right to wash your hands of me, deny we ever met, if there is any trouble. Those are major wants and for those wants you have to pay because it seems any little wants of mine, like assurance I won't get killed, could get very lost among all your wants. The starting price is $50,000. Take it or leave it."

He started walking towards the door.

He had his hand on the knob when Vanderhoof spoke again, his anger thinly veiled.

"Very well, Mr Slat. You drive a hard bargain so be assured here and now that you will earn and be accountable for every penny of this money. I get value and more for my money. If I didn't I wouldn't be enjoying my considerable wealth and success."

He crossed to a rosewood secretary desk, slid back the roll top, pulled out a leather folder, sat in a delicate chair with an embroidered seat, and started writing.

He rose, walked to Slat, still at the door, and handed him the piece of paper.

The cheque bore the embossed crest of the Vanderhoof family and was made out to Mungo Slat in the amount of $75,000.

"I'll see you and raise you one," Vanderhoof said, walking past Slat into the foyer where the butler was approaching to see the visitor out.

Slat looked again at the cheque, rubbed his jaw in amazement, then stuffed it and the cigar, which had gone out, into his jacket pocket as he set out behind the pallid minion towards the front door.

As he followed the striped trousers and black waistcoat he observed the firm definite tread, feet planted slightly to the sides so that he waddled like a duck.

"You must be doing all right here, old butler. You put your feet down like ready money, a sure sign of a man with few worries."

Before the astonished butler could respond he was down the steps heading for his little car. The rain was still teeming down.

He started the engine, released the hand brake and set off down the long lane.

At the gateway he stopped, relit the cigar, rolled down the window and drove off, trailing a small cloud of blue smoke in his wake.

Alone in the Vanderhoof library the butler was speaking softly and urgently into the telephone.

CHAPTER FIVE

By the time Slat reached home his excitement was beginning to abate.

After all, he still had established no connection between Vanderhoof and Marge McCracken's death.

Thanks, however, to the advance payment, he now had the time and the means to get to the bottom of that mystery.

The irony that he could be using the killer's own money to expose him was not lost on Slat.

He stopped at the credit union close to his office and deposited the cheque, having to visit the manager's office since the teller, unaccustomed to anything other than overdrafts on his account, was skeptical about its origins.

Once the manager saw the embossed lettering and the signature on the cheque, and made a verifying call to the Ashwarren mansion where he was informed in no uncertain terms that the cheque wouldn't bounce and that future calls of this nature could be fatal to his professional health, he treated Slat with newfound courtesy bordering on fawning which would have done Uriah Heep proud.

Since it was common knowledge that Vanderhoof company profits were above $5million a day there could be no problem with a trifling amount like $75,000, the manager gushed, writing out the deposit slip with his personal gold fountain pen and stamping the cheque before offering last week's recipient of an overdraft warning notice a short, cheap cigar.

Slat stuck the stogie in his jacket breast pocket and shook the banker's flabby white hand, marvelling at the power of Vanderhoof's name and money.

Born in the industrial north of England during the Second World War, he had been hauled around the globe by parents seeking a fresh start in life and security for their children that the United Kingdom would never provide. They had always been poor and he had never had much money.

After Clare died he lost interest in the work of the police and opened the small detective agency more as a matter of occupying himself than earning much. The few cases that came paid the bills and he soldiered on, hoping the wounds of her departure might one day heal but knowing in his heart they never would.

Now here he was with $75,000 in the bank, working for an eccentric millionaire and solving a murder which happened in his own kitchen.

At seven the next morning the shrill ringing of the telephone shattered his dreams.

"Slat," said Clement Vanderhoof's plummy voice, "you have a problem. Have you read today's Tribune?"

Slat hadn't. It lay on the doormat where it had been shoved through the letterbox at some godforsaken hour while he slept.

"Well you'd better look at it closely, my man, because you have a huge, huge problem and I want you here today with an explanation."

The receiver was slammed down with a resounding clang.

Slat shook his head, got out of bed and reached for the newspaper to see what the hullabaloo was about.

The front page headline sickened him on sight. THIEVES STEAL PRICELESS PAINTINGS. Below it kicker headlines proclaimed VANDERHOOF ROBBED and POLICE CLUELESS.

The byline on the story was Regis Yakabuski.

The phone rang again as he was shoving bread into the toaster and brewing coffee. Warily he picked it up, expecting it to be the irate Vanderhoof.

This time the caller was Regis Yakabuski, writer of the news story that seemed to spell doom to his ownership of the 75K in his bank account.

"Mungo, I'm glad you're home. I called to thank you for what turned into a lucky break on a story. You called last night about information regarding Cornelius Krieghoff, remember? Thank

God you did. It saved me hours of research when this story broke. I bet old Vanderhoof is just livid that we got the story before one of his own newspapers. Looks good on him. By the way, why did you need that information on Krieghoff last night?"

The question was thrown in casually, designed to catch him off guard.

Slat knew better than to fall for that trap.

When Yakabuski was hot on the trail of what promised to be an international story he would have no compunction in using Slat or anyone else for information to cut corners, provide leads and steer him into avenues of investigation like a bloodhound on the scent. This story could be one to make a reporter's career and Slat knew Yakabuski would be mercilessly persistent if he thought his old friend had any information about the paintings prior to the theft.

Any mention of his trip to Ashwarren Grove or the advance payment for services would aim the journalistic spotlight directly on him and would interfere with his own murder investigation, if he survived his next encounter with Vanderhoof.

All this flashed through Slat's mind in the instant between the question being asked and his formation of a plausible lie to throw the reporter off the trail until it was safe to tell the truth.

"That was for an art teacher friend of mine with a class on Canadian artists at a community college. Krieghoff was on his curriculum list and when he mentioned he needed information on the man I volunteered to get it for him. It was for a surprise. How's your story going, by the way? Any more news yet?"

The casual question was to let Yakabuski know Slat saw through his opening gambit. If the reporter disbelieved Slat's yarn he showed no sign of it. He had just written the scoop of the day and he wanted to celebrate.

After twenty years of divorce he had no family to contact. He lived a reclusive life in a converted warehouse where he made his own pottery and produced some presentable charcoal drawings of historical characters. His major entertainment was grabbing a beer on a Saturday night and watching foreign films at a specialty cinema, the kind of pictures Slat found deliberately repulsive or artsy-fartsy.

He chatted about his editors' reactions to the story and how he just happened to be in police headquarters when the story broke. He often dropped in at odd hours and this being the middle of the night was no exception. He had called the editors and demanded they hold the front page as he fleshed out his story. In typical fashion he had spurned offers of help from other staffers, working alone and at high speed. He had been helped by the research he had done for Slat the previous night.

If Yakabuski was one thing, it was careful. He knew from experience that when Mungo Slat called and asked for information there was usually a very special motive even it was not obvious. That is why he had kept the file on the Krieghoffs for future reference, having no idea he would need it so quickly.

He knew that Slat was evading his question but appreciated there was a good reason for his doing so and that he would be given the real story as soon as it was possible, with the usual restrictions.

He ended the call, making a note to himself to call again the next day, and set out on foot in a fine drizzle for his attic lair.

Slat wondered what the reporter already knew or might have surmised, grabbed his briefcase and trench coat and a battered pack of Camel filters, lit and inhaled one, thought better of going out and flung himself into a chair for a quick read of the story which had tied Vanderhoof's girdle in such a knot.

Yakabuski's story said the theft had taken place in the early evening of the day on which Slat and Vanderhoof were cutting the deal for the protection of the paintings.

Police had no idea how fifty priceless works of art had been secreted from a climate-controlled private gallery on the penthouse floor of a downtown office building without someone seeing something. They had no witnesses, leading to speculation that the theft was an inside job. The theft had been discovered by a secretary seconded from one of Vanderhoof's other companies to work on projects too sensitive for regular staff.

The millionaire trusted nobody outside of his immediate family and so he split his work among secretaries drawn from various units of his empire, each eager for promotion and none aware of the others' existence. In that way no one of them knew more than a single component of the project they were working on.

This secret army was used by Vanderhoof to buy and arrange for delivery of the works of art be purchased for his growing gallery which was not solely restricted to the Krieghoffs though they were his favourites, his children as he called them in rare mellow moments.

This particular secretary, Ted Reynaldson, had innocently entered the gallery in search of a few pamphlets about Cornelius Krieghoff which he wanted to give to a friend writing a book about a fictional art heist.

Seeing the walls bare he had panicked and, contrary to instructions, called the police.

Vanderhoof had a simple policy that he would be informed first about any irregularities in his empire and he alone would decide if and when the police would be contacted. It was the same instruction he had issued to Mungo Slat.

According to Yakabuski's story the paintings had been spirited out of the building while police were searching all modes of transportation for clues to the GO train massacre.

He wrote "the fish had slipped through the net and were headed for deeper waters".

The rest of the story was filled with speculation and offered few facts of interest to him. It would provide some relief to readers from the ongoing stories about the train massacre, readers who, Slat thought wryly, would never have heard of either Cornelius Krieghoff or Clement Vanderhoof. The former because he was simply not that famous in the world of art and the second because the millionaire shunned the limelight and his presence in Toronto was almost a secret other than to the few wealthy contacts he maintained. All business was conducted at arms length from his clients and he was blissfully, deliberately, oblivious to the sordid little lives of the minions who toiled to maintain his prosperity, or to the sometimes morally doubtful transactions they conducted on his behalf.

As Slat read the story for the third time he became aware of some startling gaps in the logic.

Yakabuski had written that the paintings had "apparently" been spirited out of the building in broad daylight. This was not the kind of assumption the reporter was prone to make.

Then there was that interesting turn of phrase that the fish had slipped through the net and were heading for deeper waters. Surely the reporter would usually have written something like "evaded pursuit and may already be out of the country".

Baffled he read the account again. There was something not quite right about it and it was nagging at him. He needed a clue to help him if he ever got the chance to work on the case at all but there was nothing in the story except that one enigmatic phrase about fish and deeper water.

He considered asking Yakabuski outright what he knew but figured that for a waste of time which would probably jeopardise his new relationship with the man he suspected of having a hand in the murder of Marge McCracken.

Finally, exasperated, he tossed the newspaper onto the couch and set out for he knew would be an uncomfortable meeting at 1547 Ashwarren Grove.

As he drove he tried to reassemble all the pieces of this bizarre puzzle which seemed to be growing exponentially without his input or control.

A strange voice had summoned him to a meeting in the upper crust enclave of the city.

Within hours of the call his landlady was killed in his apartment.

A massacre on a morning commuter train tied up the city and its police for days.

Within minutes of both events two young men in hockey jackets had crossed his path.

A millionaire gave him one hundred and fifty per cent of his advance to ensure paintings which were being stolen as they spoke would not be stolen.

A reporter working on the theft had provided information to Slat about their painter hours before the theft.

It looked to Slat like a classic case of being a day late and a dollar short and he didn't like it one little bit.

He decided to take a circuitous route, using Highway 427 north to Rexdale, then slanting east across Etobicoke and southerly into the Rosedale area.

All the way he kept a wary eye on his rear-view mirror watching for unmarked police cruisers and the rust-brown Saab the reporter sometimes drove, figuring Yakabuski might well have decided to set up a surveillance on him.

Their relationship had grown out of mutual admiration stemming from the day a cheeky young reporter strolled into Slat office at police headquarters and asked if he was still working on a case the department had publicly declared officially closed six months earlier.

Slat was working on the case and said so. When he asked the reporter how he knew he was told it was an instinct coupled with disbelief that a detective of Slat's calibre would abandon a case of such importance.

The official line about closing the case had been broadcast to lure suspects into a false sense of security while Slat and Andy Hocking kept relentlessly working, following leads and maintaining a low profile while doing so.

Slat had admired the reporter's chutzpah and his willingness to share information in return for an exclusive story. He was a rebel cut from the same cloth as Slat and that made them natural allies, if not quite friends.

As he drove he kept comparing the events of the past two days, searching for some interconnecting thread, however tenuous, which he could unravel to solve the murder, the massacre and the art theft in one fell swoop. He knew the likelihood of that was extremely remote but needed something to believe in and somewhere to begin which was better than the nothing he had at the moment.

If Marge McCracken's murder had been designed to throw him off the trail it hadn't worked. Still, there seemed to be no connection between her death and the offer of $75,000 for work on an apparently unrelated project. So why did he feel so uneasy?

That thought led to another question. Why would someone pay him to prevent an art theft unless he had specific knowledge that such a crime was in the offing?

Could Vanderhoof have engineered the theft of his own paintings to drive up their value and collect the insurance money at the same time? He had, after all, alluded several times to the price of the paintings when they met.

Was the reporter from The Tribune involved in this messy scheme? Vanderhoof had made it a very specific condition of employment that he not speak to Yakabuski of all people. Were they in cahoots? Was the news story written to mislead the police and to actually inform the thieves about what the police were doing?

Could the story actually contain coded messages from Vanderhoof to his accomplices?

That sounded far fetched, thought Slat as he signalled his departure from the highway, but he had to consider all possibilities no matter how outlandish they seemed.

The more he thought about these questions the less valid they seemed. The one credit Yakabuski had with Slat was that he was an honest reporter, perhaps the most pure reporter in the city. His talent was legendary and his dedication to finding and presenting the facts as accurately as possible to OK precedence over all else in his life.

So how did the attack on the GO train fit into any scheme to defraud the insurance companies and add to Vanderhoof's wealth? If it was a ploy to draw police attention from the theft of the paintings it had to be the most costly and dangerous red herring in Canadian history.

Had the massacre taken place in Israel, Beirut or even somewhere in Europe it might have made more sense. Those places were home to a great deal of violence already while Toronto was virginal in the danger department by comparison.

If the deed had been committed by an organization like Brigata Rossa or Bader-Meinhoff someone would have called a newspaper or radio station to claim responsibility, an act which always infuriated him, imagining the killers laughing at the carnage and at the bumbling efforts of the police to find them.

As he drew closer to Pearson International Airport at Malton he concentrated harder on his driving because of the congestion being caused by police searches of all vehicles.

Slat usually solved his cases though an alchemic process of allowing all the facts he gathered to filter through his mind like water through limestone. Their random impacts on his conscious and subconscious minds usually resulted in some insight, some constant which connected the details.

Armed with that insight he tried to climb inside the minds of the suspects, working forwards and backwards, unravelling the tangled skein of facts and events until the end was found and a new garment could be woven which would reveal all.

For the second time in as many days he parked in front of 1547 Ashwarren Grove, pressed the doorbell and listened for the telltale shuffle of feet as the doyen of the serving profession made his unhurried way to the front door.

This time the tread was firm and brisk and the door was pulled open with vigour leaving Slat staring into the face of a ruddy-cheeked young man with reddish hair and a salt-and-pepper moustache.

"May I help you, sir?" he inquired in a polite voice with a strong Canadian accent.

Slat was momentarily nonplussed.

"Where's the butler who was here yesterday?" he asked without introducing himself.

"Henry, sir? He was taken suddenly ill last night and I was called in to replace him. Now, sir, what is your business here?"

This new man was so obviously unstuffy and open that Slat warmed to him immediately even though he had desperately wanted to kick the former butler in the pants just to start his day off right. He stifled his disappointment and smiled at the new man.

He had an appointment with Clement Vanderhoof, he said, gave his name and followed the slim waistline and shiny shoes down the foyer to the library.

As the rosewood door opened he could see Vanderhoof pacing the fireplace rug, his faced flushed and angry. He was clenching and unclenching his fists and obviously fuming.

"Mr Slat," he said through gritted teeth as the door closed, "please sit down. We have a major problem, you and I, and I need some answers here and now."

It was obvious to Slat from the outset that Vanderhoof was exhibiting all the behavioural traits of a parent whose child has been kidnapped.

He was in genuine physical and mental pain over the loss of his paintings.

He tossed away any idea of Vanderhoof being part of a conspiracy to steal his own works. This man loved those paintings with his very soul and would do nothing to endanger them for any reward anyone could name.

"I am well aware that the theft of my paintings took place shortly after, or even during, the time you were with me yesterday, being so pecuniary if my memory serves me, Mr Slat. What I want to know now is if you, contrary to me very specific instructions, contacted that reporter Yakabuski at The Tribune."

"No. I didn't. The first I knew of the theft was when you called and told me to read the newspaper story. That's when I learned that the job I had been hired for was over before it even started."

His answer seemed to satisfy the millionaire.

He offered brandy and a cigar and they started to outline a plan of action based on the information Slat had gathered, which wasn't much.

CHAPTER SIX

The bell rang summarily three times then stopped.

After a moment of silence it rang again.

The short fat man rolled over on his cot, realising it was the evening Angelus and he was due in the chapel for vespers in five minutes.

He tucked his grimy undershirt into the top of his grey shorts and reached for the single hook behind the door where hung the brown habit of the Franciscan friars with its thrice-knotted cord symbolizing the vows of poverty, chastity and obedience he had made twenty years earlier.

As he reached he rubbed at his bloodshot eyes with his free hand, trying to knead the wrinkles out of his forehead. He was very tired. He was also very worried.

It had been a week since he gave the orders for a special operation to begin and still he had heard nothing from his partners in the field.

He rubbed his chin, covered with tough, white stubble, and pulled the habit over his head with a single motion born of doing the same thing in the same way for many years.

He straightened the cowl on his shoulders and smoothed the six-decade Franciscan rosary dangling from the cord at his side then sat on the edge of the horsehair pallet and reached for his sandals, cursing softly because only one was visible beside the cot, its mate nowhere to be seen.

As he rummaged for it underneath the cot his fingers came into contact with a piece of paper. Pulling it out he saw it was an envelope with Canadian postage, addressed to him.

Cursing the stupidity of the brother porter who had slipped it under his door with such force that it had drifted under the cot, he slit its flaps, wondering how long it had laid there in the slut's wool.

As he tugged at its contents the bell sounded again and he stuffed the unopened letter into the copious sleeve pocket of his habit and set off towards the chapel where the friars were gathered for the prayers of the divine office prior to their evening meal.

For the last twenty years Fra Pasquale had lived in the tiny convent perched above the cliffs near Sorrento, south of Naples.

His father had been the head of a crime family whose tentacles pervaded almost every element of Italian life from the gilded halls of the Vatican to the Neapolitan slums.

Thanks to the family wealth, at whose origins he could only guess, he had been educated in fine art at the University of Bologna. Now, using his education and talents to the fullest, and the talents and contacts made by the family, he was operating a highly successful art smuggling and counterfeiting ring from the convent of San Girolamo, far from the prying eyes of the law and beyond suspicion in the simple brown habit of the sons of St. Francis of Assisi.

Entering the order had not been difficult for the young man of twenty who devoted himself for a year and a day to the novitiate and the following three years leading to his final vows, during which time he gave neither the father guardian nor the novice master any doubts about his religious calling.

Once out of training and free to operate within the rule of the order, a rule read aloud every Friday in the refectory prior to lunch, he renewed his acquaintance with his old family comrades, finding among them operators who had no compunction in doing whatever it took to steal the works of art he commissioned them to gather.

His task was to mastermind the thefts, accept the incoming goods and paint fake copies which were then sold for millions on the markets of the art world. The family pocketed the proceeds while keeping the priceless originals. His own fat fee went into a bank account in Madrid, far from the prying eyes of his superiors who would be aghast at the very thought of a Franciscan owning property of any kind, especially money.

The original paintings were carefully and lovingly stored in deep caves below the convent, catacombs for the bones of generations of friars. The more accessible caves were left sealed and unvisited, assuring eternal peace to their inhabitants. The most inaccessible of the caves, discovered by him ten years earlier while on a reconnaissance disguised as a retreat, had been opened by a family member and the paintings were stored there, guarded by the bones of saints and sinners from the convent above.

The cool, dry air of the catacombs provided perfect storage conditions for oil paintings which would remain there for years with no diminution of their pristine beauty.

Only one other human being knew of the location of the paintings. By keeping this location secret he thus avoided the temptation for other members of the clan to double cross him. His father was the lone confidante and he was bound by the double laws of blood and omerta, the silence he swore to maintain to his grave about family business.

Once their duties in the chapel and the convent were completed for the day the friars were free to go into nearby villages and towns in search of food and alms. Their rule forbade them from owning property and handling money and enjoined them to work for their food where possible and to take their gifts back to the convent to be shared by the whole community.

This freedom provided the perfect cover for Pasquale. Visiting the homes of his cronies he would return to the convent laden with foodstuffs bought to order in the market so he wouldn't have to waste his time begging when he had more lucrative work to do.

Kneeling in the choir stalls he could feel the letter from Canada burning a hole in the rough wool habit. He tried to concentrate on the words of the psalm Dixit Dominus but to little avail.

As his body went through the motions of the office his mind wandered to the order he had given for the theft of a collection of paintings by Cornelius Krieghoff far away in Toronto, Canada.

His accomplices were told to enter the country at different points, one through Montreal in Quebec, the other through a border crossing with the United States.

They were to meet in Toronto where precise details of the operation would be agreed.

Pasquale issued no instructions himself, figuring that by paying high prices to the best people he could leave the details to them so they could compensate for emergencies he could not foresee from his remote convent.

What he had done was issue instructions that once they had stolen the paintings they would hide them aboard a Spanish freighter standing by in a Great Lakes port on the pretext of making emergency repairs to essential machinery. Exact details of where and when the contact was made with the ship was left to the participants. Family agents had already bribed the Spanish captain for doing what was needed.

The ship would traverse the St. Lawrence River to the Atlantic Ocean, bound for Barcelona, where its precious cargo would be offloaded to a small coastal freighter which would bring them to Sorrento.

At no time would anyone handling the cargo know its content or its value. Bribes would be paid and official palms greased to prevent mysterious mishaps which sometimes befall mysterious shipments when too many people know too much.

The two men chosen for the mission to Canada were known and personally vetted by Fra Pasquale.

Tony Royce had been known since his birth by Pasquale and his father Egidio Ferragami since his birth as a result of the Italian occupation of Abyssinia during the Second World War when Royce's father and Egidio had both been wounded and were cared for in the tents of the Dursa people of the western desert.

The second man, Abdel Salam, was of the Dursa people, son of the man who saved the lives of the former enemies.

Their pedigrees were assured and they were ripe and ready to be used in the operation, probably the most dangerous work they would undertake in their lives.

Failure would mean certain death, if not at the hands of the authorities, then from family members of the organization which had reached into the halls of power of almost every nation in the Western world.

CHAPTER SEVEN

Tony Royce had one passion throughout all his years at school. He was a fanatic about art, especially painting.

His ability to create fresh new works was limited but he had a highly developed sense of appreciation for the works of the great masters and an uncanny ability to copy them to flawless perfection.

That passion and skill led him to the University of Bologna to study fine arts. That and a chance meeting with a beautiful young woman in a church in Rome.

His father, a colonel in the British Army, had retired after the sudden death of his young wife when the boy was two years old and had found refuge in the bottle, having little to do with his son until he reached puberty when he took him to a remote Lincolnshire estate and trained him in all aspects of military and guerilla warfare.

The younger Royce became fascinated by the machinery and tactics of war and worked assiduously, soon surpassing his father in knowledge and practical ability.

During a summer vacation away from the farm he travelled to Italy and rented a small room in a pensione close to St. Peter's Basilica in Rome. He lived, slept and ate alone, prowling the Eternal City, sketching and memorising all he saw.

On a sketching visit to the church of San Pietro in Vinculi, while copying the famous statue of Moses by Michelangelo, he met the girl.

He watched and sketched, one eye on the most beautiful creature he had ever seen. She was small, fine-boned, with olive skin and lustrous brown eyes which captivated his soul.

Within an hour they were chatting softly and she told him she had wanted to see the famous statue but had to come alone because her father refused to enter an infidel temple.

Farida bin Salam was an art student from the University of Bologna, tutored by the famous professor Pasquale Ferragami, the world's greatest living expert on Renaissance paintings.

While Royce, fascinated, wondered about the cost of tuition at Bologna, she spoke about her father, Abdel Metwallah Salam of the Dursa tribe.

"I must meet your father as soon as possible," he said urgently.

The young woman panicked.

"You must not. That would lead to a terrible anger. My father is very jealous and protective of his only daughter and might kill you. I beg you not to do this. I see from your eyes that you have the same feelings for me in your heart that I have in mine for you. Allah alone knows what my father might do if he realized how we feel. Let's stay friends and stay in Italy when he returns home after this trip. I will be at the university for one more term. Perhaps we could find a way to meet there."

She quickly rose and walked out of the church.

Tony Royce watched through a slit in the door as she entered a long black limousine bearing a flag with a crescent moon on it and the emblem of what he took to be some emirate in the Middle East. Soon she was lost to sight in the Rome traffic.

That evening he called home and asked for permission to enroll in the University of Bologna to study fine arts. His father agreed to make all the financial arrangements immediately so he could start his studies in September.

Six weeks later Tony Royce walked onto the famous campus of the ancient university.

At Bologna art was not merely a subject for study, it was a religion.

Above the front door was carved an inscription from Dante and Royce asked the first student he saw what it meant.

His translator was a Canadian, Casey Vanderhoof from Toronto. They chatted briefly and agreed to meet for coffee after their classes.

For the first three weeks Royce immersed himself in his studies and in searching for the beautiful young woman he had met in Rome.

She seemed to have vanished into thin air. Becoming more desperate by the day he finally decided to finish the term and visit her father, risking his displeasure in his eagerness to see Farida again.

Under tutelage of some of the finest art minds on the planet he learned all he could about colours, texture, balance, anatomy, pigments, perspective, techniques and even the models used by the great artists of the past.

His copies of some Michelangelo frescoes from the Sistine Chapel, taken from his summer portfolio, brought him to the attention of one professor, a Franciscan friar called Pasquale Ferragami, who invited him to his rooms for a chat after classes.

When he knocked on the door and walked into the room the first person he saw was Farida bin Salam.

She was sitting on a couch next to a young man who had to be her brother, so complete was the family resemblance. He was introduced as Abdel Salam, son of a sheikh from North Africa.

The friar, standing in front of the fireplace in his simple brown habit, notice the adoration in Royce's eyes as he looked at Farida. He noted the response, followed by a demure lowering of the eyelids.

"Mr Royce, it seems you have a rare appreciation of beauty both in art and in humankind. These young people came to me because of my friendship with their father who saved my father's life during our country's campaign in North Africa. That is part of the reason for your being invited here today. You wanted to meet Farida again and she wanted to meet you. Her brother is opposed to your desires. He fears you may want to take his sister away from her ageing father and from her land, culture and religion. Through my intercession he has agreed that the two of you may spend some time together in Bologna. This will not be reported to her father but should your behaviour prove in any way less than circumspect you will answer to her brother. He is a jealous guardian of his sister's honour and quick to anger, so be warned. You will also meet their father one year from now. The price for these favours is, of course, high. What you will be asked to do in return will stretch your considerable artistic talents to their limits and may enable you to earn sums of money beyond your wildest imaginings.

I am acting here as an agent for your father, their father and our common interest in great art. I am also your supervisor in the delicate and highly secret work you are to be asked to perform in return for the above favours. So, Mr Royce, are you in or are you out? I need an answer now. If you are out, you will never see Farida again. What do you say? I know this is all a great shock to you but what we wish to reveal to you can only be done under the promise of secrecy and if you are one of us."

"OK, father, count me in," said Royce, knowing he could not refuse when the penalty for doing so was never seeing Farida again.

During the ensuing short silence he saw a smile flit briefly across the corners of Farida's mouth. Even Abdel looked less tense though he was far from smiling.

The friar walked to a small table and poured four glasses of thick red liqueur from a decanter and handed one to each.

"Saluti and good luck to our work," he toasted and they tossed off the sweet liquid which warmed their throats.

The formalities over, the meeting became somber again.

The plan which Ferragami unfolded to the group was for Tony Royce, with his posh English accent, to pose as an art expert, visiting owners of priceless collections, asking if they would be interested in selling some or all of their works. That being unlikely but the works having been seen and the locations memorised and filed, he would return with Abdel Salam, an expert burglar with worldwide contacts in shipping and transportation.

They would steal the works, ship them to Italy, and Royce and the friar would copy them for sale on the black market through a chain of the friar's 'friends' whom he spoke of kindly as God-fearing people, managing to leave Royce with the distinct impression that they were anything but.

If he had any second thoughts about accepting the deal they were overshadowed by his desire for Farida and the fact that he had no future prospects in life which excited him half as much.

Once his initial consternation that a man wearing the habit of St. Francis would be involved in such a scheme had evaporated, he began so see the venture as his chance of a lifetime.

He nodded his agreement once more, solemnly, with commitment befitting the most serious decision he had ever made.

This was the moment the others had been waiting for. The friar strode over and clasped both Royce's hands in his own. Abdel shook his hand with a smile. Farida stayed on the couch where her flashing smile and shining eyes showed her contentment. He was in.

Now instructions for the first project began in earnest.

The three students were ordered to cultivate the friendship of Casey Vanderhoof of Toronto, son of the art connoisseur Clement Vanderhoof, owner of the world's largest collection of Krieghoffs, valued at more than ten million dollars.

Ferragami wanted them for resale in Germany and northern Europe.

Once they were firm friends with the young Vanderhoof they were to wangle invitations to Toronto to find out where and how the paintings were kept and how they could be removed.

Then they would steal the paintings and ship them to Sorrento, taking refuge for a while with the Dursa tribe governed by Farida's father Sheikh Abdel Metwallah Salam.

Their methods of operating were their own to evolve but had to be approved by the friar who would arrange all necessary contacts and communications for them.

Only the initial stage of the plan would involve Farida. The friendship made and the plans secure, she would retire to her desert home, far from suspicion, to await their return with the paintings.

After the meeting they departed separately and Royce walked slowly to his rooms.

Opening the door he found a white envelope ion the mat inside. Inside was a message.

"Your contact in Toronto is the butler at the Vanderhoof house. He knows nothing of the plan but will ease your way a little. Good luck. Dottore F."

CHAPTER EIGHT

The trio spent the next two weeks wooing the young Vanderhoof.

Based on his initial meeting with the Canadian student it was easy for Royce to make contact and, over coffee with the shy young man, find out that his sole passion was art and that, although utterly incapable of producing it himself, he was appreciative of any insights he could gain from those with broader knowledge than his own.

He was in Bologna because his father sought for him a knowledge of art to add to the patina of culture Casey would be expected to display as heir to the largest fortune in Canada.

Clement Vanderhoof had no time to acquire that patina for himself, having started from nothing, building his vast empire by the work of his own hands and his sharp business acumen. To make up for his own lack of formal education he had sent the boy to the best schools in North America and Europe, hoping to achieve a veneer of respectability through that means.

Casey wasn't particularly bright. He was totally uninterested in sports and was seen by his peers as dull, lacking in personality and a poor conversationalist. His sole passion was art.

He was well aware of his father's ambitions for him and found them burdensome. Wanting to study art to the exclusion of all other subjects, he dithered, seeking the right moment to ask his father's permission. Telling Clement that collecting art treasures was a sure ticket to greater wealth, especially if one collector could control the works of one or two masters and set world prices for them, was the argument he used that ensured his enrollment at the University of Bologna.

His father, pleased at what he saw as his son's burgeoning business initiative, promised to set up a $250,000 capital fund so Casey could start collecting whichever artists' works he believed would increase in value over the years.

From meeting Casey to introducing him to his friends was a small step for Tony Royce.

Despite the Canadian's shyness and awkwardness with people he was fascinated by Farida and when she suggested they all attend a Mozart concert he not only accepted but insisted on treating them all to dinner afterwards.

The evening was a resounding success for the conspirators and, having dropped the unsuspecting Casey off at his modest apartment, they retired to their rooms to discuss their next move.

During the evening Royce had been disturbed by the attention Farida was paying to Casey Vanderhoof. It was apparent she found him charming and equally apparent that he was falling under her spell.

Within a week she announced that she had been invited to Toronto to stay at the Vanderhoof home, a change of plans which at first upset her brother and Tony Royce but which she convinced them was beneficial to their project if she could be working from the inside of their victim's home.

A quick note was sent to Dr Ferragami appraising him of the change in plans and giving him a new timetable for the trip to Canada which had been moved forward into November.

Casey had been summoned home by his father, needing input into plans for a new hotel he was building in the Caribbean. While Clement was in Aruba, Casey was to hold the fort in Toronto, completing transactions which would affect the hotel and negotiating the purchase of goods and services needed to create the best possible milieu for the wealthy snowbirds who would spend their winters, and vast sums of their money, in it.

The timing was perfect. The old man would be out of the country and Casey would be alone in charge with Farida there to wind him around her little finger.

A return note from Pasquale Ferragami informed them that a Spanish freighter would be in Canada traversing the Great Lakes, its captain already paid a large sum of money to be in the right place at the right time, accepting without question or scrutiny a cargo which he would offload in Barcelona.

Responsibility for planning the actual theft, escape and delivery of the paintings to the ship would belong to Abdel Salam, the note said.

Royce, it continued, with his superior knowledge of English, would help Salam avoid any pitfalls his lack of familiarity with nuances of the language might encounter.

A post script on the note said the name of the vessel was La Coruna.

Permissions had been arranged and tariffs paid for the journey through the St. Lawrence Seaway system with its locks and canals linking the Atlantic Ocean with the Great Lakes more than a thousand miles inland.

La Coruna was small as Seaway freighters went. A scant five hundred feet long and with fifteen thousand tonne capacity she would be able to slip in and out of the locks and canals with ease, making good time to Lake Erie where she would stand by for word from Salam.

Captain Enrique Verdugo y Torrero, known as El Serpiente from his uncanny ability to smell out potential problems and slither around obstacles which would have destroyed a less wily sailor, was well suited to the task at hand.

Under constant pressure from the vessel's owners to make better time, complete more voyages, carry more tonnage and maintain the smallest possible crew complement, he was not above accepting any graft or bribes which came his way.

He had a wife and three children in Barcelona and a mistress in Tenerife whose financial demands had to be met if his wife was not to learn of her existence.

Contact with El Serpiente had already revealed that La Coruna could be tied up in the harbour at Port Colborne, entrance to the Welland Canal from Lake Erie, for three days in late November while repairs to its hydraulic winching system were carried out.

The time was set. There could be no turning back.

Tony Royce now had to contact the butler at the Vanderhoof mansion to plan transportation of the paintings from Toronto to

Port Colborne, a journey of about a hundred miles. He was also in charge of buying weapons, ammunition and disguises in Toronto and making any other arrangements he deemed necessary on the spur of the moment. He would also help Salam plan their escape route out of the city of three million.

Within a week plans began to take shape rapidly.

La Coruna set sail for Canada. Fra Pasquale approved their plans. Casey Vanderhoof bought two first-class tickets for himself and Farida from Bologna to Toronto via Roma.

Tony Royce bought a return ticket from Bologna to London and from London to Detroit, Michigan, on the Canadian border about two hundred and fifty miles west of Toronto. For Abdel Salam he bought train tickets from Bologna to Milan and Paris and return air fare from Paris to Montreal, about three hundred miles east from Toronto.

The day before she left Bologna Farida received a phone call from the butler at the Vanderhoof mansion.

News of art thefts in Europe had made Clement Vanderhoof leery of leaving his paintings while he worked in the Caribbean and he was about to hire a private detective to guard them in his absence.

The detective's name was Mungo Slat and he was reputed to be the best in the country.

"Don't worry about Mungo Slat," Abdel said, clicking the safety catch on the revolver he always carried. "He'll never know what hit him."

CHAPTER NINE

Mungo Slat was worried.

A whole day had passed since the theft of the paintings and he still had no idea where to start.

His instincts told him the GO train massacre was somehow part of the picture, as was the murder of Marge McCracken, but he could not connect the dots to produce a clear picture no matter how he racked his brains.

Without a plausible explanation or theory he couldn't contact the police so he decided to work alone, hoping to find something, anything, that would shed some light on the mystery.

He had called Andy Hocking but his former partner was as much in the dark as he was. All the pair of them knew was what they gleaned from newspaper reports and most of that appeared to be speculation.

Hocking shared with him one fact that the newspapers didn't yet have. A standard issue gym bag had been found on the train. It was the type available at any sports store and was free of fingerprints.

Police inquiries showed that a bag like it had been bought the previous day at a downtown department store by a bespectacled, studious young man accompanied by a stunningly beautiful young woman with dark complexion and glorious brown eyes. Neither was known to the store clerk. The transaction was paid for in cash and, since the purchase was made during the start of the pre-Christmas rush, descriptions were sketchy at best.

That bag, dropped between the first and second coaches of the train, became a momentary source of hope for Slat, a hope which faded quickly in the reality that it offered no clues as to the identities of the killers.

It looked as if the two men in hockey jackets either had two accomplices or the bag simply wasn't theirs in the first place.

After banging desultorily about his office for an hour in sheer frustration, Slat decided to go for a walk so he could marshal his facts and try again. He decided to take Sebastian the bulldog with him.

They waddled down the street and found a street vendor's wagon where he bought two jumbo hot dogs, one for each of them.

The dog mangled its meal in its giant maw as he thoughtfully chewed on his, distracted suddenly when the animal proceeded to belch loudly, then relieve itself beside his feet.

"You dirty bugger," he yelled. "Last time I bring you out for lunch, you ungrateful bastard!"

He turned away from the dog in disgust and his eye caught the window of a travel agency where a poster showed a bright picture of a cruise ship gliding through the turquoise Mediterranean.

It brought back with a jolt Yakabuski's article and the line about the fishes slipping the net and heading for the open seas.

Slat chortled with delight at the possibility that the Tribune reporter might have unwittingly handed him his first concrete idea about the robbery.

He patted Sebastian's wide skull, stepped to the cart and bought a second hot dog for the beast.

"Sometimes you're such a clever bugger, Sebastian, you make me sick," he told it as he handed the food over, watching his fingers as they almost joined the sausage entering the gaping mouth.

They headed back to the office, Slat to start make phone calls, Sebastian to fart and belch his way through the rest of what for him had been a rapturous two-wiener day.

Slat threw his crumpled and muddy trench coat over a chair, lit a cigarette and set to work tracing the names, registration and destinations of every ship that had been in the St. Lawrence Seaway system in the past five days.

His first call was to the chief of water police at Ontario Provincial Police headquarters beneath the Gardiner Expressway on Lakeshore Boulevard.

While his call was being routed to the correct office he scanned the business pages of The Tribune hunting for the daily shipping register of all vessels entering and leaving the port of Toronto.

He was halfway down the list when the officer answered. Slat made his request but received little help other than advice to contact the St. Lawrence Seaway Authority office in Cornwall, Ontario, close to the Quebec border and across the river narrows from Massina in upstate New York.

"You could also get your hands on a copy of an annual book listing all ships entering Canada and the United States by Greenwood and Dills of Cleveland, Ohio. It contains information such as the names, registration, tonnage, ports of origin, names of captains and chief engineers, flags flown under, companies owned and so on. You can get one at any decent bookshop," the officer said before hanging up.

Slat grabbed his coat again and marched out unto the street in search of a decent bookstore.

He finally found what he wanted in a small specialty shop three floors above Yonge Street above a picture framing business named Well Hung.

Elated with his find he trundled back down the stairs, rushed straight across the road, oblivious to the honks and shouts of angry motorists, and beetled back to his office.

He was halfway down the index page of the new book when he realised he wasn't alone.

Sitting in the corner, a cigar between his teeth and an amused look on his face, was Regis Yakabuski of The Tribune.

"Man, you scared the liver out of me," Slat shouted.

It had been a year since the two men had seen one another in the flesh and that only briefly at the funeral of a police officer gunned down while attempting to arrest two petty thieves.

Yakabuski looked older, thinner and more tired than Slat remembered him. His sandy hair was thin to the point of baldness and there were deep bags beneath his watery blue eyes. Those eyes were always devoid of expression. Shark eyes, Slat called them.

Yakabuski was forty five, ten years younger than Slat. Born in Saskatchewan to Ukrainian parents, he had worked at a series of local and metropolitan dailies all owned by Corey Newspapers until he was poached away by The Tribune where his career had blossomed as he produced his finest work to date.

"Hello, you old buzzard," he smiled at Slat. "How about a cup of coffee and some small talk? My God, that dog stinks. Is he yours? He's been bubbling and farting since I arrived. Some watch dog, too. He never blinked an eye when I knocked and walked in and he hasn't woken up yet. I figured if your door wasn't locked you couldn't be too far away so I decided to come in and wait. I hope you didn't mind?"

"In answer to your questions, no the dog isn't mine. Yes he stinks, Yes you can have coffee but we will go out for it since that pot is due for its annual scouring and the stuff tastes like hell."

They ambled round the corner to a swanky French patisserie which served coffee in glass mugs along with a variety of breads and pastries.

After a round of reminiscences over coffee and cigarettes the talk turned serious as Yakabuski asked about the GO inquiry, fishing for information he could use in his next report.

Slat told him, poker faced, that all he knew was what he had learned from reading The Tribune.

"I know you are probably right but I think the police are getting nowhere fast with their inquiries. In my book you are the best man to solve it, with or without their help. I want a story, all right, but I also want this crime solved and I want you to know you can trust me on that. If there is anything I can do to help you, please let me know."

Slat chewed the end of his cigarette and pondered that in silence. He had no reason to doubt the reporter's sincerity and, to face facts, he had little to go on at this stage. Perhaps two heads would be better than one after all.

"All right, Regis, but on one condition. If you hear anything that even remotely impinges on this case I want to know about it before it gets into print and I don't want to see it in print until we mutually agree to release it. I know that's a lot to ask but time is of the essence and a break of an hour or two could be vital. Deal?"

"Deal," said Yakabuski with a smile, turning to order two more mugs of coffee.

Slat launched into a full account of events since the mysterious call asking if he would like to earn a large sum of money, ending with his purchase of the Greenwood and Dills shipping directory.

As the reporter listened Slat could almost hear the wheels turning as each piece of information was sorted and filed by the human computer lurking behind those watery shark's eyes.

When Slat ended, Yakabuski lit a cigar, stared into space for what seemed like an hour to the restless investigator, then started speaking softly and slowly.

"You know, you might be onto something with the idea of the paintings being taken out of the country by sea. I never thought of that when I used the metaphor in my news story but it may have been a happy accident, what's the fancy term for that? Synchronicity? Yes, that's it. Karl Jung would be proud of us. You will have to do a lot of cross-checking on the movements of Great Lakes shipping even when you know the name of the vessel you are looking for, which you don't. I can do some of that through my contacts at The Tribune if that will buy time for you to check into the sudden change of butlers at Vanderhoof's house. To be honest, I can't make any connection between your landlady's murder and the theft of the paintings, let alone the murders on the train, but your instincts always seem to be right and think we should go with them at least until something better crops up."

He got up, paid for the coffees, walked outside and hailed a taxi for the newspaper offices, leaving Slat bemused but relieved of at least one burdensome chore.

He was also elated at a clue which had popped out of his recitation of events, one he had forgotten until Yakabuski picked it up. There had been a change of butlers at 1547 Ashwarren Grove.

Why had the butler been replaced at that precise time? Was there some connection between the butler and the theft of the paintings? Was the butler's illness coincidental and nothing more?

There was only one way to find out and that was to call Vanderhoof and ask him outright.

Back in his office he dialled what was becoming a familiar number and heard a guarded voice ask what he wanted. It must have been a police officer stationed at the mansion to guard the Vanderhoofs and to intercept any ransom demands that might be made.

"Mr Clement Vanderhoof, please. This is Mungo Slat and I may have some news for him."

There was a click on the line which warned Slat his call was being recorded. After a long pause, which he knew was to allow the police and Bell Canada to trace the call to his number, the plummy voice of his client came on the line.

"So there you are, Slat. Where the hell have you been? Have you found my paintings? What's the news you have for me? Speak up, man, I want answers and I want them now."

When the tirade ended Slat calmly said he had a matter of some importance to discuss and asked permission to visit the mansion.

"Why can't you tell me now? Why do you insist on wasting my time and patience by coming here?"

"Frankly, sir, I don't want to take the chance that your telephone may be bugged. I want to speak with you in private. I thought it was the butler who answered the phone and I wanted to make sure this call got straight to you. It took long enough as it was," he added maliciously for the benefit of the eavesdropping police.

"Very well, come if you must. But know that I want answers and I want action. I paid you $75,000 to do something and it's high time you started to deliver," snarled Vanderhoof and slammed down the receiver in Slat's ear.

Slat scribbled a few notes reminding himself to check on Vanderhoof's son, who he thought was out of the country. He wanted to know where he was exactly, if he had returned, who was with him, and precisely when he returned to Toronto.

Then he grabbed the trench coat and car keys for his third foray into Nob Hill north.

He was greeted at the door by the same young butler as before. The man looked quizzically at him as he tossed his coat onto a deacon's bench in the foyer and set off briskly towards the library without waiting to be announced.

The butler was three paces behind him when he arrived at the rosewood door.

"Too bad you're not as fast on your pins as old whatsisname, your predecessor," Slat whispered as the butler reached for the door handle.

"Yes sir. But Ashley is still ill so I will have to learn to walk more quickly," the man smiled.

"Do you happen to know where he lives? I rather liked him and would like to send him a get-well card," said Slat.

"Sorry, sir, I don't know. His full name is Herbert Ashley and that is all I know about him. Perhaps Mr Vanderhoof may be able to assist you with that. May I show you in now?"

Slat stepped aside and was shown into the library.

This time Vanderhoof was not alone. Seated to the right of the fireplace, which was crackling cheerfully, was a sallow skinned young man in horn-rimmed glasses. He was wearing a grey suit with a conservative navy blue tie.

Standing behind him with one hand on his shoulder was the most strikingly beautiful woman Slat had ever laid eyes on.

Clad in a winter white wool dress with a cowl neckline on which rested a single pearl brooch, she perched on the arm of the couch as he approached, allowing him a glimpse of shapely legs, olive skin and flashing deep brown eyes whose loveliness and lustre made him ache.

The master of the house was behind a bar pouring glasses of Scotch whisky which he topped off with a squirt of soda.

Refusing the butler's request to serve the drinks, he asked him to hold all incoming calls and admit nobody until further notified.

"Now then, Mr Slat," he said as the rosewood doors closed behind the butler, "what do you have to say for yourself?"

Slat looked pointedly at the young couple by the fireside before responding. The millionaire, divining his meaning, told him they would be staying and would be privy to anything he had to say.

"This is my son, Casey Vanderhoof. The young lady is a fellow student from the University of Bologna who is visiting for a few weeks while I am engaged in other business while waiting for you to resolve this horrible mess."

Slat smiled at the young woman who barely nodded her head. He nodded to young Vanderhoof who returned his nod with a reserved smile.

"To make a long story short, I have been following two lines of inquiry. The first concerns the sudden departure of your butler, Herbert Ashley, at precisely the same time as your paintings were stolen. The second involves the possibility that your paintings are already on a ship and on their way out of the country."

There was a pregnant pause before Vanderhoof exploded with rage.

"That's it? That's all I get for seventy five thousand fucking dollars? You came all the way out here to tell me you have two stupid guesses about where my paintings are? Really!"

Slat was not about to take any more abuse from this petty tyrant.

"Listen, Vanderhoof. I came all the way out here, as you put it, to find out where your butler lives, when he booked off sick, how long he worked for you prior to the theft. I can work the rest out for myself without the assistance of your sarcasm or overworked emotional outbursts," he said, omitting the fact that Regis Yakabuski was working for him in direct contravention of Vanderhoof's orders in return for an exclusive story. That would have been adding insult to outrage but he was considering it in view of the tycoon's behaviour.

"Ashley worked here for about three months," Vanderhoof said through gritted teeth.

This shabby, stout, short detective was starting to get seriously on his nerves and he had the feeling he had seen not only the last of his paintings but the last of his money as well.

"He lives in a tenement building somewhere on Jarvis Street but has a room here in case he is needed for late night duties or if the weather is inclement. Unlike you, Mr Slat, he came to us extremely well trained, well recommended and well mannered. He is quite missed around here and will be welcomed back with open arms when he recovers from whatever ailment he may have contracted in the lower quarters of the city."

The allusion to Jarvis Street, the former red light district of the burgeoning downtown, was not lost on Slat.

"Yes, you old swine, I bet you know your way around that quarter well enough," he thought as he squirreled the information about the butler away in his brain cells for later retrieval.

Since the room had degenerated into a brooding silence, he started explaining his theory about the shipping, telling Vanderhoof he was checking on all ship movements in the St. Lawrence Seaway system and that he would alert the police when he had something concrete to report so they could apply for a search warrant and, with help from the Canadian Coastguard, board and search the vessel in question.

"Thanks to the great length of the Seaway system most vessels will be in the waterway for a few days yet," he concluded.

In spite of his bravado in the face of his client's anger he was very unsure of himself at this moment. What if the paintings had not been smuggled onto a ship at all but had simply been spirited across the border with the United States where there was, after all, a massive market for works of art?

He had to admit to himself that there were many imponderables.

Even if a ship were used, it could have sailed to Buffalo, Cleveland, or some nearby port in the United States where its cargo could have been offloaded and floated on the black market already.

Worse still, the paintings could still be in Toronto, being held until police interest waned before being shipped elsewhere later.

"Well, Mr Slat, what if none of your theories holds water? What if they are all dead wrong?" the voice of the millionaire cut through his thoughts.

Slat had to admit to himself that the man was no fool. It takes more than good looks and contacts to amass more than a billion dollars and keep that fortune growing.

"I assure you I am not putting all my eggs in any one basket at the moment. Sooner or later some information is bound to surface and I am confident that someday your paintings will be returned to you safe and sound."

There was another protracted silence.

"Very well, Mr Slat, you have precisely three days to find my paintings. If they are not in my possession in seventy two hours from this minute you owe me seventy five thousand dollars and will receive in return my assurance that you will never work in this city again. Is that a deal?"

Slat had his back to a wall and he knew it. This crafty businessman was used to playing high stakes poker with other peoples' lives and he was used to winning. He was left with two stark choices. He could either fold and cash in his chips now or he could hold out and wait for a better hand.

"It's a deal. The money is being held in a trust account and will be paid back with interest if your majesty demands it. Since we are playing a game of intellectual poker here, how about adding a little more excitement to the ante? I will get the paintings back within seventy two hours. Then I will see you and raise you another seventy five thousand dollars. It's double or nothing. How about it, Mr Vanderhoof?"

He heard a gasp of disbelief from the young woman and saw a slight blush tinge Vanderhoof's ears.

"You're on, Mr Mungo Slat. I'm not in the habit of giving away any of my money and I don't propose to start doing so now on your behalf. I'll double the fee if you succeed. If you don't, you lose seventy five thousand dollars plus your future career. That seems fair enough to me."

Slat smiled amicably. He had wanted to observe the reactions of the son and the visitor and to make sure Vanderhoof wasn't playing some insurance scam. He was now sure he wasn't.

At the same time, he wasn't sure he had won anything himself, either.

He had seen his landlady dead, more than a hundred people gunned down on a commuter train and the police and himself baffled by it all. Now he felt as if he were facing an army tank with Vanderhoof at the controls, steering straight at him as he sat in his tiny Renault 5.

He turned to face the lovely young woman.

"So how do you like Canada so far? Is this your first visit?"

She coloured slightly as she answered.

"Yes, this is my first visit and I like this country very much."

Her English was impeccable with only the slightest trace of an accent.

Slat could tell she was as nervous as a gopher on a hotplate but had no idea why.

As she turned to look out of the window a flash of silver on her right wrist intrigued Slat and, rising to leave, he crossed towards her.

"That's a very charming bracelet," he said, smiling. "It appears to be inscribed with some sort of lettering or runes. Is it for good luck?"

She coloured again and her eyes flashed as she replied.

"The bracelet was given to me by my father. Its words are in an ancient language called Aljamiado. It's a family heirloom but I don't know what it signifies or where my father got it."

"What did you call that ancient language?" Slat asked innocently.
"Aljamiado," she replied.

At that moment he heard the library door open and heard Vanderhoof's voice asking the butler to escort Mr Slat to his car.

"Remember, Mr Slat, you have seventy two hours and then all hell is going to break loose over your unworthy head unless I have my paintings back," Vanderhoof said pointedly as Slat left the room.

In the foyer he found the butler holding his trench coat with some disdain.

As he fastened the buttons he asked the young man if he had ever heard of Aljamiado.

"No, sir. Is it some kind of cheese?"

"Sorry, you lose," said Slat, opening the front door and heading for the driveway.

CHAPTER TEN

With two new avenues to explore Slat felt relatively optimistic in spite of the seemingly impossible challenge he had issued to himself and to the newspaper magnate.

The missing butler, the mysterious bracelet with its ancient script and its wearer's obvious discomfort when he mentioned it, gave him a sense of elation at the precise moment when the millionaire thought he had him by the short hairs.

It was typical of Slat to see possibilities where others saw only problems. That had been the secret of his success and it came to the fore now as he faced either the loss of his fat fee or the doubling of it if he found the paintings within the deadline he had just agreed to.

Not that money was much of a motivator for him. Far from it. Since Clare's death he had given away most of his possessions, choosing to live like a modern hermit, an anachronism in the age of greedy affluence. He did, however, plan to buy a new trench coat from his earnings.

He drove straight from Ashwarren Grove to Port Credit and his favourite doughnut shop where he could ruminate among the coffee and pastries.

After two cups of strong java and a plain doughnut, still devoid of ideas, he flung himself off to the house in Troy Street to think in his own room. He had no appetite for the silver screen in front of which he also liked to mull over his problems.

He felt certain he would stick with the ship theory. He would also try to find out more about the young woman's bracelet. He didn't know why but some inner voice was telling him it could be connected to the case. After all, she too had arrived on the scene at or about the same time as the paintings were stolen. He would also check out the address of the conveniently vanishing butler.

After a brief rest, a quick shower and shave in the now silent house, devoid of its former superintendent, he donned a warm sweater and cords, flung on the trench coat, grabbed two packs of Camel filters from the carton he had just bought and reached for the telephone directory to suss out the Jarvis Street address of one Herbert Ashley.

In his coat pocket he stuffed a torch, a box of matches, a small revolver and a clip of bullets.

Then he drove to the Port Credit GO station and caught the train to Union Station.

This time the ride was uneventful but he could see the strain on the faces of the few riders as the train rumbled through the Mimico rail yard and past the grey bunker which housed the death car, still under wraps and still being examined by forensic experts from the police department.

The fear was intangible but it was omnipresent throughout the train.

Passengers studiously avoided eye contact with their fellows but this time it was from fear, not the usual morning and evening rush hour aloofness. They perched on the edges of their seats as if ready to flee at the first sight of anything unusual or threatening. Nobody dared to read a newspaper or magazine lest their attention waver from what they feared most, a repetition of the horrendous massacre of two days ago.

The whole city of Toronto had become gripped by fear. It was evidenced in the scant number of passengers on an evening when the Toronto Maple Leafs of the National Hockey League were playing their archenemies, the Montreal Canadiens, in the Gardens on Carlton Street.

At Union Station Slat rode the elevator to the east end of the main concourse and caught a subway train to Queen Street where he alighted two blocks from Vanderhoof's office tower and a few short blocks from Jarvis Street to the east of Yonge Street which was the central street between east and west.

It was a damp November night with a fine rain turning to sleet.

Pulling his coat collar around his short neck he set out for Jarvis

Street, crossing Church and Parliament streets, looking for the number on the street sign which would send him south or north of Queen Street.

He found the address he wanted about two blocks north of Queen Street. The building, a shabby tenement, was in darkness, its dirty exterior reflecting wet and slimy under the streetlights.

Slat climbed the four wide front steps to a large unpainted wooden door with broken stained glass in its top half and, seeing no bell or buzzer, turned the doorknob and stepped inside.

The hallway was three storeys high. Its right hand wall was covered with black metal mail boxes, some bearing names scrawled on pieces of paper stuffed into their front panels. Others had numbers and no names. Still others were devoid of identification of any kind.

Slat peered in the gloom at the names looking for Herbert Ashley's. It wasn't there.

The hall stank of stale urine and the odour of cooking cabbage came from a ground floor apartment. Two bicycles were in the middle of the hallway and he had to step around them as he groped down the dim passage looking for a door which might belong to the landlord or superintendent.

At the every end, under a grime-encrusted chandelier with four of its six bulbs missing, he found a hand-written sign saying "Superintendent. Apt. #6".

He rapped three times on the door and stood waiting in the fetid aroma of filth, decay and neglect which seemed to seep from the very walls.

He could hear the sound of a television set, a baby wailing and a man and a woman fighting on an upper floor.

The door opened a crack revealing a heavy chin and a baleful brown eye which stared unblinkingly at him.

"Yeah, whattaya want?" a deep make voice growled.

"I'm looking for Herbert Ashley's apartment. His name isn't on the mailboxes out front so I thought you might be able to help me," Slat said evenly, determined not to let the grim eye and all-pervading filth upset his equilibrium.

"If his name is gone then so is he," growled the voice and the door started to close.

"Wait," Slat said firmly. "How do you know he was ever here, then? Perhaps he has skipped out and owes you back rent. Have you considered that?"

The door stopped and the eye returned to its post.

Slat figured he had better keep talking even it meant looking like a vacuum cleaner salesman desperate for the commission that would buy his next meal. He lowered his voice confidentially.

"I have reason to believe that Mr Herbert Ashley is not really who he pretends to be and that he may actually pose a danger to the residents of this fine building."

That worked. The chain was unsnapped and the door opened to reveal an unshaven middle-aged man with a pot belly. He wore a filthy grey undershirt and black trousers with his braces dangling at the sides. His filthy feet were bare. His face was a mass of jowls and wrinkles. Tousled hair and pink creases in his left cheek indicated he had been asleep when Slat banged on his door.

A glimpse of the interior of the apartment revealed an almost bare room with a colour television blaring and the remnants of a chicken takeaway dinner in a spindly metal tray.

There was a filthy blanket on the couch and three empty beer bottles were strewn on a scatter rug in front of it.

The floor was covered with newspapers and what looked like junk mail which had been tossed aside after being read.

The superintendent stepped into the hallway, closing the door on his detritus, and whispered confidentially to Slat.

"You know, sir, I thought the same thing myself when he first moved in. Funny fellow that one. Spent a lot of time alone but when he did have visitors they looked foreign and jabbered away in some strange language. Could have been Italian, Portuguese or something like that."

"Truth of the matter is," Slat said, "I need to see inside his apartment since he is still listed as living here and you don't seem to think he has moved out, do you?"

"If he has moved out he bloody well owes me rent. I'll take the bastard to court to get what's owed to me, you can count on that," the man growled.

Slat had no patience with this man who lived in a flat like a landfill site, ate slept and worked in his own filth yet was dangerously quick to use the law to his own advantage to fight everyone else for wrongs real or imagined. He was not the neatest of people himself but this dedication to filth and ordure offended his every sensibility and he wanted to throw up at any moment.

Forcing a short smile to his lips he asked again if he could have a peek at Herbert Ashley's abode.

They climbed a flight of dank, greasy stairs to a floor which was an exact replica of they one they had just left. The theme of its decor was filth piled on rust and decay. Grimy yellow walls were stained with mildew and the smell of urine in the air was pervasive and sick-making.

The landlord led Slat to an unpainted wooden door with the number 12 marked on it in white chalk.

He cowered in the hallway, barely visible as his grimy attire blended in with the decor, camouflaged by filth and, despite his protestations, not quite the brave fellow he had been on the floor below.

Slat rapped heavily twice on the door then stepped quickly to one side. He had once lost a partner in the police force when a hail of gunfire came from inside such a door, killing him as he was poised to knock again.

This time nobody answered.

Motioning the superintendent over with his head Slat ordered him to open the door using his pass key.

As the filthy wooden plug swung open the pair of them gasped in amazement.

The spotless interior had plush carpeting, classic furnishings, a huge television set, hanging baskets of exotic house plants and a push-button phone on a glass table beside a French provincial couch with needlepoint cushions and a stylish coffee table in front of it holding a huge book about the history of the Hudson's Bay Company.

The walls were lined with bookshelves laden with volumes by authors ancient and modern, some mysteries and a set of leather-bound classic which must have cost a fortune and were surely a collector's item. A pipe rack contained four good briars next to a humidor of blended tobacco.

This was obviously the home of an affluent, educated and tasteful man, fastidious about his surroundings and, by extension, about his personal habits.

The filthy rent-collector gasped.

"This bastard lives like a king! And to think of the cheap rent he gets away with. I could have been charging him at least another hundred a month for such luxury."

He rubbed his hands together greedily, no doubt contemplating how to squeeze more money from this tenant is he ever resurfaced.

Slat started a meticulous search of the apartment, careful to replace anything he touched to its exact position and angle.

He was no Sherlock Holmes peering into jars and taking samples of tobacco or scrapings from shoe soles. He felt if there were any clues to the role of the butler in the theft of the Kreighoffs they might not be well hidden in what the tenant obviously saw as a safe hiding place amidst the squalor of the slums.

His search showed him only that the refrigerator and the kitchen cupboards were all empty.

The anomaly of an empty, spotless, expensively furnished apartment in a tenement building which should have disappeared beneath the wrecker's ball decades ago was puzzling. It was like King Solomon choosing to live in a leper colony.

It was obvious the bird had flown and this confirmed his suspicions that Ashley was connected with the theft. Without him Slat had zip, zero, nada, bugger all to work with. He was back at square one and the clock was ticking.

He picked up the phone at the small table and found a dial tone. The line had not been disconnected, which meant the man couldn't have been gone for long.

He dialled his home number to test the line.

As he did so he idly rubbed the point of pencil over the telephone message pad on the table. He rubbed and rubbed absentmindedly until he began to see the outline of a word begin to form itself on the page.

He kept rubbing until it was clear.

The word, in upper case letters, was KRIEGHOFF.

Incredible and excited he rubbed some more, covering the entire page with graphite.

Not until he reached the very bottom of the sheet did two more words appear, again in upper case letters.

LA CORUNA.

He grabbed the sheet from the pad and flung himself onto the couch, excited and perplexed.

Someone had written those words on the page above the one he had doodled on. The pressure of their writing had created an imprint on the page below, to be released when he rubbed it with the pencil point.

Now he had a connection between the missing butler and the stolen paintings. Why else would the name Krieghoff be written on the man's telephone message pad at home?

The only problem in the short term was the fact that the butler was nowhere to be found.

And what about the words La Coruna? What the hell was that, Slat asked himself. Was it the name of another painter? A place? The title of a painting? The name of the person the butler was contacting about the Krieghoffs?

Those two new words stayed uppermost in his mind as he made his uneventful way home. The name La Coruna baffled him. He tried to remember the names of Cuban cigars and even ancient goddesses whose names he could barely dredge up from the silt of his student days.

As he walked to his car in the Port Credit station parking lot he recalled the words of a poem from his high school days in the misty beginnings of time.

"Not a gun was heard, not a funeral drum as his corse to the rampart we hurried," he said aloud, wondering what the hell a "corse" was and failing to remember the title of the poem or the name of the poet.

It came back to him in a flash as he sat in the doughnut emporium beside the Credit River. The Burial of Sir John Moore at Corunna. Or was it Coruna? Perhaps the Spanish name for Corunna was actually La Coruna with that little squiggle over the N which would make it sound like "corunya"

So now what did he have? A reference to a Victorian poem on a note pad in a slum. That didn't make much sense, he thought.

If La Coruna is the name of a place, could it mean it was the ultimate destination of Vanderhoof's paintings? That was a possibility, even it it was vague.

Then he remembered that he had been looking for shipping information in the St. Lawrence Seaway earlier in the day. Could La Coruna be the name of a ship?

"By George, he's got it," he shouted out loud, startling staff and customers. He got up, paid the bill and walked back to his apartment elated.

"La Coruna may well be the name of a bloody ship. I was right after all. Thank you, Regis Yakabuski," he said as he walked.

He waltzed down the tricky stairs to his basement abode and heard the phone ringing. This time he turned the light on as he entered. This was not the night for more surprises.

The tired voice on the other end of the line belonged to the Tribune reporter.

"I have a list of all shipping passing through Lake Erie, Lake Ontario and entering Toronto Harbour in the past week. Can I bring it to your office in the morning so we can go over it for ideas? What time would be good for you?"

"Listen, Regis. Can you check that list right now and see if the name La Coruna is on it? La Coruna, that's right."

There was a short pause then Yakabuski's voice.

"Sorry, nothing by that name. I have a couple with exotic names like Northern Cherry and Rembrandt. I thought the last one might be useful since it is called after a famous painter. La Coruna, eh? How did you come up with that one?"

Again the last casual and artful question. Slat decided to duck it, still not totally sure he could trust the reporter.

"Nowhere special. I saw the name, or one like it, on some cigars and thought it sounded like great name for a ship, that's all. Call it a hunch."

He made his goodbyes, promising to meet Yakabuski at 9:30 the following morning, and hung up.

That night he slept little and that fitfully, tossing and turning as the words Krieghoff and La Coruna wove their way in and out of his dreams.

By four he was wide awake and cranky. Tossing on his clothes he walked back to the all-night doughnut shop and settled in with a strong coffee and a humongous cinnamon bun to chew the problem to death once and for all. It didn't work.

Four hours later he was on the morning GO train keeping an eye open for the two men in hockey jackets, wondering if their appearance a few days ago had been simply a coincidence after all.

He even sat in the carriage directly behind the engine, shunned by most commuters who were now superstitious about it since the massacre.

When the conductor poked his head in he was surprised to see a lone figure sitting silently by the window, hoping some form of osmosis would break through the logjam in his mind.

Before he left the conductor dropped a copy of that morning's Tribune on the seat next to Slat. Olav Palme, prime minister of Sweden, had been assassinated while leaving a Stockholm theatre with his wife. The killer had escaped without a trace.

President Ronald Reagan was trying to convince the U.S. Senate to give him $100 million for aid to the Nicaraguan Contras in their battle with the Sandinista government.

The Canadian dollar had slipped below 74 cents U.S. and interest rates were falling.

On the Metro page was a story by Yakabuski stating police still had no leads in the GO train massacre. It said ridership was down by fifty per cent in the wake of the event as commuters switched to buses, trolleys and private vehicles, car pooling where they could.

There was no mention of the theft of the Kreighoffs. A news blackout had been imposed by the imperious Clement Vanderhoof who was keeping all information very close to his diamond-studded vest.

There was some crumb of comfort in that for Slat. The case was still his alone. It also meant that Yakabuski hadn't betrayed his trust and slipped the story to the city editor.

The fewer people who knew about the case the better, Slat thought, as the train rattled through the Mimico rail yards where police still hovered over the shrouded death car in its tomb-like bunker.

The victims had all been identified, removed and handed over to distraught relatives. Many would be buried today or tomorrow by shattered wives, uncomprehending children and grieving grandparents.

Within months many of the widows and children would wend their way away from the Golden Horseshoe back to their small towns of origin where they afford to live modestly on their insurance money, raising their children in a safer, kinder environment than Toronto could afford them.

At the office he found Yakabuski waiting with coffees and a bag of bagels with cream cheese. He was playing with Sebastian, tossing him bits of bagel.

As they ate he told Slat about his search through the shipping lists and the problem he was having keeping an inquisitive city editor off his back while he researched their project.

Typically, he had called the harbour master in the middle of the night for some facts and received an ear roasting for his trouble. The man loved to hate the Tribune and wasted no time in unleashing his hounds of venom. In spite of all that, Yakabuski managed to get the list he wanted.

The list was long and detailed with names of vessels, cargo tonnage, times of arrivals and sailings.

Monday: Stephen B. Roman, cement carrier, bound for Chicago; Chicago Tribune, newsprint cargo, bound for Montreal; Paterson, grain carrier, bound for Thunder Bay; Algorail, stone carrier, bound for Lachine; Canadian Century, bound for Duluth; William J. DeLancey, bound for Buffalo; Golden Hind, bound for Montreal; Consumers Power, bound for Montreal; Frankcliffe Hall, bound for Detroit; Sam Laud, bound for Sarnia; Jean Parisien, bound for Port Colborne.

Similar information was listed for every day of the week. Not one name seemed to offer a clue and there was no ship called La Coruna on the list.

Slat threw the list down in frustration, reaching for another cigarette from an already dwindling daily ration, then swivelled round in his chair to face Yakabuski.

"Somewhere out there, my lad, there's a ship called La Coruna. I'll bet my licence on it. Now, how the hell do we find it and where it has been and where it is headed?"

The reporter looked at him quizzically.

Slat continued: "We need to call the Seaway Authority in Cornwall. They know the names of all vessels passing through their locks and canal because they charge the buggers a fat fee for the privilege. If they have the name we can pinpoint its direction and progress through the system and find out if it was within striking distance of Toronto on the date of the robbery."

While Yakabuski called the operator for the number of the Seaway Authority, Slat turned his attention to the strange bracelet he had seen on the wrist of the young woman visiting Clement Vanderhoof in his library.

CHAPTER ELEVEN

Once plans for the operation were set in motion the three conspirators moved quickly.

Farida bin Salam had little to do but wait for the call from Casey Vanderhoof then meet him for the taxi ride to the airport and the flights to Canada.

The young students had become infatuated with her and was attentive to her every whim, catering to her like a faithful retriever, satisfied with the slightest of smiles or a small pat on the hand for his reward.

She found his solicitude unnerving and would have preferred a man who acted in a more customary fashion, seizing her at the first opportunity and making mad passionate love to her. This man with his courtly demeanour did not force his attentions on her but seemed to want to serve her rather than possess her, a concept she found hard to swallow.

It wasn't that he didn't want her. He simply wanted to bide his time until she would come to him freely, offering pleasures he would not want to refuse. So far she had given no indication that she shared his feelings but supposed it was because of the control exerted over her by her father and brother. Because of that he decided that rather than compromise his position and hers he would wait for a more propitious time to declare his feelings to her. Perhaps when they were alone in Toronto he could make his move.

Farida knew her brother would expect her to do whatever was necessary to gain this man's confidence but her feelings for him were so confused that she decided to wait until the job was safely done before advancing her own cause with him, if that was what she really wanted.

Once she was safely on her way Abdel called Tony Royce and confirmed that he would be leaving that same evening for Montreal.

He left orders with the concierge that their rooms were to be left untouched until their return from attending a family emergency in their homeland, locked the suite and caught the minibus to the airport.

He had with him enough money for a six month sojourn in Canada, a Canadian visa obtained under the guise of his being an art student going to Toronto for research purposes and staying with family friends from Benghazi. This family had been recruited by Fra Pasquale's friends, paid well for their silence, and threatened with dire consequences should they ever disclose their visitor's identity.

Tony Royce left the same day, headed for Detroit and the Canadian border via New York City.

On the flight he was seated beside a young woman with vivid red hair who soon engaged him in conversation to pass the long hours.

She was an art student in New York City and had been in Europe to view some of the treasures of the Vatican Library before taking a side tour to Bologna to see the city's architecture.

She gave Royce her address and phone number in New York and he promised to call her if he was ever in that city.

He had to change flights in New York and had two hours to spare. He decided to walk outside the terminal for a breath of fresh air. The bedlam outside was staggering even to a traveller used to airports such as London's Heathrow and Gatwick. He was intrigued by the traffic chaos and the sheer pace and noise of the place and decided on the spot that since he had two days to get to Toronto to meet Abdel he had to see more of New York before he left.

Leaving his luggage to be transferred to Detroit where he would collect it later he caught a bus into Manhattan and dialled the number of the redhead from the plane and arranged to meet her for supper at a downtown eatery.

After dinner they wandered the streets of Greenwich Village listening to the music floating out of bars and cafes before wending their way to her tiny bedsit where she played Japanese flute melodies on her small record player before they made love on the living room floor, on the couch and again on the bed until they fell asleep exhausted as the new dawn lightened the sky.

About two hours later Tony Royce awoke, befuddled, not knowing where he was.

He looked at the girl, whose name he had learned was Sylvia, lying next to him in a tangle of sheets and remembered he needed to call Abdel in Toronto to confirm the time and place of their meeting.

He rose, dressed and walked into a tiny kitchen with a miniature herb garden growing in window boxes, the girl's best memory of her late mother, she had told him last night.

Finding an old-fashioned coffee percolator he made a brew, scrambled eggs and toasted bread before waking the girl.

As he worked in the kitchen he pondered his options. He had not planned to meet this young woman but she was a welcome diversion until he could get to Toronto and see Farida again. In a jam, he thought, she might provide a base for hiding in New York should anything go awry with their plans.

He still had to get to Toronto, five hundred long miles away. He toyed with the idea of buying a weapon in New York where they were readily available but discarded the idea.

He remembered he had to cross an international border and must not be found with a weapon in his possession. Besides, Abdel was buying weapons in Toronto, probably at this very minute.

He carried the breakfast into the bedroom and set it down beside the sleeping girl, tickling her toes with his free hand until she stirred, then awoke with a jolt, afraid he was an intruder, then remembering their evening of love and smiling, blue eyes flashing beneath her Titian hair.

As she reached for the food one of her ample breasts slipped out of her nightie. She blushed, then giggled. "Oh, for Chrissakes, you've seen more than that already, haven't you?" she said, leaving the breast out as she tucked into the breakfast, cramming toast into her mouth and spilling coffee onto the sheets.

After eating she grabbed her watch and shouted in panic that she was late for the first class of the morning. She asked if she could leave him alone for a few hours until she returned. He nodded, amused, and she was off like a shot, still dressing as she walked out of the front door.

Two minutes later he was in a pay phone on the street outside, calling the number in Toronto where he was to contact Abdel Salam.

Abdel told him there had been a hitch with the accommodations in Toronto. The Benghazi family had changed their mind at the last minute and he was now in a room at the Blue Lantern Motel on Lakeshore Boulevard West, close to the Humber River on the shore of Lake Ontario.

Other than that the news was positive. Farida was a guest at the Vanderhoof mansion and has already learned that the Krieghoff collection was kept in a private gallery atop the Corey Building about ten miles from where Abdel now was. She had also learned that surveillance of the gallery was minimal since access to the top floor of the building was restricted to a chosen few people. Because of this there were no electronic monitoring devices such as were used at public galleries.

The Spanish freighter La Coruna would be in Port Colborne harbour on Lake Erie, close to Buffalo, New York and about a hundred miles from Toronto by the end of the day.

Thanks to some Camorra connections from Italy, Salam had bought black market weapons and Farida had bought sports bags to carry them in.

All that remained was for Royce to get to Toronto and link up with Abdel at the Blue Lantern Motel about five miles from Port Credit.

Then Salam dropped the bombshell which rocked Tony Royce.

"Vanderhoof is hiring a private detective to guard his paintings. He seems to feel they are ripe for stealing. The butler said the detective's name is Mungo Slat and he will be invited to the mansion to be offered the job in the next day or so."

Tony Royce had just found out that his hostess of the previous evening was named Sylvia Slat and that she was from Toronto. Surely there couldn't be many people in Toronto with that unusual surname.

"So what about this Mungo Slat?" he asked. "Is he likely to be a problem?"

"Not at all. I have plans to eliminate him before he even knows what the job is all about," replied a cheerful Salam. "I already know his address and will be checking on where he works and his daily travel habits. When he gets home from work tomorrow we will be in his house and...kaboom."

"Kaboom," said Royce, sick at the stomach, angry at his foolishness and bad luck.

In a nearby restaurant he ordered coffee and sat to ponder his next move. He had to get out of New York and into Canada today. He decided to head back to the flat, pick up his hand luggage and be gone before the girl came home from her class.

As he quietly opened her front door he suddenly came face to face with a breathless Sylvia Slat.

"Thank God you're all right! I was worried you had gone for walk and been mugged or something. You could be lying in a hospital and I wouldn't know where you were."

Royce hugged her gently and asked why she was home so early.

"The damned bitch model called in sick at the last minute and now four of us won't finish our projects on time and will lose marks. I could strangle that cow!" she said with unexpected vehemence.

"So I have the day off and decided to spend it with you. Let's go back to bed, Tony," she pleaded, unashamed lust in her eyes, rubbing her body against his.

As he watched her undress Tony Royce knew he had to kill her.

"Are you coming or are you just going to sit there looking into space all day?" Her teasing voice jolted him back to the moment.

Slowly, reluctantly, he undressed and climbed into the bed beside her. As she stroked his skin he began to stir with longings and decided to postpone her death until they had made love one more time. "Who knows how long it will be before I get another chance?" he asked himself.

Afterwards, while they lying peacefully in each others' arms, he slipped the pillow from under his head and held it firmly over her face. As she kicked and struggled he held it there until finally her thrashings stopped. He removed it and checked her pulse and breathing. There were no signs of life.

"There, Mr Mungo Bloody Slat. Let's see how you like that one for openers," he hissed through his teeth as he dressed.

Before leaving he wrote a note in large looping strokes which he attached to the outside of the girl's front door.

"Please do not disturb. I'm working on a major project."

He attached the note with masking tape from a roll under the kitchen sink, dropped the key on the table and walked out with his bag, making sure the lock snapped shut behind him.

He left the building by the back stairs and wore dark sunglasses. Two blocks away he hailed a yellow cab and was on his way to the Port Authority bus terminal at 8th Avenue and 42nd Street in Manhattan. His plan was to catch a bus to Buffalo, enter Canada at the nearest crossing point and proceed to Toronto. The luggage in Detroit would have to be abandoned.

With any luck the girl's body wouldn't be discovered until he was well out of the country. Then he would have to deal with her father in Toronto. Keeping it in the family, he thought grimly.

After a short wait at Gate 68 he boarded the bus and in half an hour was out of the city on his way towards Albany, the state capital.

The sun shone on his face through the window and he started to relax, realizing that he had, for the moment, escaped detection for the murder of Sylvia Slat.

CHAPTER TWELVE

The first leg of the journey lasted two and half hours.

Royce had to share a seat with a tall, young black man holding a huge ghetto blaster across his knees. From time to time his fingers fiddled longingly with the controls and once he looked at Royce as if pleading for permission to turn it on.

Royce had an almost pathological hatred of popular music, a hatred which made him quite bloody minded at times. He scowled at the innocent man and at the radio and turned his face to look out of the window.

If at that moment he had wanted to listen to any music it would have been Shostakovich#s 11th Symphony, subtitled 1905, which depicted the slaughter of quietly protesting Russian peasants in front of the Czar's palace in St. Petersburg, the summary shooting of hundreds of them being the precursor to the Russian Revolution of 1917 and the eventual downfall of the house of Romanov.

In Albany, where he saw unkempt men leaning against run-down buildings, drinking liquor from bottles scarcely concealed inside brown paper bags, the bus stopped for a rest break.

Afraid at first to get off the bus and risk drawing attention to his presence, Royce had eventually to yield to the insistent urgings of his bladder and alit to seek the toilets.

When he returned with a coffee and a bagel he found his erstwhile companion had moved to sit beside a young woman and the two were listening to the now softly playing radio.

For a few moments he enjoyed the space of an empty seat beside him but in a few minutes a large man with two days' worth of stubble on his face plopped into the seat. He rummaged in a shopping bag for a book, stuffed the bag under the seat in front, crossed his legs, leaned towards the aisle and was soon engrossed in what looked like a detective novel.

It was a short haul from Albany to Schenectady through some of the most beautiful scenery Royce had ever viewed.

He found Schenectady a delightful town with clean buildings and the peaceful air of a community untouched by the hustle and bustle of the larger cities. The bus passed a large church and Royce smiled at the sign which proclaimed it as Second Presbyterian Church. It was a sign of local honesty, he thought, that they had chosen not to compete with the thousands of First Presbyterian churches which dotted the continent.

After a brief halt at the bus station, where he noticed the diner was called Terminal Lunch and decided not to get coffee there, his companion left and was replaced by a small man in green trousers who stared fixedly ahead all the way while Royce dozed briefly on the route to Syracuse.

He awoke groggily and saw the man beside him focussed intently on the road ahead as if he were driving the bus from back there. He would have stared a lot more fixedly, Royce thought, if he knew the passenger beside him had strangled a woman in New York City that same morning.

Slightly before Syracuse the bus swung off the highway into Utica, whose sign proclaimed it as the city which "has it all". The downtown looked unimposing but the bus station had a toilet and Royce was glad to use it.

At Syracuse the bus stopped for a half hour meal break and the driver was replaced by another. There were police officers in the bus station but they seemed more interested in eating than in Tony Royce who shrugged down in his seat to avoid being seen.

After Syracuse the bus stopped in Rochester, home of the Kodak company, then suddenly he was on the final leg, headed for Buffalo on the shore of Lake Erie, his body aching from the journey, his mind racing in preparation for the crossing into Canada.

On the outskirts of Buffalo in a suburb whose sign announced it as Depew N.Y., he saw a large factory with an airfield and the name Italcottero on a blue neon sign atop the buildings.

He recognized it as a branch plant of the massive helicopter manufacturer in Turin and tucked away the location and the thruway exit number in his mind for future reference.

Within minutes the bus was pulling into the depot at Buffalo and the driver was announcing a half hour rest break before it proceeded to Erie in Pennsylvania and the Ohio cities of Euclid, Ashtabula and Cleveland with connections to points west.

Royce alighted and inquired at the terminal about buses to Toronto, being told the next one was leaving in thirty minutes via Fort Erie, taking the Queen Elizabeth Way through St. Catharines and Hamilton.

He bought a ticket, found a hamburger stand and ate his evening meal to kill the time.

When he boarded the bus he smiled quietly. All he had to do was sit tight and in a couple of hours he would be in Toronto.

The bus wove its way through the streets of Buffalo and onto the Peace Bridge which spanned the Niagara River where it rose out of Lake Erie on its way down over Niagara Falls into Lake Ontario.

At the other end of the bridge the bus suddenly left the main roadway and drove around the side of a building emblazoned with the sign Canada Customs.

Fortunately the stop was brief and cursory. The official looked at his passport, asked how long he planned to stay in Canada, then nodded him back to the bus where he sank, trembling with relief, into his seat.

Two hours later he was in Toronto where he called the Blue Lantern Motel, received directions and was soon in a taxi speeding down the Gardiner Expressway and onto Lakeshore Boulevard, the waters of Lake Ontario on his left.

In the motel Salam quickly told the two girls in his bed they would have to leave, regretting his partner's impending arrival when he was in the throes of such pleasures.

He gave each one a $50 bill and spent five minutes cleaning the room and dressing to welcome his partner.

When Royce walked in the smell of perfume almost made him puke.

"You've had women in here, haven't you, you old bugger?" he said as he hugged Salam.

"One has to pass the time somehow in this cold hole. Besides, women are my hobby and loving their bodies is what I do best," smiled Salam., puffing on a Turkish cigarette.

"So how is Farida?" Royce asked, trying to keep his voice casual.

"She's doing her job and keeping that rich boy occupied as ordered."

The reply annoyed Royce who had mental images of her lithe body in bed with the pasty-skinned Casey Vanderhoof.

He wasn't far off the mark in his imaginings.

At that moment Farida and Casey were enjoying a shower together in the Rosedale mansion where she had promised to teach him things he had never before imagined, let alone seen or done.

There was no question that she was assiduous in following her brother's orders.

To best achieve her aim of gathering intelligence for her brother and Tony Royce she had decided to seduce Casey and occupy his mind and body so completely that he would forget his natural caution and tell her what she wanted to know.

They had been left alone for the evening and, after dinner served by the new butler, who withdrew discreetly, she made her play for the inexperienced young man.

She had prepared for the siege by dressing in an iridescent gold sheath gown which revealed deep cleavage and well-rounded breasts. The dress clung to her slim hips and thighs ands glittered and glimmered when she walked, which she did in a manner no normal man could possibly resist.

Highly-piled shining black hair, exquisite make-up on an unblemished face, subtle perfume on her wrists and neck completed a package designed to lure Casey Vanderhoof to a fate much better than death.

By the time dessert was served, he was hers.

By the time the last wine was sipped, she was beginning to be his, surprising herself by her reaction.

This man was completely different from the men of the Dursa tribe of her desert homeland. They saw women as necessary for breeding future generations on and for helping with the menial tasks without having any say in the major decisions which were taken by a council of men.

This man showed gentle, genuine affection and when he made

love to her he raised the physical union onto a mystical plane which left her breathless and awestruck.

By the time dawn came they were both exhausted and happier than either had ever been before. As light crept through the curtains she watched his boyish sleeping face and began to believe she really could love him forever.

In his suite down the massive hallway Clement Vanderhoof was already stirring. He always rose early and he had a lot to do that day.

He had returned to a darkened house late last night and had gone straight to his rooms. He would tell Casey all about the Caribbean hotel deal at breakfast.

After a short shower he re-entered the bedroom to find the butler had left a carafe of coffee and the early editions of The Tribune, The Globe & Mail and the Wall Street Journal, his usual morning reading.

He settled into a large armchair with his coffee, put his glasses on and scanned the dailies. There was nothing in them of importance to his empire.

Disgruntled, he set them aside and sat for a moment in deep thought.

His eye rested on a photograph of his late wife, Margaret Corey, daughter of a Presbyterian minister from Guelph, the woman whose maiden name he had used for his newspaper chain. She had always abhorred his indifference to religion but loved him in spite of that for his other attributes.

Now she was gone, carried off by that damned cancer for which there had been no cure despite the hundreds of thousands of dollars he had donated to research.

His thoughts drifted to the day their son Casey was born. In most respects the boy favoured his mother and was more like her than Clement liked to admit.

Where Clement was acquisitive, bold in business and a tyrant in controlling his staff, Casey showed little enthusiasm for the world of money, more interested in art than in the cold, hard cash his father worshipped.

At least that interest in art could be converted into money, Clement mused, if one were to corner the market on a certain artist or genre.

But in the end even that interest comes with its own set of problems.

You spend years amassing a collection of original works, increasing your net worth as you enjoy the hunt, the acquisition and the knowledge that you have exclusive access to them, only to become a target for those wanting to steal what you have worked for.

The theft of the Krieghoffs had been a blow to the Clement Vanderhoof pride and it hurt like bloody hell.

As one of the sharks in the business world he prided himself on a keen sense of impending danger. He seemed to be able to spot problems weeks ahead of his competitors and it was that insight which had caused him to contact police chief Andy Hocking to ask for the name of a private investigator who would best be able to prevent the theft of his paintings.

Hocking had no hesitation in passing on the name of Mungo Slat.

The disappointment he had felt when he met Slat had done little to dispel his worries. He felt the man was past his prime, sinking into middle age as a useless, washed-up former professional. That first impression had been slightly changed when he saw Slat in action in his library, raising the stakes on the deal and showing a degree of intelligence and self confidence belied by his scruffy appearance.

All the same, he sighed, he would be lucky to see his paintings again. He didn't buy Slat's shipping theory but had nothing better to offer, his instincts remaining strangely silent for once.

For the first time in his life he felt dirty, raped, sullied by the theft and he didn't like it.

Someone had actually penetrated his sanctus sanctorum, filched his most precious possessions and got clean away. He hated that and wasn't about to suffer those feelings much longer.

That was why he had promised Mungo Slat (where did he get that outlandish name?) twice his fee to solve the matter within seventy two hours. He had already decided that if Slat failed he would resort to more drastic, probably illegal means of getting his own paintings back.

For a man used to being very objective about people and business dealings, even in his relationship with his wife and son, Clement Vanderhoof was far from objective about the loss of his paintings.

In a way he admired Slat for being able to see the situation objectively, even humorously at times, while working out a plausible solution free from the angst Vanderhoof was suffering this morning.

He reached for the coffee carafe, glancing at his watch, annoyed to see it was already seven and he had passed two full hours reading and musing.

"Not my style at all. I must be getting old," he muttered as he reached for his clothes.

At that same time Casey and Farida were untwining themselves lethargically from their sleepy embrace and soon were passionately making love, this time more deliberately as the newly confident Casey rose to the occasion, driving Farida to new heights of satisfaction.

Finally, sated, they rose and showered together in his suite then parted, she for her room and the toiletries she needed, he to call the butler and order a full English breakfast.

When the pair entered the dining room, twenty minutes later they were surprised to find an ebullient Clement Vanderhoof waiting for them, his plate filled with bacon, sausages, mushrooms, tomatoes, beans and eggs, a rack of toast in front of him.

Once their plates were filled he launched into details of his highly successful hotel deal, then presented Casey with a list of instructions for the day, a list so long it was apparent he would have to leave Farida to amuse herself for most of the day.

That was exactly what she wanted to hear. She desperately needed to contact Abdel but had wavered because of her involvement with Casey and out of fear the butler or some other member of staff might be eavesdropping on her calls, possibly at Clement's behest.

The minute breakfast was over, a meal during which she nibbled a piece of toast and drank a single cup of coffee while the two men wolfed down great quantities of food, the twinkle in Clement's eye betraying his suspicion of the reason for his son's newfound appetite, she set out for her room where she changed into street clothes and asked the butler to arrange for a car and chauffeur to drop her off at a downtown department store, collecting her again at three that afternoon.

The minute she was out of the car, a few blocks from city hall, she headed for a bank of telephones at the subway entrance and called the Blue Lantern motel.

An ecstatic Tony Royce answered and arranged for the three to meet for lunch so they could fill her in on their progress and listen to any news she may have to offer.

Over the meal they laid out their plans while Farida, starting to be of two minds about the mission because of her new affection for Casey, listened uneasily.

She did say she thought she should leave the Vanderhoof mansion while Casey was occupied and join them on their assault on the Corey building. They told her she was needed where she was since by diverting the Vanderhoofs she was creating the perfect opportunity for them to get inside the building and steal the paintings.

Royce told her he would be casing the building that afternoon, watching staff movement, finding the best way to get in and out quickly and unnoticed.

At the same time Abdel would phone the captain of the La Coruna. She should be laid up in Port Colborne by now with welding and other work starting on the hydraulic winching equipment, work that would go on all day and well into the night.

Since the Seaway system operated around the clock the ship could sail as soon as the captain notified the authorities his repairs were completed and he wished to depart for Barcelona.

The call made, Abdel would rent a van, paying cash and using a false name, parking it close to the Corey building, ready to spirit the paintings out of the city and to the decks of the La Coruna.

Leaving Farida and her brother discussing family matters in the restaurant, Tony Royce walked the two hundred yards to the Corey building. Once again he was alone in a strange city.

Abdel told his sister he was concerned that she leave very soon for Bologna. She assured him she was being extremely careful, arousing no suspicions, and that she and Casey would be returning to Italy to resume their studies within a week.

She had done her part by finding out where the paintings were kept, which floor they were on and she even had some idea about their protection, or lack of it as it turned out.

She still had one important function to perform. She needed to decoy the Vanderhoofs away from any stray visit to the gallery by staying on as their house guest.

To avoid being conspicuous, the three had eaten in the basement restaurant of the department store in full view of thousands of shoppers who would think nothing of three young people sitting together chatting animatedly in a foreign language, an everyday sight in the cosmopolitan city which Toronto had become.

After lunch Farida entered the store for some small purchases to justify her visit, then waited for the car and headed back to Ashwarren Grove.

Within an hour Abdel Salam had rented a small, white panel van and left it in the cavernous parking lot underneath the city hall.

That done, he found a telephone in a secluded corner of the city hall grounds and placed a call to El Serpiente, captain of the La Coruna.

When Tony Royce arrived in front of the Corey building he was astonished at its size.

Sprawling over two city blocks the huge edifice with windows of spun gold glass reeked of opulence, putting some nearby taller bank towers to shame by its splendour.

Once that exterior was penetrated, however, the interior was all business and far from luxurious. Corey executives did not loll on padded chairs and possess keys to the executive toilets. If you worked for Clement Vanderhoof you worked hard and you worked long and you earned every penny he reluctantly paid you.

Royce sauntered into the lobby and stared at a bronze statue of a dollar sign, a fitting emblem in an enterprise whose god it was.

A security guard in a blue uniform sat behind a lighted map of the building which showed all the tenants of its twenty five storeys by name and suite number.

A continuous hustle and bustle of people flowed in and out of the bank of elevators which comprised the centre core of the building.

To the right of the elevators Royce noticed a back door where people came in and went out to an adjoining street. Beside it was a smaller door with the word Concourse written on it. Through that door people came and went carrying bags of food and cups of coffee.

He walked across the hall to the lighted map, testing to see if the security guard would challenge him. The man was reading a pocket novel, oblivious to the throng.

Standing and reading the map, Royce noticed that Clement Vanderhoof's suite was on the twenty-fifth floor. He also noticed that the elevators only had numbers to the twenty-fourth floor and that floors twenty two to twenty four were occupied by Corey Newspapers.

Seeing a procession of young women, whom he took to be secretaries, heading for the concourse door, he followed them through it and down a steep, narrow staircase, walking crabwise to allow room for the line of ascending people with trays of food in their hands.

A door at the bottom led into a massive underground shopping concourse with signs pointing the way to Union Station, a mile to the south. He realized he could actually walk from where he was to the station all the way underground through shops and offices without ever stepping outside into the fresh air. Had he realized how bitterly cold the wind from Lake Ontario blows up the canyons of Bay Street in January and February he would have been lavish in his praise of the architects who had the foresight to build this remarkable structure.

He strolled along the smorgasbord of earthly delights, amused at the sight of slim-waisted secretaries tucking into huge platefuls of food before scurrying back to their desks for an afternoon of drudgery.

Worried that Farida may have made a mistake in her description of the building, he sauntered back into the lobby and checked the legend on the sign once again.

He already knew in his heart that if she had made a mistake, either innocently or deliberately because of what he feared were her growing feelings for young Vanderhoof, he would kill her, and her brother with her, if he had to. Should he make a mistake his life would be worth nothing at their hands, so explicit were their instructions from Fra Pasquale Ferragami.

He figured there had to be a special, unlisted elevator, linking the top two floors of the building.

That meant there had to be a special pass key or coded device to gain entrance.

There was security in place, after all. How could Farida have missed that vital piece of information? She had visited the building with Casey and should have been aware of it. Maybe she had been taken to the twenty-fourth floor and led around in circles before being taken to the special elevator to the top.

That was it, he told himself. She had been duped. Security had been tighter than they imagined.

Chewing on that gristly problem he walked outside the back door for a breath of fresh air.

He dare not spend too much time in the atrium for fear of being recognized by the security guard.

A small concrete patio led down into an alleyway behind the building linking two cross streets. Two bicycles and a motorbike were chained to a lamp standard in the alley.

A stroll to the end of the building showed him Bay Street, Toronto's financial thoroughfare, running north and south. At the other end the building stretched towards Osgoode Hall where budding lawyers were trained.

The walked back inside, entered an elevator and noticed the floors were numbered one to twenty four but there was no thirteenth floor since that number was considered unlucky by architects and builders.

He pressed twenty four and the doors slid silently shut. The ride, unimpeded by stops at intermediate floors, lasted exactly twenty seconds. He also noticed there were no lighted displays over the elevator doors telling people where the machine was at any given time. That was a plus for the heist.

As the doors opened, Royce stepped into a narrow hallway with wood panelling on the walls and deep gold pile carpet underfoot. Two more elevator doors were in the hallway and, far to the right, a solid wooden door without number or identification markings.

To his left a receptionist sat behind a huge electronic typewriter, filing her nails while chatting on the phone to one of her friends or co-workers.

On the wall behind her hung an oil painting of a man in his early fifties with a solemn yet sly look on his ruddy-cheeked face. It was Clement Vanderhoof, founder of the empire on whose property he was trespassing.

Before the secretary could see him he ducked back into the elevator, which was still open behind him, scanning the hallway for signs of an entrance to the top floor.

Then he saw it.

Tucked into a corner, looking more like a cupboard than an elevator, was a small lift built to transport no more than two people at once, and preferably just one.

Beside the door was a small, round, brass disk with a keyhole in the middle. This was the way to the inner sanctum. His gut instinct to reconnoiter had been correct.

As he stared at the small door, a large wooden door at the end of the hallway opened and another security guard in blue uniform with bright shirt and black tie emerged carrying a bag of mail which he dropped beside the secretary's desk. He did not seem to notice Royce.

He walked past the elevator and towards the small door in the corner, pulling from his pocket a small key on a long silver chain attached to his broad black belt. He inserted the key into the lock and turned it once to the right.

The door slid silently open to reveal a small compartment with rosewood paneled walls. Halfway up the walls was a burnished brass handrail. The floor was covered with deep grey pile carpet.

The security guard entered the elevator, reached for a button and the door closed.

Royce closed the door to his own lift and descended to the foyer.

He had noticed that the guard was elderly, with white hair, and that he was unarmed. He did not carry a mobile radio or phone.

Royce walked across the street and bought a hot dog and coffee from one of the perennial street vendors who clutter the area around Nathan Philips Square in front of the city hall. Finding a copy of The Tribune stuffed under a bench he scanned it as he ate.

There was nothing of interest in it so he stuffed it back under the bench

By the time the coffee was finished, the cup hurled into a garbage container, he was starting to shiver from the cold wind blowing up from Lake Ontario.

"I wonder why anyone chooses to live in this godforsaken climate. They should have left it to the Indians and gone somewhere warmer," he muttered, shrugging his neck down inside his coat collar.

He crossed the street and walked around the Corey building perimeter once again looking for entrances he may have missed on his first sweep. There were none.

He was worried that if he stayed too long he would be noticed by the police patrols which regularly patrolled the area, their yellow cars looking like New York taxicabs. He needed to stay unnoticed but he still had to find some way of getting to that elusive top floor. He had about two hours until the doors closed at five, his watch showed him.

At a little after four a van drove up and stopped at the end of the alley behind the building.

A crew of cleaners in navy blue uniforms, carrying handfuls of folded black plastic garbage bags, climbed out of the van and walked inside the building.

"That's it! If Abdel and I can join the cleaners we can gain access to the top floor and at the same time to bags to carry the paintings out in. Brilliant!" he said to himself, smiling at the good fortune.

The concept of using the cleaners grew as he circumnavigated the building once more. By the time the theft of the paintings was discovered he and Salam would be well on their way Port Colborne. The cleaners would be the first suspected and would be closely questioned, allowing more time for their escape.

As he decided he had seen enough and was about to walk out into Bay Street he saw a man wearing a charcoal grey suit emerge from the back door of the building. He had a black briefcase attached to his right wrist by handcuffs.

"So that's how they do it! The crafty buggers do their banking by sending out a flunkey handcuffed to the money. I'll bet my last dollar the only one with a key to those handcuffs is the bank manager himself. Not, bad, Mr Vanderhoof, not bad at all. But still not good enough to prevent what I am going to do to your finances once I get those paintings back to Sorrento."

Ted Reynaldson, handcuffed to the briefcase, crossed the square, walked slowly down the alley and disappeared around a corner. Royce was about to follow him when the back door opened again and he jumped quickly around the corner of the wall. He was just in the nick of time. Casey Vanderhoof, his erstwhile companion in Bologna, walked outside accompanied by the same elderly security guard Royce had seen on the twenty-fourth floor. The guard was carrying a courier pouch.

The two men walked around the same corner as Reynaldson, taking the same direction. Royce wondered if the guard was employed as a personal bodyguard for Casey Vanderhoof but then realized from his age that the opposite was more likely and that Casey could be guarding the guard. That thought amused him and a brief smile flitted across his features as he set out to follow the pair at a safe distance, using the teeming pedestrian traffic for cover to avoid being spotted.

He had little trouble staying close in the throng of shoppers and sightseers who barged across the street regardless of the colour of the traffic lights, displaying the manners of city dwellers everywhere.

As they passed beneath the canopied awning of a building being renovated, Casey suddenly stopped in his tracks, turned and stared behind him as if aware he was being followed.

Royce ducked into a store doorway until his prey resumed his walk.

At the entrance of a branch of the International Bank of Canada the elderly guard bid his companion goodbye and entered the building.

Royce watched from his doorway as Casey Vanderhoof waited at the kerb for a traffic light to change before striding across the street to the entrance to the Toronto Club which, Royce could tell from its stately facade, was the haunt of the rich and mega-rich who would use its premises for clandestine business meetings, political maneuvering and other affairs among the brandy, cigars and blessed, if expensive, privacy.

Once the door closed behind Casey, Royce sauntered unobtrusively past the front of the bank through whose plate glass windows he could see Ted Reynaldson just leaving the manager's office, no longer chained to the briefcase, nodding to the elderly guard who was sitting outside the office in a chair.

As Reynaldson walked out of the bank the guard entered the office at a signal from the manager.

Royce watched as the manager, a short, stout, pink, fawning man unwilling to allow any other staff member at his branch to wait on the personal minions of the great Vanderhoof, who sat on the bank's board of governors and without whose accounts their stature and profits would be greatly diminished, ushered the guard inside and closed the door.

Less than a minute later Royce saw the guard leave the office, folding a receipt for the contents of the pouch he had carried and slipping it into his shirt pocket. He and the manager were laughing at some joke, doubtless told by the banker as part of his ongoing campaign to keep Vanderhoof's staff happy and maintain the account at his branch.

As the old man walked slowly towards the front door of the bank Royce could see the fatigue on his face. From the bulbous nose with its red swollen purple veins he also noticed that the old man liked a nip or two of what his grandmother used to call "the cure". This was his cue and he was quick to act on it.

As the guard opened the door Royce launched himself into the entrance and crashed into the old man, knocking him clean off his feet.

In a flash he was there to help him back to his feet, apologising profusely in the most clipped of British accents, claiming to have been bumped by a shopper with an armful of parcels as he walked around the corner beside the bank.

He helped the oldster dust himself off and, taking him by the elbow over his mild objections, directed him through the door of a small pub next door to the bank. There he insisted on buying him a meal and a couple of drinks to help him recover from the shock to his system and by way of apology for his own part in it.

He asked the man his name, without revealing his own, and learned he was called Basil James.

Despite the suddenness of their meeting James took an instant liking to the young Englishman. Originally from England himself, he had been in Canada for more than sixty years, arriving as an orphan from a Dr Barnardo home in Sussex, sent into the provinces to make something of himself and gain the head start denied him by his natural parents.

Now in his early seventies, Basil James lived in a small apartment near the city centre which was within walking distance of the job which was his mainstay and helped eke out his meagre pension.

Royce learned all this during the first pint of beer which Basil downed like a trooper, to Royce's amusement as he sipped slowly at a soda water with a wedge of lime in it.

The old man said he had never married. He had worked at a variety of jobs all across Canada since running away from his first foster home on a farm near Gatineau, Quebec, where the skinflint farmer and his wife beat him, starved him and treated him like a mute slave since he spoke no French and they no English.

After spells on the transcontinental railroad as a gang foreman then later a train conductor he had stopped off on the prairies one night, missed his train due to drunkenness and was fired. In desperation he had crept into the YMCA in Moose Jaw, Saskatchewan and next day found work as a newspaper vendor at the corner of Main and Fairford streets there.

It was there that he had met Clement Vanderhoof, new owner of the local daily newspaper which he sold.

Vanderhoof had an eye out for hardworking people who could enhance his profits and the sight of Basil James at his stand in every kind of foul weather the prairies could throw at him eventually led to the vendor being offered a full-time job in the circulation department of the Prairie Advance.

Vanderhoof had no idea he had a drinker on his hands and, worse still, an employee for whom organisation and supervisory skills were a complete mystery. Bill James was an absolute disaster at the job.

In spite of that the normally ruthless Vanderhoof remained impressed by the simple dedication and loyalty of the man and decided to take him with him when he opened his new corporate offices in Toronto.

He figured he needed a factotum who would do what he was asked without question and could be relied on to keep his mouth shut.

If asked, he could probably never explain to himself, or to anyone else for that matter, his rare episode of benevolence towards this young man in dire straits but he knew he would give him a job until he was either unwilling or unable to work for his keep.

So Basil James arrived at the ivory tower of the Corey Building as security guard and personal messenger for his crusty benefactor. He even had a uniform to go with the position.

The uniform was the real clincher for him. For years he had mourned his loss of the railway conductor's uniform. Now here he was, decked out in navy-blue slacks, blue shirt and black tie. He even had a peaked hat with the Corey corporate crest on it. Best of all for his British pride, he even had epaulettes on his shoulders.

He had worked in the building for thirty years when he met Tony Royce. He was called in for odd shifts and at odd hours as Vanderhoof demanded, rarely off work on weekends or holidays yet always wearing a faithful smile like an obedient dog whose sole reward would be a bone or a pat on the head.

As Royce plied Basil James with drinks and a plate of steak and kidney pie the information poured out in torrents between bites and sips. When the old man faltered Royce invented adventures of his own, adding enough drinks to sink the Spanish Armada.

The trip to the bank had been Basil's last job for the day. He felt obligated to the young man who had saved him from what he believed had been a brush with death in the bank doorway.

Two hours later the booze began to get the better of the old man and his eyes started to flicker, close, then pop suddenly open again, accompanied by slurred mutterings of "I'm awake. I'm up."

Two drinks later he pitched face forward onto the table top and started snoring his brains out.

Slowly and silently Royce moved to Basil's side, on his knees, and gently started to remove the elevator key from the ring on the chain attached to his belt.

Once the old man stirred, flicked at his side impotently as if disturbed by a mosquito, then lapsed back into a stupour while Royce held his breath.

On the third attempt Royce finally unclipped the entire chain from the old man's belt and slowly slid the chain, ring and keys into his hand.

He walked to the toilets and called Salam, explaining his lateness and telling of his good fortune. Then he walked into the street without paying the bill, leaving Basil James to face the music when he finally came round.

While Royce was having his afternoon adventure, Salam had been tracking the movements of one Mungo Slat.

Later, over supper at a restaurant in Mimico with bad food and high prices, they compared notes.

Salam now knew where Slat lived and had seen the house, saying it appeared empty for most of the evening except for an old woman he could see through the front window wandering around aimlessly looking half drunk.

They decided they would call on Slat that night, eliminate him in a surprise attack, and travel to the Corey Building where, armed with the elevator key, they would join the ranks of cleaners, steal the paintings, drive to Port Colborne and install them on board the La Coruna.

Then Royce would find his way back to New York City for his return flight to Italy while Salam would drop off the rental van in Montreal and fly from there to Tripoli and the lands of his father. Farida would return to Bologna with Casey Vanderhoof, then slip away to her native land shortly afterwards.

They left the restaurant and Salam directed Royce to the Troy Street house where they waited in the darkness of his kitchen for Mungo Slat to return home from the salt mines of divorce investigations.

That was when they heard the clumping of heavy feet on the stairs.

That was when Marge McCracken went to meet he maker.

CHAPTER THIRTEEN

The murder of the old woman had infuriated Tony Royce.

He was quite prepared to eliminate Mungo Slat as a necessary part of the operation. Now it had all gone badly wrong and the man they wanted to kill was not only alive but would be on the hunt for them.

Ever since his brief sojourn with Sylvia Slat in New York City he had known he would have to kill her father if they were to have any hope of stealing the Krieghoffs and making a clean escape.

Now they were on the verge of removing the paintings and Slat was not dead. That was a complication neither of them had foreseen.

Royce was angry that Abdel Salam had botched his surveillance of Slat's home. Neither could have known that Slat would ask his landlady to rescue his burning supper while they lay in wait.

They decided to travel into the city on the GO train and bumped into Slat in the doorway of the train, though neither one recognized him.

They had seen a man staring at them as they say by the window and had moved away to avoid recognition. Only after the train was pulling out the station did Royce remember the man's face from a photograph in Sylvia's apartment in New York. They had missed a second opportunity to kill the one they were hunting.

Worse still, he had seen them and would be able to recognize them again if their paths crossed.

That series of near hits was too much for Tony Royce. He decided to part company with the inept Salam at the first opportunity, even if it meant he would never see Farida again.

His rage became explosive and he wanted to strike out and hurt someone, anyone, to avenge this humiliating series of failures, especially the murder of an old woman.

He left the train at Mimico and, followed by an abject Salam, walked angrily back to their motel where they heard on the radio that the old woman's body had been discovered and police were asking for witnesses to come forward and aid their investigation.

That frightened Salam. He said he would not speak in English any more and demanded to be taken to the airport and put on the next flight to Italy after calling Farida so she could get to the airport and travel with him.

"Sure, chickenshit!" Royce shouted. "You come here with a scheme to make millions, drag me into it through some goddam friar at the university, tempt me with your sister, drag me halfway around the world, kill an innocent old woman, then you want to hightail it out of here and run back to your bloody desert leaving me to pick up the pieces. No way, Jose! You started this and we will bloody well finish it or I'll kill you myself."

He took the revolver from his jacket pocket, clicked the safety catch and pointed it at Salam.

"You'll get this right between the eyes if you so much as think about not finishing this job. Got that?"

Salam, pale and sweating, nodded his agreement and the gun was lowered.

For the next hour they planned their strategy as peace returned.

Shortly after midnight they called a taxi, packed their bags and in less than half an hour were outside the Corey building.

In the toilet of an all-night coffee shop they changed into cleaner's overalls and caps, rags hanging from their back pockets concealing the revolvers they carried there.

Each had a balaclava in his pocket and they wore gym shoes to muffle the sounds. Their watches were synchronised to the second.

They dumped their clothing behind a bin in the alley and strolled to the back of the building where they found a sea of activity with cleaners coming and going with full and empty garbage bags. They walked inside and found another security guard sitting at the desk in the lobby ogling the Page 3 girl in the early edition of The Sun while listening to a football match from Los Angeles on the radio. He looked up, nodded at them, and returned to his pursuits.

Cleaning staff came and went at all hours of the night and he knew he could recognize a couple of cleaners at ten paces if he had to. They all looked pretty much alike.

Besides which, there had never been an incident in this building in the ten years he had worked there so why would this particular night be any different?

Royce and Salam walked briskly to the bank of elevators, stepped into an empty one and pressed the button for the twenty-fourth floor.

When the cabin halted they tiptoed across the plush carpeting towards the narrow door which housed the private elevator to the penthouse.

Royce was sure there was nobody on the floor above. He had checked the lights as he approached the building and noticed they were only lit from the tenth floor down. That meant the cleaners had already finished the top floors, working their way downwards to the foyer and then to the concourse beneath the building where they would end their shift at seven in the morning with coffee and pastries from an early restaurant down there. This was about the same hour that the first conscientious executives would stumble into the concourse for cups of coffee and bagels in paper bags which they would consume at their desks as the work day began.

For some the early start was vital for dealing with colleagues in other time zones, especially in Europe and the United Kingdom where it was already lunch time. Others simply wanted to beat the rush-hour traffic by starting earlier and leaving earlier in the afternoon for a more hassle-free journey.

In front of the small door Royce took out the key he had filched from the drunken Basil James, inserted it into the lock and turned it to the right. The door slid silently open and they stepped inside. Within a few seconds the door hissed shut. He looked for the control button but there was none. The weight of their feet on the floor triggered sensors which started the elevator and it slowly started to rise without their having to do anything.

By the time they reached the top floor beads of sweat were visible on Salam's brow. He was worried that there might be someone waiting for them up there.

Royce, on the other hand, was icy cool, almost shivering from the cold and the excitement.

He felt this iciness in his veins when he was in complete control of his senses and alert to every danger. The coldness enabled him to act without panic or anxiety in times of stress. The need for a cool head and a steady hand had been instilled in him by his father who taught him the physical and mental attributes necessary for guerilla warfare.

He had no doubt they would succeed in their mission. His only doubt was whether he could trust Salam and his sister. The incident at the motel had convinced him Salam would cut and run at the first sign of danger.

He had already decided that if he had to he would kill Salam and leave his body in the art gallery, escaping alone with the paintings. Unfortunately he did not know where the van was parked, nor did he know the name of the ship they were to meet, or the name of its captain. He needed Salam alive until the paintings were safely stowed aboard that vessel and on their way to Italy.

Since his feelings for Farida had cooled considerably since her visit to the Vanderhoof mansion and the false information she had supplied about the security system he knew he would have little compunction in killing her, too, if she got in the way. He always harboured a secret fear that the brother and sister would kill him if they could once the job was done.

The lift slid to a silent halt and the door opened revealing the reception area.

Royce stepped out silently, revolver at the ready, finding the area in darkness other than a narrow shaft of dim light from inside the lift whose door was already starting to close.

He flicked on his pinpoint torch, making sure it shone away from the windows, and beckoned Salam out of the lift.

They had no detailed plan of the layout of the floor but Royce assumed it generally followed the contours of the floors beneath because of the central position of the elevator shaft.

They donned their balaclavas and surgical gloves and started a cautious tour, moving to their left, opening and closing each office door and cupboard as they went.

Most desks were bare, their mahogany surfaces shining richly in the narrow beam of the torch. Each had a brass plate on its front engraved with the name and title of the executive who worked behind it.

Three quarters of the way around the floor they opened the door to the corporate boardroom. Salam whistled softly when he saw the massive rosewood table with red leather chairs for the twenty directors, all family members and relatives of the Vanderhoofs.

He was amazed at the way in which wealth was flaunted in North America, an unfamiliar custom to a desert dweller whose wealthy father still lived in tents, counting his wealth in camels, sheep and goats. He did not know that his father was many times wealthier than Clement Vanderhoof thanks to his wartime connections and to the discovery of oil under his land for which he received considerable royalties about which he told nobody.

He was yanked from his reverie by a sudden tug on the sleeve. Royce grimly whispered to him that he should pick his feet up and get on with the job.

The followed the hallway until they reached an ornate door with the name Clement Vanderhoof affixed to it on a brass plaque.

It took a few second for the deft Abdel to open the locked door. Immediately to their left they saw another door which had to be the entrance to their mecca, the art gallery.

While Salam carried out a methodical search for hidden wires and microphones, Royce scanned the ceiling and walls for closed circuit television cameras and other hidden eyes which might alert the guard below, or the police directly, that there were intruders in the upper chamber.

They found nothing. Other than the secret lift, the gallery was unprotected.

"At least your sister was right about this part," Royce hissed to Salam.

In the middle of the first office was a huge desk carved from a single piece of hard wood imported from Africa. It had to weigh at least a ton, Royce guessed, and wondered if had been installed in the building before the roof was completed since it would have been impossible to fit it in the narrow lift they had used.

The shiny surface of the desk was bare except for a framed photograph of a middle-aged woman. From her eyes Royce knew she was Casey's mother, Clement Vanderhoof's late wife.

A tiny door off the office revealed a small en suite bathroom complete with shower and a wardrobe filled with expensive suits, new shirts still in their wrappings, and about a dozen pairs of brand new shoes, all the accoutrements a rich tycoon needed for a quick change of clothing in the privacy of his inner sanctum.

It had been said of Clement Vanderhoof that the greatest symbol of his wealth was his penchant for being able to wear a brand new shirt every day of his life. He never wore a shirt twice, never had one laundered, starched or pressed.

The rack of shirts and suits filled Royce with anger and disgust. While people down below on the streets were starving to death, their guts twisted in hunger and pain, this rich bastard was throwing away new shirts every day of the year. He wanted to shred them all in his anger and despair.

It never occurred to him that someone might well be reaping the benefit of what he saw as wanton waste.

Basil James, the old security guard, was one such beneficiary, as were many of his fellow drinkers at the Nag's Head where he sold them on for a fiver each, contrary to his instructions to drop them in the garbage hoppers in the basement.

It seemed very strange to Royce that in a city the size of Toronto there would be such an art gallery and that it would be so completely unprotected.

It had never occurred until very recently to Clement Vanderhoof that his paintings would be the focus of attention for thieves. If he had a safety concern it was that he might be kidnapped, grabbed on a city street and held for ransom, a ransom his relatives had already been sternly instructed not to pay no matter what the outcome.

All his protection devices were installed in his home and in his cars. He and Casey lived solitary lives, prisoners of their wealth, rarely appearing in public, always keeping their fingers on the pulse of the business world through a battery of highly secretive and intensely loyal intermediaries.

Their only social activity was in belonging to the Toronto Club and that was for business purposes since through their contacts there they heard every financial rumour at least an hour before it hit the streets.

Opening the door to the art gallery, Royce shone his torch on the list of paintings given to him by Fra Pasquale Ferragami in Bologna what seemed like weeks ago.

He fished six garbage sacks out of his pocket, filched from the supplies used by the cleaners still working below.

Not that there was much rubbish generated in the executive suites. All paper was meticulously shredded after use after an earlier scandal erupted into print and cost millions in damage limitation after an enterprising reporter from a rival company searched the company rubbish bags ands found incriminating evidence of crooked dealings there. The reporter was Regis Yakabuskli from The Tribune, the man Clement Vanderhoof hated for his success and admired begrudgingly for his talents and audacity.

Royce had no idea of the market value of the paintings on the list which he held in his left hand as he juggled the slippery plastic bags in his right.

They were worth $7.7 million on the open market but would fetch many times that amount on the black market when copied by Ferragami and his associates beneath the convent in Sorrento.

He squinted at the names on the sheet, hoping he could recognize the works which corresponded to them.

"What if this guy has all the names memorized and hasn't put little plaques under them like they do at public art galleries?" he asked himself. Mistakes could be costly and would be repaid with interest by the friar and his Camorra contacts.

Inside the door they repeated the process of searching for trip wires, electronic eyes and other devices which would alert the guard to their presence. There were none.

Royce allowed his pinpoint beam of light to traverse the walls and hover over each painting. He whistled at their number and obviously pristine quality.

The reds, golds and oranges used to depict the Canadian forests in autumn glowed softly under the tiny light and he felt his skin tingle at the experience of seeing the works of a master for the first time.

Better yet, each painting had its name and the year it was painted on a small embossed plaque attached to the bottom of its frame.

He smiled at Salam and tugged off his balaclava to get some

respite from the warmth of the building.

His partner was giggling at the ease with which they had been able to penetrate this hidden treasure trove. It was not his first assignment for Dottore Ferragami, unlike his novice accomplice with the fast gun. He recalled working much harder to disarm protective devices in some galleries they had raided.

He, too, was amazed at the glow of the paintings under the tiny light. They seemed as freshly burnished as if they were still wet, painted that same afternoon by a ghostly master at the command of a secretive and acquisitive patron.

It was difficult to imagine that the painter of these jewels had died in 1872 at the relatively young age of fifty five. His ghost must stalk this gallery at night, paint brush in hand, constantly refreshing the paintings.

The Krieghoffs lined the gallery walls which was a simple rectangle. In the centre of the floor were huge display cases containing delicate jade and ivory carvings from China, wooden carvings from Africa and soapstone carvings by the Inuit craftspeople of the Canadian Arctic. Statues, busts and ornaments stood on pedestals. Some were obviously Victorian but some, much older, were from Pompeii and Troy.

Royce thought the quality and presentation of the collection was impeccable and smiled grimly at the thought of removing some of it.

He walked round the collection, affixing a small piece of masking tape to the frame of each painting on Ferragami's list.

Salam followed, delicately removing each work from its frame, rehanging the empty frames in the wall afterwards. Both wore surgical gloves over skin-tight lycra gloves. Neither spoke a word.

As Salam removed the paintings from the frames he propped them against the wall and Royce started a second circuit, gingerly placing them into the plastic bags, careful not to touch the surfaces or damage them in any way.

First on the list and into the bag was The Morning After the Merrymaking in Lower Canada. Then came Falls of the Little Shawinigan; Bargaining for a Load of Wood; Village Scene near Longueil, 1850; Hurons Camping Near the Big Rock, Longueil, Quebec 1858; Steelers Supper Depot on a Frozen River; Playtime,

Village School; Bilking the Tollgate (said to be the parsimonious Vanderhoof's favourite); Sleigh Racing on the St. Lawrence; and Before The Kill.

Since Salam's work was slow and precise Royce had time to wander the gallery, still marvelling that such treasures were kept atop a downtown Toronto office tower for the sole gratification of one man. He contemplated adding a few other pieces to the haul for his own benefit but fear of reprisals from Ferragami stayed his hand.

After about two hours all the paintings on the lists were in the bags. They donned their balaclavas and headed for the door.

Their departure was more rapid than their arrival, mostly because they now knew how to enter and activate the private lift. They were in a hurry to get own to a lower floor as quickly as possible to mingle with other cleaners carrying bags of refuse out to the waiting van behind the building.

They carefully closed all doors behind them, latched all latches and locked all locks which would be locked from the outside. They carefully rubbed all knobs, handles, table tops and chair backs they may have touched so as to eliminate fingerprints. Not that any prints could have been matched to them. Neither had a police record.

The exit went incredibly smoothly.

On the twenty fourth floor they removed the balaclavas and took the elevator to the eighth floor. Royce guessed that the cleaners he had seen on the tenth floor would be at least two floors lower down by now.

He still had the key to the penthouse elevator in his pocket. He contemplated dropping it under a desk guessing that if the old security guard could be seen to have lost the key he would get the blame for the theft and that would take the heat off them until they were well out of the country.

They saw a cleaning woman on the eighth floor scrubbing an office wall. They waved to her and she called to them in what sounded like Portuguese. Around the corner they walked straight into the path of the security guard who stood aside and nodded to them as he inserted the key of his watch clock into a wall timer.

They descended to the foyer and crossed to the small door

leading to the underground concourse, following the route Royce had staked out that afternoon.

Resisting the urge to run, they walked calmly past padlocked shops and coffee bars until they reached the alleyway leading underneath the street to the parking lot below the city hall.

Once in the tunnel they burst out laughing at the ease with which they had made their escape, so long in the planning and so close to disaster in its initial stages.

"I'd like to see the look on that sucker's face when he gets to work tomorrow and finds his treasures gone," Royce laughed.

"What would you have done if I hadn't been able, or willing, to get those paintings out of their frames?" Salam asked evenly, not smiling.

The laughter stopped abruptly. After a silence which seemed eternal Royce said "I would have killed you on the spot and left you there."

That stifled all further attempts at conversation.

They walked in silence to the van, paid the fee at the entrance booth and drove out into the cold night air on their way to a rendezvous with El Serpiente, captain of La Coruna.

Back at the Corey Building the cleaning staff was descending to the seventh floor and the security guard was opening another cup of coffee. He had an hour to kill before his next rounds.

In Port Credit, ten miles to the west, Mungo Slat was leaving the all-night coffee shop, returning to the apartment where a few hours earlier he had found the dead body of Marge McCracken.

At the house on Ashwarren Grove, Farida bin Salam was curled in the arms of Casey Vanderhoof. They were both naked and both fast asleep.

CHAPTER FOURTEEN

Royce and Salam had a lot of ground to cover that night.

Their schedule, now amended to include the assassination of Mungo Slat, meant driving to Port Colborne, returning to Port Credit for that item of unfinished business, then the flight from Canada.

The double trip was a major inconvenience for Tony Royce. As he scanned the map under the passing lights of the city he realized Port Colborne was only twenty miles from the United States border with Canada at Fort Erie where he had entered the country. To be so close to his escape route and to have to return to Toronto to kill Mungo Slat, the man whose daughter he had smothered to death in New York City only yesterday seemed stupid but he had to obey orders.

During the planning of the theft of the paintings he had been the leader. Now he was in the hands of the man he had already threatened with a gun and told he would have killed if they had failed.

Procuring the van and driving to the ship was Abdel Salam's role and Royce had to sit back and allow him to perform it even if he found it galling, especially when he didn't trust Salam and found his sister a source of worry.

Until Farida was out of the Vanderhoof mansion and back in her own country he was not sure she wouldn't turn them both in if the going got rough.

It had been Salam's idea to bring Farida along, over some strenuous objections by Royce at first. Then their roles became reversed as Royce realized she would make an admirable decoy for the young Casey Vanderhoof and could gain inside information to aid their entry to the Corey Building. At that point the protective older brother objected but was eventually persuaded that she would be both safe and useful in Canada.

Salam was an excellent driver and, with Royce navigating, they were soon on their way out of Toronto, going west towards Hamilton, from where Royce would find them a back highway across the Niagara Peninsula through Stoney Creek and Smithville. Their route would take them past the historical battlefield from the War of 1812 when the Americans were defeated by the Canadians.

As they crested the Niagara Escarpment outside Stoney Creek a bitter wind buffeted the van. They soon turned eastwards on a highway which meandered through farmlands barely discernible on a relatively moonless night.

Soon after leaving the town of Grimsby they reached the village of Smithville on a series of sharp curves in the road which caused Royce to stiffen as Salam hurled the van into them, one eye on the road, the other on the mirror, looking for police cars.

They were between Smithville and Bismarck when the first flashing red light appeared in the rear view mirror.

Royce contemplated telling Salam to make a run for it but knew that in a white van in unfamiliar territory they would stand little chance of escape. He motioned to Salam to slow down to the speed limit and drive on, waiting for the inevitable.

As they waited in agony Royce took out his revolver, attached the silencer, loaded and cocked it, and waited, his face strained and white.

By now the reflection of the police lights were flashing inside the van and they stiffened as a blue and white Niagara Regional Police cruiser drew alongside.

They exhaled large breaths of relief as the police car accelerated past them, obviously interested in other matters, oblivious to the stolen cargo it was leaving in its dust. The red lights vanished around a corner, reappeared again at a distance, then turned off down a side road and disappeared from sight.

Royce noticed that Salam was hunched over the steering wheel sweating profusely, a loaded gun in his right hand.

"You can put the bloody pistol away now, Abdel," he grinned.

The nearness of the miss hit them both at the same moment and they started laughing uncontrollably, Salam's body shaking so violently that the van swerved sharply across the road.

Royce sat there, tears streaming down his face as he recited his version of the traffic cop telling his superior officer now he had driven past a van loaded with more than seven million dollars worth of stolen paintings but had managed to catch the son of a bitch who ran a stop sign at St. Ann's corner.

After that scare the rest of the journey was uneventful.

They carried on until a sign sent them to the right and south towards Lake Erie where they took Highway 3 through Wainfleet into Port Colborne then followed high lights on the bridges across the Welland Canal's Lock 8, the longest lift lock in the Seaway system.

A ship was passing through the canal which spilt the city into two segments, and the jackknife bridge at the north end of the locks was already down again.

The twin railway and road bridges in the downtown area were both raised, looking like giant coat hangers in the sky, the tiny control cabin perched jauntily under the span of the road bridge more than fifty feet in the air.

It would take about twenty minutes for the ship to clear the bridges before they could be lowered so traffic could cross from the east side to the west side of the city.

As they drove towards the lighted twin bridges they could see the navigation lights on the traversing vessel as it sailed southwards to Lake Erie. From the derricks on its deck they knew it was a "salty" from overseas, not one of the flattened grain carriers which formed the bulk of traffic on the Great Lakes.

On the east side of the harbour, safely out of the main shipping lane, El Serpiente had tied La Coruna to the dock wall, having secured permission from the Seaway Authority and the local harbour master for a stop to make emergency repairs to the vessel's winching system.

He had been there since four that afternoon, had been boarded by customs officers and given permission for his crew to go ashore and visit the local shops and taverns.

A few unlucky mariners were grumbling at having to stay aboard to perform the unnecessary repairs ordered by their captain and to keep the engines running, ready to sail the moment the cargo was loaded.

The ship was green. Its stack markings were the red and gold of Espana Terza on a white funnel. The red and gold Spanish flag hung from the rear deck pole and a Canadian flag, red and white with a large maple leaf, flew at the top of the main mast.

The lake pilot assigned to the ship disembarked for a quick visit to his family who lived in the city, promising to return at midnight to navigate the ship through the canal and lock system into Lake Ontario.

As darkness fell, sparks from welding torches illuminated the silent deck which was also lit by spotlights, giving the ship an eerie glow in the light mist rising from the water. The rest of the ship was in darkness as El Serpiente waited for his visitors.

The Seaway Bridge was about a hundred yards north of the ship, the rail bridge another hundred yards north of that.

Both bridges were operated by massive chain pulleys weighted by immense slabs of concrete which counterbalanced the weight as the pulleys hauled the entire roadway fifty feet into the air to the sound of loud sirens and the flashing of lights on the barriers blocking traffic from approaching the area where the road had been.

As a ship neared the bridge the operator in his control tower activated the engines which lifted the office and the bridge high above the canal so the vessel could sail underneath. Since some vessels were more than a thousand feet long and at least forty feet high, traffic could be blocked for up to half an hour as a slow-moving ship manoeuvred its way beneath the bridges and around the bend in the canal protecting the famous Lock 8.

There was a rule that all bridges across the canal could not be raised at the same time. This was critical since the fire station and hospital were both on the west side of the city. If downbound and upbound ships were in the canal at the same time, one would have to wait until at least one road bridge was lowered so traffic could cross. The lock also split Highway 3, linking the boarder at Fort Erie, twenty miles to the east, with Windsor on the western border across the river from Detroit, Michigan, almost three hundred miles away.

During the winter months when the system was closed because of ice and the lock was drained and repaired, ships were moored along the canal walls either for storage or for repairs, their crews laid off for two months of life with their families.

Royce and Salam approached the Spanish freighter, crossing the southern bridge and turning right immediately at its end, entering the dock through a coal yard. As they bumped across the rough ground they could see the spotlights on the deck and the sparks from the ersatz welding operation, being conducted as realistically as possible because the bridge operator was equipped with powerful binoculars and must not be allowed to suspect that anything out of the ordinary was happening on his patch.

As Salam drove alongside the small green freighter, which now towered above them, its orange derricks reflecting the spotlights, a door opened on the bridge and Royce saw the silhouette of a large man standing with arms folded, watching their approach.

This was the infamous El Serpiente. Royce felt a shiver pass through his body as he heard the man's name on the lips of the smiling but still grim Abdel Salam.

They parked the van at the foot of the gangway and Salam went aboard, leaving Royce in the semi darkness with the paintings.

High above his head he watched Salam climb to the bridge where he heard voices speaking indistinctly in Spanish and saw a white envelope change hands. The captain vanished inside the bridge, presumably to count and recount the bribe before accepting the cargo.

He reappeared after a few minutes, spoke a few words, then Salam retraced his steps down the gangway and opened the side door of the van. Together they carried the bags of paintings onto the ship, handing them to a sailor who carried them aft to a small area behind the bridge where the pilot would not notice them.

Finally the Krieghoffs were on their way to Barcelona and soon after that to Sorrento.

Immediately after the paintings were handed over, Royce headed back down to the van while Salam entered the bridge for a drink with the captain of La Coruna.

Ten minutes later Salam emerged and walked down the gangway. Royce could hear the "buenas noches" of the mariners at the rail as he descended, climbing into the van with a toothy grin on his face.

"Well, my friend, that's that over with. Now we go looking for our friend Mungo Slat."

The engine roared to life and they turned the van around for the return trip to Toronto.

From the control tower on the bridge a pair of eyes glued to binoculars followed them and a hand wrote down the licence plate number of the van and the name of the rental company emblazoned on its side.

An hour later the welding ceased on La Coruna, its siren blasted once and the bridge swung upwards to admit it into the canal on its way towards the St. Lawrence River and the Atlantic Ocean.

CHAPTER FIFTEEN

With Regis Yakabuski doing the legwork on the shipping register search, Mungo Slat was free to turn his attention to the mystery of the bracelet he had seen on Farida bin Salam's wrist at the Vanderhoof mansion.

For some reason that bracelet kept nagging at his brain no matter how he tried to shut it out.

He had a notion that somewhere in that language called Aljamiado he would find a clue that might unravel the mystery of Marge McCracken's death, the slaughter on the GO train and the theft of Vanderhoof's masterpieces.

Time was now very much of the essence and he couldn't afford any wild goose chases. He felt sure this was not a wild goose chase but something he had to find out about and had to do right away.

The disappearance of Herbert Ashley, the Vanderhoofs' butler, Yakabuski's insistence on the shipping angle and the appearance of that young woman wearing the bracelet seemed too coincidental to be any hunt for wildfowl.

He flipped through a box of recipe cards where he kept names of his contacts behind recipes for Chicken Tandoori, Darwin Steaks and Sole Meuniere, meals he would never cook but whose recipes served as camouflage, thanks to Clare, whose it has been, for an excellent portable filing system.

He was looking for someone who was an expert in ancient languages, especially Arabic and other Middle Eastern tongues.

He drew a blank.

Lighting another cigarette, his fourth that morning he reminded himself, he tickled the slobbering Sebastian behind the left ear as he ran the problem through his memory banks.

He had two days left to find the paintings. Not much time, but he had worked under tight deadline pressure before and wasn't about to chuck the towel in now.

Besides, he reminded himself, his deal was to recover the paintings within seventy two hours. Bringing the suspects to justice was not part of the deal. Even the unreasonable Clement Vanderhoof couldn't expect the recovery of his full monte of paintings and apprehension of the thieves within that time frame. Not even for the princely sum of $75,000.

He poured coffee from a thermos bottle. As he hunted in his desk drawer for a sachet of sugar a small memory stirred in his brain.

Clare had been studying Spanish at the University of Toronto on a part-time basis, purely for interest and to gain familiarity with the language and culture of the newest batch of immigrants to Toronto from South America, many refugees from wars in their home lands. The university boasted the best Spanish language faculty in North America.

Clare never did things by halves and would only study where she could be exposed to the best teachers and could learn the most.

He recalled her retuning home one night, tired and happy, full of information about the Moorish conquest of Spain and their eventual ouster by Ferdinand and Isabella, their Catholic majesties of Aragon and Castille.

Later she missed two weeks of classes through an illness and the professor kindly invited her to his lodgings in Massey College where, over black coffee sweetened with honey, he helped her catch up what she had missed.

"Now what was that professor's name?" he asked his memory as he rummaged for the sugar.

In a moment it came back to him. It was Ottmar Wallenstein, an improbably sounding name for a Spanish expert, he thought.

"He must be from Argentina or somewhere like that," he muttered to himself.

He reached for the phone directory, eager to find out if Wallenstein was still at the university.

Given the tradition for professors to work for tenure, bringing the brightest and best students to their classes once they were regularly published in learned journals on their subjects, he thought it likely that Wallenstein would still be there.

He had impressed Clare so much that she had planned a trip to Spain to see the Alhambra and the other historical sites of that wonderful country with which she had fallen in love.

The trip had never happened. It was just one more goal shattered by her death.

All Slat recalled from her classes was that Spanish contains many words of Arabic origin as a result of the seven hundred year conquest of the Iberian Peninsula by the Moors. He hoped this professor would be able to fill some of the chasms in his knowledge.

He flung himself back in the chair, which groaned and creaked in protest at the weighty attack, then dialled and asked for the number of the faculty of modern languages at the University of Toronto.

"I'm very sorry, sir," a departmental secretary told him, "Professor Wallenstein died two years ago. The new man is Professor Diego Vasco Ibanez. I will be happy to connect you if you wish."

Slat did wish and was soon speaking to another secretary who said the professor was in his classroom but would be free in the afternoon if he wished an appointment. He was pencilled in for three, leaving his number in case of conflicts, and hung up, elated at finding a source for his inquiries.

With a few hours to kill he decided to pursue some other leads, searching for common threads in the case. This would call for legwork and lots of it.

First he called Regis Yakabuski at The Tribune.

There the going had been slow. Calls to the Seaway Authority in Cornwall had seen him referred to the computer firm in St. Catharines which logged all local shipping movements by the hour.

Their records showed that five ships had made unscheduled stops in Port Colborne for emergency repairs after severe storms on lakes Huron and Erie had lashed them for two days. Their names were Paterson, J.W. McGiffen, La Coruna, Rubens, and Willowglen.

Finally the name La Coruna had surfaced on a shipping report. It was a ship after all. Yakabuski had been right in his guess about the paintings leaving the country by sea.

It should be a simple matter, Yakabuski said, to find out where the ship was now and precisely where it could be apprehended in the Seaway system. As soon as he received that information, Slat would have it too.

Slat hauled out a battered map of the province and found Port Colborne. He wondered why that port had been chosen for a layover. Did that mean the ship was headed for open water on Lake Erie, bound for some port in the United States?

Yakabuski's list had also showed that the freighters Algosoo and Algowest were both in dock at Port Colborne, the former for repairs to a broken bow bulkhead, the latter for installation of a new feeder belt to its self-loader. Since Algoma Marine which owned them had a yard in the port it made sense to carry out these extensive repairs, which would take most of the winter to complete, at that location.

Considering that the Seaway would close in two weeks, the list of vessels still in the waters was extensive.

Yakabuski counted seventy four ships strung out between Thunder Bay and Montreal, a distance of some 1,500 miles with dozens of ports and terminals long the route in two countries.

It was a massive amount of material to sift but the meticulous Yakabuski was attacking it with gusto while waiting for the call he needed on the direction and destination of La Coruna.

What had started to look like a search for a contact lens in a tank of jellyfish was beginning to show signs of success at last, even if the going was tedious.

All this was based on the premise, Slat reminded himself, that the stolen works of art were actually aboard that ship.

It seemed an easy task to find a 10,000 tonne freighter in the lakes when they started but when they realised the sheer size of the country and the seemingly endless combinations and permutations of lakes, rivers, canals, ports and terminals which comprised the system, the immensity of the task was almost overwhelming.

Slat still hadn't told Yakabuski that the name of the ship he wanted was definitely the La Coruna, the name written on the notepad in Herbert Ashley's apartment on Jarvis Street.

He needed to confirm that the ship was in port on the day the paintings were stolen and, if it was, its time of departure and its destination. He wanted to intercept the vessel during its voyage and before it left Canadian waters. Until he had all that information he was prepared to keep Yakabuski in the dark a while longer.

He still harboured a few niggling doubts about the reporter's loyalties to his city editor and his career while his silence was paramount to the success of the hunt.

What he was doing to Yakabuski was totally unfair, he admitted to himself. He was causing the man a great deal of hard work for no apparent purpose but until he felt sure of the information the reporter might uncover, he could not afford to tip his hand too soon.

By now Yakabuski had left for his home, reams of computer printouts in his satchel. There he would brew strong coffee, sip his favourite Scotch and, foregoing meals and all but the most basic bodily needs, would hunker down to study the list until he uncovered a reasonable number of possibilities.

He promised he would call Slat at any time of the day or night when he thought he had what they wanted.

Slat's next call was to Inspector Andy Hocking of the Metro Toronto Police to check on the status of the hunt for the GO train killers.

Hocking was out and the call was pushed through to Scotty Jackman, information officer, a left-over from Slat's junior days in the Lakeshore detachment where they had been partners on the night shift.

"Slat, you old bugger, how are ye?" Jackman still retained the burr he had brought from Glasgow thirty years earlier. "The GO case? Aye, well listen, Mungo, the official line for the shit-disturbing press is that we are following all leads and will report when we have a solid case. But between us girls, the department is nowhere on this one and the old man is getting g very shirty about it. He wants answers and he wants them today. The only clue we have it a sports bag we found but even that is clear of prints and is so common every kid has one today. Your best bet is to call the old man tomorrow. He's in Ottawa just now answering to the prime minister because some MPs are creating a stink about slow action on the case. Some of them are trying to make political hay out of this massacre and Brian Mulroney needs answers so he called Andy. Call tomorrow. In the meanwhile, leave your number and if I hear anything I'll call you, off the record of course, and fill you in. OK?"

Slat felt the cold hand of despair gripping his windpipe. With the best police force in North America stumped after deploying three thousand officers on this case, how was he to solve it within two days?

Perhaps he should come clean with Yakabuski, pool their information and brains? He still dithered about that.

He decided to grab lunch before his appointment with Professor Ibanez and walked round the corner to Sam's delicatessen.

Sam was an immigrant of indeterminate origins. Slat knew he was from somewhere in the Middle East but had never heard Sam claim the same place of origin twice.

They had met years ago when Slat was in uniform on the beat. They formed a bond which allowed for the exchange of information which would never go beyond the walls of the small deli with its red-checked plastic tablecloths.

Sam had seen and done things which Slat could never imagine. In the process he had gained insights into the human mind and heart which had proven invaluable to Slat when he was stumped by some aspect of a situation. Sam was a force to be reckoned with in his own right.

The deli was almost empty when Slat walked in. He parked at a bar stool and ordered corned beef on rye with black coffee. He was thirsty for a cold beer but decided to forego the pleasure lest he arrive at the university smelling of drink.

Sam served him, making the usual small talk about the weather, the economy, the murders on the GO train and U.S. foreign policy in the Middle East, efforts he said would benefit nobody but the arms dealers, most of whom just happened to be American.

The sandwich eaten and a second coffee poured, Slat broached the subject of the train killings.

"I tell you, Mr Slat, that was a planned job. I also believe it was connected to the theft of the pictures from that millionaire, may Allah have mercy on his unworthy soul! Just this morning I was talking with a man who worked for that rich bastard. He was the guy who found the paintings had been stolen and who called the police. For his trouble he was fired on the spot. For a good deed he lost his job. If he worked for me, found a robbery and called the cops right away he would have got a free meal and a day off, at least."

Slat's ears perked up at this news.

"Do you know this man very well?" he asked cautiously.

"Well, not well. I know he was an accountant for Vanderhoof. I also know he was on that train that got shot up. I think he's a very lonely man. He told me once he is unhappy at his work. I think he likes to talk a lot to get attention and that turns some people off. I don't remember his name but if he comes in again, and he might because he loves my cabbage rolls on special, I'll call you right away."

His voice trailed off as two police officers entered and sat near the window.

He served them coffee and muttered to Slat as he walked part.

"Specials, specials. All my life is made up of cheapskates eating my specials. How can I make a living feeding people only on specials?"

Slat pulled out a business card and wrote on the back of it. He handed the card to Sam and asked him to give it to the accountant if he came in. Sam stuck it on the side of his cash register so he would remember.

Slat caught the College streetcar and headed for the university.

Professor Ibanez, trim and small, was about forty five. He wore a dark suit, a neat black moustache and gold wire-rimmed glasses.

Once they were seated in comfortable armchairs, Ibanez puffing at a briar pipe and Slat on a Camel filter, he broached the reason for his visit.

"I would like some information about the Moors in Spain, a brief history of that time and anything you can tell me about a language called Aljamiado, if that makes any sense to you."

Ibanez smiled, knocked the dottle from his pipe into a large ceramic ashtray and began.

"That's a tall order and most of it would be available to any student in the library so they would be told to go there and read it. But you're not one of them, are you? The language Aljamiado was once used by Jews expelled from Spain in 1492. That's an easy date to remember since that's when Cristobal Colon sailed to discover what you call the New World. It was also in that year that Ferdinand and Isabella drove all the Jews from the Iberian Peninsula. Many fled to North Africa and to hide their identity from their Arabic neighbours for obvious reasons, adapted the Arabic script of writing to phonetic Spanish, thus enabling them to preserve their language, religion and culture in a hostile environment. If you have seen something in that language you may have met either a descendent of those Jews, someone from Libya, Morocco or even Ethiopia, or a very lucky antique dealer. Now how can I help you further?"

A secretary brought cups of steaming black coffee which Ibanez sweetened with dark amber honey from a jar in his desk drawer. Then, settling into his chair, he began his history lesson.

CHAPTER SIXTEEN

While Slat was closeted with Ibanez, the La Coruna was traversing Lake Ontario between Hamilton and Toronto.

It had taken the remainder of the night and most of the morning to clear the Welland Canal through the Flight Locks at Thorold and Port Weller to gain access to Lake Ontario.

As dawn broke and the crew arose for their breakfast of pan y chorizos, El Serpiente was listening to the radio for news from on shore.

The CBC report, which he understood passably, though his spoken English was execrable, gave a weather synopsis for places he had never heard of, discussed upcoming municipal elections in Toronto, gave overnight scores from hockey and Canadian football games, traffic details of highways into the city and even cricket scores from the West Indies where the English team was locked in mortal combat on the manicured turf of the Kingston Cricket Club in Jamaica.

There was no mention of a theft or the name of his ship and for that he was grateful even though he didn't know exactly what his mysterious cargo was.

With clear weather forecast, just a slight chance of flurries the radio said, and his course set for the length of the lake to Iroquis and the locks leading to the St. Lawrence River, he decided to keep the radio on and try to improve his comprehension of the English language.

By mid morning the news reports were full of shock at a massacre on a commuter train earlier that day. Two men were being sought and police had closed airports and seaports, cordoning off highways in and out of the city.

"The fools!" El Serpiente snarled. "If something like this ever happened in Spain the Guardia Civil would have the criminals behind bars by now."

He smiled in patriotic pleasure, knowing he was probably wrong but feeling better for having said it.

Of all people he had the most to fear from the Guardia Civil but could afford this small patriotic sally since he was thousands of miles away from their jurisdiction. He was born in the slums of Barcelona and his nodding acquaintance with the police came from time in a reform school after he and a school friend were caught stealing chorizos from a butcher and selling them on the black market for a healthy profit.

His mind turned to the sealed packages in green plastic bags brought aboard the ship in the middle of the night. He wondered if the massacre on the train had anything to do with the contents of those bags.

While he was contemplating the news the first mate had taken the bags from their aft position and, opening one of the smaller grain holds in the deck, lowered the bags, now in hard canvas sacks, on a rope into the sea of red Durum wheat below. He tied the end of the rope to the inside of the metal lid of the hold. There the paintings would stay, cushioned by the grain, safe from prying eyes until they reached Barcelona, about twelve sailing days away.

The small green freighter, followed by a smudge of black smoke, chugged solidly along the shipping lane marked on the navigator's charts through the upper portion of Lake Ontario.

The engines thrummed steadily, the bow thrust doggedly into the waves and, despite the ship's low attitude in the water due to its cargo, two seamen in winter parkas were painting the deck stanchions and the lower half of the derricks.

At noon the weather report was amended, now calling for severe snow storms and brisk northerly winds as a high pressure cell was forcing cold Arctic air into the Great Lakes basin. The worst time would be late afternoon, about the time the La Coruna would be in the widest section of the lake where winds sweeping from Ontario across to upstate New York would create hazardous sailing conditions for smaller vessels

It was at this time of the year that the freighter Edmund Fitzgerald had foundered and sunk in Lake Superior with the loss of all hands. The disaster was engraved on the Canadian collective memory through a spate of books and a song which catapulted a singer from Orillia to international fame. El Serpiente knew nothing of any of this.

He did know he would have to be extremely alert as the storm approached. Sudden squalls could send his ship to the lake bottom before rescuers could arrive.

He wanted to get clear of the Great Lakes as quickly as possible and cross the Atlantic to his own country where he could deliver the mysterious bags, collect a fat fee, offload his cargo of grain and spend a week with his wife and another one with his mistress in Tenerife before sailing south of the equator, the preferred destination for Spanish mariners in winter.

After a simple lunch in his cabin he retired, as did crew members not on duty, for his siesta. He rested uneasily, aware of the dangers of these cold, deep Canadian waters.

He ruminated about the cargo within his cargo. He had no intention of double crossing the people who had paid well for its delivery. He simply wondered what it was that necessitated his delay in Port Colborne, a delay which could now result in severe implications for his crew and himself if the vessel came to harm in the impending storm.

All his seafaring life he had made a good living by carrying unofficial cargoes across international boundaries. He had even smuggled the occasional criminal from one country to another for the right fee, hiding the man from the crew by sharing his cabin with him. The only one to guess at the presence of a guest was the cook who was asked to prepare double portions for the captain. Even then the betting was that the captain had brought aboard some toothsome female for his own delectation and was keeping her strictly for himself.

Carrying illicit cargo had never been a moral issue for El Serpiente. He liked money and the fees he charged for doing such work outweighed the wages he collected from the shipping firm.

Often he suspected that one of his crew was planted aboard as an agent for the fee payers as insurance that he would keep his end of the bargain but since he always did he had never bothered to find out which member of his crew it was.

Below decks Andres Padilla, first mate, knew exactly who that man was. He also knew El Serpiente was no fool and was not about to ask questions whose answers he might not like. So long as the ship stayed on course and on schedule he had no worries.

Once in the past a sailor had asked a question about some cargo taken on at an unscheduled stop. His body was never found. All records of his ever having been on the ship were erased.

For all his guile and greed, El Serpiente had never thought to question his orders. He simply didn't care that much.

His policy was to change as many members of his entire crew as possible between voyages. This was on the pretext of allowing them extra time with their wives and sweethearts but the reality was that it prevented familiarity with the movements of the ship lest they perceive a pattern to the voyages and the stops at various ports, sometimes for unscheduled repairs in the middle of the night. He wanted to avoid the possibility of being blackmailed by a seaman seeking an opportunity to increase his net wealth.

An hour after lunch the captain was back on the bridge watching the shoreline through binoculars. He saw plumes of filthy smoke rising from what looked like a smelting plant where blue flames from neighbouring smoke stacks licked their chops at the sky.

He saw a large double-spanned arched bridge with rows of toy cars crawling along its black suspenders. At one end was a building with a large blue H on the wall. This was Joseph Brant Memorial Hospital in Burlington.

As La Coruna rounded the bay, called the Golden Horseshoe, the captain's attention wandered to other matters.

The crew had been grumbling about the length of this voyage, the absence of shore leave and the lack of women. He had tried to mollify them by allowing them ashore in Port Colborne but they were still uneasy and that worried him.

By now the sea lanes were busier as La Coruna joined a convoy of freighters moving out of the bay, fighting their way past a few brave fishing smacks risking a swamping for a final catch of perch or walleye.

One or two ships were headed towards the entrance to the Welland Canal, hoping to snatch one last cargo of grain from the ravening jaws of winter at the risk of becoming stuck in the ice and trapped until spring. They would be rescued in late March by a doughty little Canadian Coastguard icebreaker with its cheery red and white insignia and its chopping, thrusting bow which would smash the ice pack to jelly so the ships could slowly push their way to freedom.

This was not the fate El Serpiente wanted for his little ship.

La Coruna could be crushed by the winter ice of the Great Lakes, its hull battered, seams split, propellers sheared off under the pressure of frozen water moved by winds and currents into fields of grinding destruction.

The thought of such weather made him shudder and he contacted the engine room for more speed then hailed a pair of lounging sailors on the deck and berated them for their idleness when they had stanchions to paint and hatches to secure.

As he left the bridge for his cabin an icy spray hit his face and he could taste the first snow in the wind as it bit his lips.

Outside the cabin door he suddenly stopped. He could hear the high-pitched whine of a small plane somewhere behind the ship.

The sailors on deck watched as a small plane veered sharply away to the east where another freighter was plying the same shipping lane two miles ahead.

Inside the Coastguard spotter plane Regis Yakabuski was writing furiously, a notepad on his lap.

He had listened to the Coastguard receive notice that a freighter named La Coruna had been visited briefly by a small white van in the early hours of the morning, that two men had carried some bags aboard and the ship set sail an hour after they departed. The call came from the bridge operator in Port Colborne.

Failing to reach Mungo Slat when he called his office, he decided to take action himself, wangling a ride on the spotter plane on the pretext of surveying the shipping rush for the ocean for his newspaper.

From the information provided by the Seaway he now knew she was heading for Spain with a cargo of durum wheat loaded in Thunder Bay, the major grain terminal for the prairies.

He knew he should have waited for Slat's approval before setting out but, since he promised the city editor a story with aerial pictures of the last vessels clearing the Seaway, he convinced the newspaper to pay for the flight and to smooth his way with the Coastguard officials.

He wasn't sure what he was looking for but wanted a closer view of the ship. Perhaps he would be able to tell if the crew was armed and what the layout of its decks was.

While waiting for the flight he had found out that the van, its number recorded by the bridge operator, had been rented the previous day from an agency in Toronto by a swarthy young man with lots of cash to pay for the silence of the agency staff. He hadn't received his money's worth.

Yakabuski was well aware that Mungo Slat didn't completely trust him and wanted to bring in a piece of plum information that would sway the detective in his favour. He also wanted an exclusive story more than anything else.

For that he had to earn Slat's confidence and abide by the ground rules set down at the outset of their collaboration.

As far as El Serpiente was concerned the Coastguard plane was probably counting vessels still in the system due to close in two weeks.

They would have seen that his ship was fully loaded both from reading the Plimsoll Line on its side and from the way the bow ploughed into the smaller waves while some larger ones washed right across the decks amidships as the little boat bucked and tossed in the growing swells.

As a precaution he removed a small, well-oiled revolver from a cloth bag in his drawer. He decided to keep it loaded and on his person for the rest of the voyage.

Below in the engine room Andres Padilla saw the spotter plane through a porthole and tightened his grip on the handrail where he was standing above the main engine, watching the engineer checking his controls, recording temperatures and pressures.

Padilla had a submachine gun in his cabin and would use it if there was trouble. Right now he was happy to keep the ship running for home, hoping that damnfool captain wouldn't panic, change course or make any unscheduled moves which would betray the alternate mission of the voyage.

What El Serpiente didn't know was that his first mate was also the target of a manhunt as a result of his time ashore the previous night.

While the rest of the crew enjoyed some relief in the bars and in the arms of some local women, he had slipped away from them, stolen a car from a nearby grocery parking lot and driven it to Toronto, using a map he found in the glove box.

There had paid an unexpected call on his friend Herbert Ashley, whom he had contacted at the Vanderhoof residence from on board La Coruna.

They met outside the grimy Jarvis Street tenement and walked to a nearby bar where Padilla plied the butler with drinks, praising him for his work at the mansion. Two hours later he poured him into the car and headed out of the city.

Ashley was barely awake when his bound and weighted body hit the icy waters of Lake Ontario and sank into its murky depths off the end of a pier near a generating plant in Long Branch.

Padilla drove back to the port, replaced the car where he had found it, and sauntered into the bar where his comrades were still carousing, bragging about the demon under the sheets he had been occupied with in an upstairs room.

It was that same Andres Padilla who later met Abdel Salam and Tony Royce on the deck of La Coruna and took delivery of the bags of paintings.

He had stowed them safely and for the remainder of the voyage would make sure nothing happened to them.

Woe betide any sailor who tried to sneak a peek at them, whether from simple curiosity or from thoughts of blackmail. That would be the last peek he ever sneaked.

CHAPTER SEVENTEEN

As Mungo Slat walked back into his office, filled with the wisdom of the history lesson he had undergone at the hands of Professor Ibanez and carrying samples of Aljamiado writing and the address of a bookbinder in the east end of the city who was an expert in that ancient language, his phone was ringing.

It was Sam at the delicatessen.

Ted Reynaldson, the fired accountant and secretary to Clement Vanderhoof, had come in for the cabbage roll special as expected.

Stepping over the prone Sebastian, still snoring, he set off for the deli, hoping for some insight into the workings of the Vanderhoof empire.

There is no one better to ask about an employer than someone he has just fired, especially if that person believes he has been fired without just cause or regard for his years of loyal service.

Ted Reynaldson was such a man and a garrulous one at that. Now he was filled with venom for the magnate who had sacked him on the spot for disobeying his orders.

His diatribe against the Vanderhoofs and their middle managers was long and detailed. Slat sat quietly and allowed him to vent his rage, sipping coffee and smoking three Camel filters before the tirade waned and discussion turned to the morning after the theft of the Krieghoffs.

"You know I wasn't the only one fired?" Reynaldson asked.

"Nossir, I didn't. Who else got the chop that day?"

"Well, there was this old security guard called Basil James. He has been with Clement Vanderhoof since Jesus was a cowboy. It was his pass key that was used to gain entry to the penthouse where the paintings were kept. Only four people had keys, Vanderhoof, his wimp son Casey, Basil James and me.

It was my job to check the gallery every morning, making sure there were enough leaflets handy for whoever his majesty might want to hand them to, and to keep the place neat and clean. Not even the cleaners were allowed into the gallery.

As soon as Vanderhoof found out that Basil had been out with some guy, got drunk and lost his key all hell broke loose. He fired the old man on the spot, told him to turn in his uniforms within the hour and get out of his sight forever. He even threatened to sue him for negligence unless those pictures came back safe and sound."

Slat jotted down the guard's name on the inside of his cigarette pack, making a mental note to call the old retainer as soon as he was finished with Reynaldson.

If he could get a handle on the man who had plied James with drinks he might find out who stole the paintings.

"To think that I was late for work due to some goddamn massacre on the GO train I was on and already in a state of shock. I rushed to the gallery to do my morning checks. There were about twelve blank spaces on the walls where the paintings should have been and I panicked. I called the police straight from the gallery. I was already facing trouble from the boss downstairs for being late when we were meeting the computer company about a new system for the office. Maybe I figured that if I took charge and got things started before Vanderhoof arrived at the office I might even get a promotion, or at least less of a ticking off from Attila the Hun. Vanderhoof arrived, asked me what happened and when I said I had already contacted the police he fired me on the spot, telling me to leave the building without going back to my desk for any personal effects. He shouted that I would be blackballed in the city and in the newspaper industry across Canada and that he'd see to it that I never worked again. You'd have thought he had caught me stealing the paintings myself! I never liked them anyway and it serves the old bastard right. I hope someone burns the bloody things and sends him the ashes wrapped in a copy of The Tribune. It just goes to show how you can devote years of your life to working for some miserable sod and the first chance he gets he fires you out the door and blackballs you into the bargain."

He broke down in embarrassed tears and buried his face in his cup of cold coffee.

Slat caught Sam's eye and a fresh cup of steaming brew arrived quietly, accompanied by a handful of tissues.

When Reynaldson recovered his composure Slat asked the question he had been waiting to pose since the session started.

"Did you by chance see young Casey Vanderhoof in the gallery either before or after the thefts and was he in the company of a young woman?"

"Sure did. The snotty-nosed little shit came into the office the day before yesterday and showed some dark-skinned woman around the gallery without so much as a by-your-leave to me or the rest of the staff. She was carrying a list of the paintings and she was ticking them off as they toured the collection. He seemed proud of her interest in the paintings but any fool could see she was just aching to peddle her sweet brown ass for a stake in the family fortunes. She was a real beauty, though, probably Italian or Portuguese. She had a long nose and wore a flashy silver bracelet with strange snakes carved around it. You couldn't miss it. It sparkled and shone like nothing I have ever seen before. Must have cost the little bugger a fortune to buy it for her. I thought maybe she was a high-class call girl from some Toronto hotel," he added maliciously, remembering the sight of Farida bin Salam clinging to the arm of the slight, weedy heir to the millions.

As soon as was decently possible Slat broke off the interview, paid for the man's meal and the coffees and headed back to the office, satisfied there was a definite connection between the young woman with the bracelet and the theft of the paintings. He was certain also that her accomplice was the man who had stolen the penthouse pass key from old Basil James.

His mind flickered back to the ship La Coruna. He knew it was a Spanish name and that the girl's bracelet was in Spanish phonetics written in Arabic characters by the Jews of North Africa.

The paintings had to have been stolen by someone close to the girl, someone who was now on board that ship with the paintings. It was just too much of a coincidence for the ship's name to have been on the butler's note pad and that it was in Port Colborne on the night of the thefts.

What he didn't know was that at that very moment Regis Yakabuski was following the ship in a Coastguard spotter plane, trying to contact him from his vantage point high above Lake Ontario.

Slat considered calling Clement Vanderhoof with his suspicions but realised that without proof he would be laughed off the line, his sanity being questioned at the same time. The old man had faith in his son's choice of companion and would brook no word of criticism being levelled against anyone fortunate enough to be a guest in his home.

He threw a notepad and pencil into his jacket pocket, ready to head to the nearest movie theatre to contemplate his next move regarding the dark-skinned beauty in the Rosedale mansion. Then the phone rang.

It was the excited voice of Yakabuski, partially muffled by the sound of engines.

He told the straining Slat he was in a spotter aircraft over the lake and that directly below him was the pitching deck of the Spanish freighter La Coruna, headed towards the St. Lawrence River.

Slat's heart almost skipped a beat. He thanked Yakabuski for the information and his initiative and promised to buy him dinner in a quiet Yonge Street restaurant across from the Eaton Centre where they could compare notes as they ate.

He decided to tell the reporter all he knew about the case, throwing his natural caution to the winds, allowing himself the luxury of trusting someone for the first time since Clare's death.

Tossing out the idea of the movie theatre for the nonce, he decided to call Basil James, tell him he was working for Clement Vanderhoof, and ask for a description of the man who had stolen his keys.

He called James and, after commiserating with him for his treatment by his late employer, asked about the man.

"All I know is that this man barraged into me in the bank door, almost killing me. Then he asked me out for a meal and a drink to make up for what he had done. Next thing I remember is being awoken by a waiter then being thrown out into the street for not being able to pay the bill. I went home and straight to bed. I didn't know the key was missing until the next morning when I got dressed. By then the paintings were missing and I was soon out of a job. I do know he was English, very English, white with longish blond hair down to his shoulders. I'm sorry I can't remember any more but if you leave me your number I'll contact you if anything else comes to mind."

Slat did and the call ended.

If this man was an accomplice of Vanderhoof's guest, they seemed an unlikely pair, he thought.

Two hours later he was sitting in the upper floor of Diana Sweets restaurant above Yonge Street comparing notes with Regis Yakabuski.

At first the reporter was a little miffed that Slat had known the name of the ship all along but was mollified when Slat told him precisely why he had withheld the information. That came with a promise from Slat to share all future information on the case openly for their common benefit.

They discussed the information they had and agreed there had to be a link between the girl and the stolen paintings.

They agreed that it would be difficult, if not impossible, to convince Vanderhoof to permit Slat to interview her. She was a visitor and his guest and good manners precluded such an invasion of her privacy without some extremely valid proof.

They further agreed they had no real evidence with which to persuade the police and Coastguard to stop and search the La Coruna.

Their planning lasted into the wee hours of the morning.

Slat was bothered by the fact he knew almost nothing about the physical dimensions of lake and ocean-going freighters or of the St. Lawrence Seaway. All his police experiences had been in, or around metropolitan Toronto and he knew nothing of the work of the police marine patrols who worked the harbour and Toronto Island.

They both agreed that the ship had to be stopped and that it would be best to do so while it was still in Ontario. The Surete de Quebec might not prove sympathetic to the idea of searching a vessel under foreign registry on an apparent whim. Even if they could convince them, negotiations between the provincial police forces could take days, by which time the La Coruna would be well into the Atlantic and in international waters.

That would mean contacting the Royal Canadian Mounted Police and Interpol and with the amount of evidence they didn't have, that was a long shot at best.

It took a great deal of brainstorming and consumption of a great quantity of Scotch and water before Yakabuski managed to convince Slat that the best place to board the vessel would be while she was in the narrow locks at Iroquois, Ontario, just below Cornwall and the huge Eisenhower Locks at Massina, New York, where she would be in United States waters for the next few miles of the voyage.

Once the decision was made that the ship must be stopped and searched, they made a list of all the persons they would have to contact for permission to carry out such a search. They had little evidence and would have to rely on a rare stroke of luck to convince the authorities to stop a ship in the Seaway system on such a pretext.

"We really should get Clement Vanderhoof involved," Yakabuski finally said. "He has drag with the right people and can get what he wants quickly."

Slat had to agree. The man's power would be their best ally when other routine methods would be impossible.

They agreed that Slat would contact Vanderhoof first thing next morning and convince him to call the Spanish ambassador in Ottawa, the head honchos of the Ontario Provincial Police and the Canadian Coastguard and to twist arms to have the ship stopped under any pretext he could invent.

Knowing the La Coruna would be steaming all night, they calculated she would be in the locks at Iroquois by noon the next day. That was now less than ten hours away.

As they parted for the night, Slat to his Port Credit apartment and Yakabuski to his garret bedsit, they arranged to meet at seven for the drive to Iroquois.

As he travelled home Slat realised he knew three things for sure. He was on the verge of finding the missing paintings. He was extremely tired. He was on the verge of becoming deathly ill from the myriad Scotches he had consumed in the restaurant.

He wobbled into the apartment, switched on the light, set the alarm for five in the morning and fell asleep on top of his unmade bed, trench coat, shoes, clothes and all.

CHAPTER EIGHTEEN

At the time Slat fell into his bed, Royce and Salam were leaving Port Credit on their way to drop off the rental van in Toronto.

They had already been at the Troy Street house and found the lights all out, the driveway empty and no signs of life in the building whose other tenants had all moved away after Marge McCracken's murder, feeling unsafe in the neighbourhood.

After sitting in the driveway for half an hour, during which time a yellow police cruiser toured the block twice, they decided the van might be too conspicuous and had, after a brief argument which Royce won by the simple expedient of loading his revolver and pointing at Salam's skull, decided to abandon their plans to eliminate Slat and concentrate on escaping from Canada.

They left the van in the parking lot of the Toronto Transit Commission near the junction of Lakeshore Road and the Gardiner Expressway and walked to a trolley stop at the Humber Loop.

From there they traveled back to Port Credit on a combination of trolleys and buses and waited in the station parking lot until the commuters started to straggle in. They had spotted Slat and boarded the train. Half an hour later, having killed all the passengers in the front carriage, they had jumped from the train in the Mimico rail yards and made their escape, sure they had eliminated Mungo Slat and could now proceed to their destinations.

Sure they had eluded pursuit they boarded a waiting streetcar and asked how to get to the airport.

"Get off at the bus station on Queen Street and catch the airport bus which will deliver you straight to the front door of the departures lounge at the airport," the driver said.

Tony Royce was not leaving Canada from the airport but he

wanted to make sure Abdel Salam got out. Not that he cared for his partner's welfare. He didn't trust him and wanted to make sure he was out of the country and couldn't reveal their activities to the police and make sure Royce was blamed for it all.

As they sat in the bus shelter he suddenly realised that they were still wearing the hockey jackets they had on when they boarded the train in Port Credit.

He shook the dozing Salam into action and they set off in search of a clothing store.

They found one beside a small greasy spoon restaurant and Royce sent Salam inside it to order two coffees while he bought two new jackets. They changed in the restaurant toilet and returned to the bus shelter.

When the airport bus arrived Salam boarded without a backward glance and Royce walked back to the streetcar terminus for the ride into Toronto and the start of his own escape.

Now the job was done, he and Salam found they had nothing more to say to each other.

CHAPTER NINETEEN

The persistent beeping of his alarm clock filtered through Slat's head as he lay stiff and tired on his bed dreaming of a vacation with Clare on some sunny Caribbean island.

He was wearing shorts and his stocky white legs hung down below his flabby white belly. Clare was tanned and laughing in a sleek bathing suit, her figure maintained by the policy of eating precisely the opposite to what her husband was having.

Groaning at the persistent pinging of the alarm he rolled over and shut it off then realised he was still fully dressed. He sat on the edge of the bed, fuzzy and feeling suddenly ancient. His mouth tasted as if an army had marched through it and he recalled the session with Yakabuski and the taste of Scotch.

Tottering to the bathroom he threw cold water on his face, avoiding looking in the mirror for fear of what he might see there. He combed his thinning hair from memory, staggered to the kitchen to make coffee and toss a slice of frozen bread into the toaster.

This was the day he was supposed to stop a ship in Iroquois and he felt like a dying man.

As the coffee warmed his belly and his brain started to click into gear he remembered he was supposed to contact Clement Vanderhoof. He also remembered he had done nothing more about the bracelet on the young woman's wrist, despite taking the trouble to have a private history and language lesson at the university.

"I'm about to dash off to some bloody outpost of the empire to stop a ship with my bare hands and I still have no proof. I can't even prove that woman is involved but I know bloody well she is," he muttered as he lit his first cigarette of the morning and reached for the telephone.

After about thirty rings, during which Slat fumed and raged at the delay, a sleepy voice answered, reminding him it was five in the morning. It was the new Vanderhoof butler, angry at losing an hour of sleep but trying to remain civil in case the call, and the caller, was important.

"I must speak to Clement Vanderhoof right away," barked Slat.

"Mr Vanderhoof is still in bed, sir, and I would not like to disturb him," replied the butler calmly.

"Listen, boy. You go and get that bugger out of his bed and to this phone right now or I'll drive over there, drag him out myself and break your insolent bloody neck into the bargain. You got that? Tell him it's Mungo Slat and I have found his paintings. That will get him moving in a hurry."

The line went silent. Two minutes later the plummy baritone of Clement Vanderhoof spoke.

"Slat, have you really found my paintings? Where are they?"

"Yes, I believe I have but I need your help to get at them."

As the astonished millionaire listened Slat rhymed off his findings and conclusions, asking him to contact the Coastguard top brass, the commissioner of the Ontario Provincial Police and anyone else he knew who could help. He also asked him to call the local police and have them arrest Farida bin Salam as quickly as possible and to make sure she did not leave the house prior to her arrest.

Vanderhoof listened intently in silence. When Slat stopped he agreed to do everything Slat asked.

"Mind you, Mr Slat, if this turns out to be a hoax or a mistaken waste of my time, influence and an insult to my son's guest you will suffer the consequences in spades."

He slammed the phone down and went in search of coffee and his phone book. He was not the kind of man to stand on ceremony and would not be waiting until the people he wanted were in their offices. If he had to be dragged out of his bed at five in the morning to recover his paintings, so would they.

Then he walked down the hall to his son's bedroom, banged loudly on the door with his clenched fist and ordered his pride and joy to present himself in the hallway instantly.

As he waited, pacing the carpet, he found himself smiling with grim pleasure. Using his power and influence at this obnoxious hour of the morning meant his day was going to be successful after all, regardless of its startling beginning.

As Casey struggled into pyjamas and a silk dressing gown Farida bin Salam watched fearfully from the bed he had just hurriedly vacated. Something was wrong and it was time for her to make her escape.

She leapt from the bed and dressed quickly in the clothes scattered around the room during the night's passion play. Hearing heavy footsteps in the hallway she ran into the bathroom and shut the door behind her.

It was precisely the wrong move.

Clement Vanderhoof strode into his son's bedroom, called her name and when she replied that she was in the bathroom smiled as he turned the key in the outside lock, trapping her in there.

Then he walked out of the bedroom and locked its door behind him, satisfied that bird would stay in its coop until the police arrived to collect it.

Downstairs in the kitchen a pale and shaken Casey was pouring coffee, embarrassed and angry that he had been duped by Farida but not altogether convinced of her complicity.

Clement Vanderhoof went into his study and called the commissioner of the provincial police, apologized for the hour of the call, and explained what the problem was and what he wanted done.

He repeated the process with the Coastguard commander and the commissioner of the Metro Toronto Police.

Soon the radio channels were humming and permission was granted for the ship La Coruna to be stopped in the locks at Iroquois and for Mungo Slat to board the vessel to search for paintings allegedly stolen from Clement Vanderhoof's private gallery. The pretext agreed for the search was that during the repair stop in Port Colborne a crew member had been observed buying drugs in a canal bank tavern.

For the first time in a long time Vanderhoof felt exhilarated and useful. He was part of an actual police investigation and was taking positive steps towards recovering his stolen property. He disliked sitting on the sidelines while Slat plodded on with his theories. He liked to be in control and he had regained a measure of control by dint of a few early morning phone calls. The feeling was refreshing and he really liked it.

As Farida was being locked in her bathroom Slat and Yakabuski were driving eastwards on Highway 401, officially known as The McDonald-Cartier Freeway, towards the village of Iroquois, perched on the bank of the St. Lawrence River a few miles from the historical pioneer village at Morrisburg where Slat and Clare had spent many happy hours over the years.

Iroquois was upriver from Prescott, the coastguard station home to the ice breaker Griffin and the smaller vessel Spray, both of which would be called into action in the containment of La Coruna.

Both men were silent, Yakabuski simultaneously puffing and chewing the end of a rancid black cigar, doubtless composing the lead for the story he would finally be able to write later that day. He would call in his exclusive, breaking story from a phone booth in Iroquois, his part of the bargain kept.

Slat hoped the story wouldn't hit the streets until the paintings were back with Vanderhoof and the balance of the money he was owed had been paid into his account.

At Brockville Slat turned the Renault off the freeway and headed south towards the river and Highway 2, the scenic route that would take them into Iroquois.

After a stop for coffee and doughnuts in Prescott, famous for its old fort and the cannon overlooking the river since the War of 1812 when American invaders crossed the frozen St. Lawrence to fight the battle of Chryslers Farm, they resumed the journey, carrying extra coffee for the wait ahead.

It was half a mile from the highway to the locks where a sharp turn in the road led to a parking lot and a viewing area for tourists.

Two vanloads of Mounties were already in position in the parking lot and an OPP cruiser followed them in.

Clement Vanderhoof had done his job, Slat noticed with relief.

On the river he could see a small Coastguard cutter awaiting the arrival of the Spanish freighter.

He lit a cigarette and pulled the collar of his permanently wrinkled trench coat around his neck before stepping out into the whirling snow flurries which had just begun to fall.

Yakabuski, looking casual in blue jeans and a beige cable-knit sweater under a heavy sheepskin coat, followed, a glint of excitement in his usually watery shark's eyes, thinking about the story he was constructing in his mind and gleeful at the irony of its being about his newspaper's arch rival and written by the one reporter Vanderhoof loved to hate. He thought of the rage the editors at Corey Newspapers would have to suffer knowing they had been scooped by their competition on a story at their own doorstep.

As they walked towards the police cars Slat glanced at the locks. They were empty. They still had two hours to wait if Yakabuski's calculations were correct.

After introductions were made he asked the commanding officer why the police were there so far in advance of the expected time of arrival of La Coruna.

"Last we heard she was passing under the international bridge at Johnstown near Brockville. She's making good time and could be here within an hour. Once she's in the locks we'll use our search warrant to board her and start the search. I want you to stay on the lock side until given the signal to board the vessel. Your friend here will have to stay on dry land. The ship is Spanish territory and we are risking an international incident by boarding her at all, even on the pretext of searching for drugs taken aboard in Port Colborne."

Slat and Yakabuski nodded their agreement and the officer returned to rehearsing his men for the task ahead.

They headed back to the car for coffee and Slat turned to face the river. His heart skipped a beat when he saw a small smudge of black smoke down the stream. The ship was coming and he would soon have Vanderhoof's paintings back and, hopefully, would know who had killed Marge McCracken and why.

Inside the car Yakabuski was looking a little edgy. Slat didn't know if he was concerned for his personal safety if the situation became tense or if it was the aftermath of their meeting last night.

For his part Slat was smoking furiously, smoke billowing round his head like a wreath of wrath, his mind racing over the events of the past two days, trying to project images of what the next few days could bring.

A sudden loud blast from a ship's siren behind him made his start suddenly, spilling coffee over his coat and the dashboard of the little car.

While he had been watching that tantalizing smudge of black smoke grow slowly larger, he had failed to notice a much larger vessel approaching from the east.

It would be in the locks before the La Coruna arrived.

He dashed over to ask the RCMP commander if this second ship would affect their operation, worried that the smaller vessel might be able to bypass the locks somehow and evade their attempts to board her.

"Not to worry, sir. All vessels have to enter the locks because water levels on the other side are lower and they would run aground if they didn't. We'll let the bigger vessel through first and ask the lock gang to work as fast as possible to clear her. We don't want to alarm the captain of your ship any more than we have to and need to make this search appear as routine as possible so they won't suspect we know what we are looking for."

The plan made sense. The Spanish captain would be used to having his ship boarded by various officials in various countries.

Slat hoped that during official discussions on the bridge he might be able to board the ship and find the paintings without arousing undue suspicion.

Slat relayed the information he had gathered to Yakabuski, who was now engrossed in watching the large freighter inching its way into the narrow confines of the lock.

From his vantage point he watched the massive red hull inexorably pushing its way between the narrow walls, seeming to be gripped by them and pulled forward towards the wooden barriers at the end.

The President Quezon from Manila was bound for the Toronto terminal for a load of grain to feed the people of the Philippines.

As the 30,000 ton ship slid into the lock Slat, who knew nothing about shipping, asked Yakabuski where it was from. Unable to see the port of registration painted on its stern or the flag of its nation, the reporter studied the name and size of the red ship, concluding from its derricks and cranes that it was what lake seamen called a "salty" and eventually deduced it was from the Philippines.

By this time the large square stern was inside the lock and the gates were closing behind it. Slat could now see the three bright triangles of red, blue and white with a yellow sun in the centre of the white triangle. It was the flag of the Philippines and the port of registry was Manila.

He could voices over a tannoy on board and saw men scurrying back and forth with ropes and a ladder which was lowered over the side.

"This is where the pilot gets off. There are no locks between here and the Welland Canal so she sails without a Canadian pilot," Yakabuski explained. "The language is probably Tagalog. I once went out with a Filipino girl and she said many people speak that language in her country, though not all."

As they watched a tiny figure, looking Lilliputian against the sides of the red ship, clambered down the rope ladder and stepped onto the dock, clutching a black bag. A sack of mail was lowered down the side and another one taken aboard. The ladder was hauled up and the men moved to the bow to ensure it was in no danger of banging into the concrete walls as the gates at the front of the local swung open and the ship started slowly moving forwards towards the freedom of the river.

While Slat and Yakabuski had been watching, the lock below the ship had been drained of millions of gallons of water and the ship had been lowered until they could actually look down on decks which had previously been twenty or more feet above their heads.

All was red and cream paint, spick, span and spotless to a degree he had not expected.

The deck, the size of a football field, consisted of twelve huge hatches atop grain bins in the holds. A series of four derricks were ready to remove the hatches and, when cargo other than grain was carried which was siphoned out by massive devices like vacuum cleaners, to haul other bulk cargo onto the dockside.

The ship had a crew of forty including two Chinese cooks who prepared meals for the rotating shifts who kept the vessel moving twenty four hours a day, seven days a week.

As the President Quezon inched out of the lock, its propeller churning the water behind it, Slat could see the Coastguard cutter on the far side moving into position out of its path, ready to close in behind the La Coruna when it finally entered the lock.

A glimpse downriver showed another Coastguard cutter sheltering behind a small island of rocks and stunted trees, waiting to move in behind the Spanish ship in case she attempted to move into reverse and avoid inspection.

Across the top of the President Quezon, which was pouring black smoke from its funnel as its captain ordered more power from the engine room, Slat could see a white church steeple and a row of white houses on the American side of the river and a factory chimney belching yellow pollution into the upper atmosphere.

A small blue car drove into the parking lot.

A bearded man in a safari suit under a blue parka fringed with fur stepped out. He was carrying a large bag over his shoulder.

He was introduced to Slat as Otto Pitlik, award-winning Tribune photographer, there to take pictures to accompany Yakabuski's story, a combination which might well garner more awards for the pair of them, adding to their newspaper's circulation and to Vanderhoof's chagrin.

As the President Quezon began dwindling in size as it progressed down the river, Slat suddenly realised that the black smoke smudge he had been watching earlier had transformed itself into the silhouette of a small freighter with deck cranes, a short mast at the prow and at the stern a flat-faced forecastle housing the bridge and accommodations for the crew.

Already he could tell the ship was green with yellow trim and that its funnel was red and gold.

A Canadian flag flew high on the main mast above the revolving radar dish on the bridge.

The small ship was gliding now, its bow scarcely cutting a ripple in the water as it coasted slowly forward, waiting for the President Quezon to swing into the main shipping lane so it could enter the locks.

Slat borrowed Yakabuski's binoculars and scanned the vessel.

High on the bow in white letters was the name La Coruna. It was her.

The decks were eerily empty as he swept the glasses along them and he had the uneasy feeling he was under surveillance himself from the silent bridge. He was right.

High in the bridge Andres Padilla, first mate, was scanning the locks through binoculars, wondering at the presence of police cruisers and huddles of men.

Calling the captain in his cabin on the intercom he informed him of the situation and said he was leaving the bridge. He dashed down to his own cabin for the pistol he kept beneath his pillow.

He picked up a carbine from his bag, loaded a clip into it, checked the chamber of the pistol and shoved it into the belt at the back of his corduroy trousers before running to the stern of the ship, emerging through a small hatch above the engine room where he was sheltered by six oil drums lashed together with heavy rope. He could see the men on the dock but was invisible to them from this vantage point

He planned to stay concealed there as long as possible, only emerging if there was trouble, when he could assume command of the ship and sail it the rest of the way to the Atlantic Ocean and home to Barcelona.

On the bridge El Serpiente watched through binoculars as the President Quezon left the locks and swung out into the channel he had just vacated. The large vessel was gathering speed and the crew of La Coruna could feel the throb and thrum of its massive diesel engines as it passed a hundred yards from their starboard side. Its wake moved their ship, even when fully laden, and he cautioned the helmsman to tale corrective action to stay on course for the narrow entrance to the locks.

Above the locks, Mungo Slat felt in his trench coat pocket for the Smith and Wesson gun. It carried six bullets and was accurate over fifty yards. He hoped he wouldn't need to use it but knew if he had to he would make every shot count.

El Serpiente ordered his crew to clear the decks and stay below until called for. He figured this was a routine inspection but felt the fewer of his men the inspectors saw, the better it would be for him. He preferred to deal with the authorities alone and talk his way out of potential problems over a bottle of cognac and a few good cigars.

He was confident the goods he was paid extra to carry would never be found, banking on the fact that only he and the first mate knew where they were hidden.

He thought that since his ship would be entering United States waters within a few miles this would be a routine customs and excise check.

The order to stay below made little sense to Paul Mercks, a young Dutchman on his first voyage.

He had been touring Europe and had shipped aboard quickly in Barcelona after a torrid affair with a zarzuela singer whose husband discovered her extracurricular romance and came after him with a long knife. He had fled to the port and signed on with El Serpiente, neither knowing nor caring about the destination or cargo of the ship he had joined.

Descended from maritime lineage, life on merchant navy vessels fascinated and excited him for their ability to fulfill his insatiable lust for travel and a ready escape from his frequent need to escape the wrath of some cuckolded husband in a port of call.

Mercks was enjoying the sight of the St. Lawrence River, despite the bitter cold and the blowing snow flurries. He had missed the sights when the ship came downriver weeks earlier because he had been below decks, asleep after a night shift.

Not seeing the police cars on the dock he wondered about the order to stay below and decided to disobey it, strolling astern out of sight of the bridge to where he could watch the passing scenery.

He was suddenly seized by the arm and hauled down onto the deck where he found himself looking into the tense face of Andres Padilla who was pointing a gun directly at his stomach.

"You stupid bastard!" the mate hissed through clenched teeth. "You're supposed to be below decks and out of sight. Now you're in real trouble. If there is a fight here you are the first target because if a single shot is fired you'll be the first man on deck, my dumb Dutchman. You're too stupid for your own good. This time you are in very deep water and without a life jacket.

Mercks stood silently, the gun at his belly, and nodded to the mate who, he could see, was desperate, for what reason he couldn't imagine, and who he believed would not hesitate to use him as either a human shield or a hostage in case of gunfire. He decided to stay calm and see what would happen next. He didn't have long to wait.

From where he lay he could see the long, greasy lock wall gliding by as the small freighter slid easily inside. A glance astern showed a red and white Coastguard vessel closing in behind the lock gates which were swinging towards one another in the centre. On the dock he could see a knot of policemen though none appeared to be armed.

The cutter stayed outside the lock. Once the gates closed behind La Coruna she nosed up to them, her crew on the alert for any attempt by the Spanish captain to reverse, ramming the gates and their vessel in an attempt to escape.

High on the bridge El Serpiente was beginning to feel panic. He was obviously in some kind of trouble. There was a Coastguard ship outside the lock gates ahead of his vessel and another had moved into position outside the gates astern. To make matters worse, his first mate seemed to have vanished.

Was Padilla in contact with the police and was that why the ship was now imprisoned inside a narrow lock in what looked like the middle of no man's land?

Shoving the helmsman aside, he grasped the wheel and steered the ship exactly into the middle of the canal so its sides were about ten feet clear of each dock.

He signalled for the engines to be cut, then waited to see who made the first move.

Mungo Slat, on the dock, could see what was happening and his skin tightened. This was now a stand-off of sorts with the ship in the middle of the canal, just out of reach, untied, floating free but trapped within the gates and by the Coastguard ships. Nobody could get aboard as she sat, silent, like a ghost ship.

Yakabuski and the photographer were already at work shooting some initial pictures while at the same time trying to use their night binoculars to see through the darkened windows of the bridge.

The Seaway Authority workers were lined along the dockside ready to catch the hawsers flung from the ship and to tie them to capstans to hold the vessel steady as the lock filled with water which would raise the level inside to the locks to the same level as the river to the east.

An eerie silence descended over the locks. A stiff northerly wind cracked the Spanish flag at the stern as it flapped in the snow squalls.

After what seemed like an hour to Slat, the commanding officer of the police used a loud hailer to call to the ship.

"Attention, captain of La Coruna. Your ship must be tied to the dock. Please move her to the side and lower your ropes for fastening."

The silence continued. Only a tiny flicker of light on the bridge revealed where El Serpiente was lighting another Cuban cigar.

The silence hung in the air and over the men on the dock as heavy grey snow clouds glowered at them from the north.

Shivering in his thin trench coat, Slat briefly turned his back on the ship and lit a cigarette, fighting a raw wind which numbed and stiffened his fingers in seconds. It took three futile efforts and he was on his last match when it finally caught and he could inhale a lungful of tangy, refreshing smoke.

As he took a second drag, savouring the smoke and the tiny relief it afforded, a shot rang out on the ship and he swivelled around sharply, hurting his side in the process.

A young seaman lay on the stern deck, shot in the stomach and calling for help.

His voice sounded weak and scared as it echoed across the silence. Behind some oil barrels behind the forecastle Slat could see the silhouette of a man in a blue fisherman's gansey and navy cords, training a pistol on the wounded man's head.

As Slat watched in disbelief the seaman fired at point blank range into the wounded man's head and the moaning stopped.

Paul Mercks thought he had seen an opportunity to escape while his captor was listening to the police hailing the captain from the dock. His face was averted from the wind as he struggled to hear the wind-broken words in a language he scarcely understood, especially when delivered with a thick French-Canadian accent.

That was when Mercks tried to bolt for freedom. He was too slow. The man seemed to divine his intentions and, turning quickly, shot him in the stomach, smashing his spinal column and paralysing him immediately.

Lying on the deck racked with pain, unable to move, he summoned his dwindling strength and called for help in his native Dutch, in French and in English. His third call was his last.

His final sight on earth was of the contorted face of Andres Padilla, filled with rage and hatred, pointing the pistol at his skull. As if in slow motion he saw the index finger of the right hand tighten on the trigger before he fell into a sea of blackness.

On the bridge El Serpiente had started to ease La Coruna sideways towards the dock. He heard a shot from the ship's stern and wondered what the hell had happened.

He didn't have to wonder long. A second shot rang out, followed by a volley from the police on the dock.

The phone rang and he slammed it to his ear, handling the wheel expertly with the other hand as he snarled into the mouthpiece.

"Que quiere?"

"Madre de Dios!" screamed the frightened voice of the second mate. "They have shot Andres Padilla. He went crazy and shot young Mercks the Dutchman on the aft deck and the police killed him with their rifles. We're all going to die here in this frozen place."

"Shut up! Stay below and leave the goddamn police to me," shouted El Serpiente, slamming down the receiver with a crack.

Again the voice from the dock called on the loud hailer, this time ordering the crew to stand on the deck at the railing with their hands on top of their heads and ordering the lock crew to secure the ship to the capstans.

El Serpiente slowly picked up the intercom and flicked on the switch.

"All hands on deck, all hands on deck," he shouted in Spanish. "Walk to the port side with your hands on top of your heads and there will be no more shooting."

As the men emerged from their quarters and lined the deck rail he ordered four of them to cast down the hawsers to the lock operators below so they could secure the vessel. Then he ordered them back into line with their mates and smiled as they scurried across the frozen deck to the comfort of their companions.

When the ship was secured he flicked the intercom on and called to the police on the dock.

"Ahora, senor polices, we are tied and ready. What do you want me to do now? Will you come aboard? Can I see what has happened to my mate and the Dutch sailor?"

The reply was prompt and curt.

"This is Commander Michel Challefour of the Royal Canadian Mounted Police. Your vessel is now in my custody until further notice. Please remain where you are but have one man lower a ladder so we can come aboard. What is the name of your captain, please?"

"I am Captain Verdugo y Torrera of the Spanish mercantile navy and I have aboard a load of wheat bound for Barcelona from Thunder Bay. I will be pleased to cooperate with you once you tell me why you have stopped this ship which is Spanish territory."

As he spoke one of the crew started lowering a rope ladder down the side of the ship.

By now El Serpiente's mind was whirring.

What could the police want? Was this all connected to the small airplane which buzzed the ship yesterday? Was it connected with the cargo brought aboard in the middle of the night? Why did Padilla kill Mercks? What if one, or both, was still alive and talked to the police? How would he get paid if he didn't deliver that mystery cargo? Was he going to spend the rest of his life in a Canadian jail? What about the ship and the crew? What about his future plans to use the extra money he was earning to retire and live in Zaragoza, his favourite place in the whole world?

He watched, outwardly calm but inwardly turbulent, as two police officers with broad yellow stripes down the sides of their trouser legs climbed up the swinging ladder to the deck of La Coruna.

He heard the voice of the commanding officer on the dock telling him that what had started out as a routine inspection of his ship was now a murder investigation due to the use of weapons and the presence of two dead men on the aft deck.

By the time the two Mounties clambered to the bridge El Serpiente was spitting mad. He was tempted to shoot them both, slam the ship into forward and ram the lock gates, taking his chances with the Coastguard vessels which appeared to be unarmed.

Then he remembered that La Coruna was tied to the dock and changed his mind.

He still had hundreds of miles of river, locks and canals to navigate before reaching the open waters of the Gulf of St. Lawrence and the Atlantic Ocean. Even if, by some miracle, he made it that far, there was still that two-hundred mile territorial boundary, wide enough for a speeding navy frigate to catch up with a slow-moving freighter wallowing in the swells, its belly filled with heavy grain.

Reluctantly he decided he had the least to lose by cooperating. At least that would buy some time.

After all, the mate and his victim were both dead and no blame for their actions could attach to him or anyone else on board. The worst that could happen would be their being called to testify at an inquest in a few days. After that they would all be on their way home.

All he had to do, he told himself, was blame the killing squarely on the shoulders of Andres Padilla, referring to him as a constant troublemaker pushed over the edge of sanity by the insolence of young Paul Mercks. If he made that case at the outset he might even prevent the search of his ship the commander below had referred to.

He already knew that Padilla was the man planted on his ship by the people who hired him to collect the mysterious package in Port Colborne. He was damned well glad to be rid of him.

He called to the crew, telling them to stay calm and no harm would come to them. They were huddled together on the deck in the biting cold, watching the two Mounties who had taken up positions on either side of the door leading into the bridge.

Switching to his broken English, El Serpiente called to the police that he would come down from his bridge and hand over control of the ship to them on condition that he be allowed to contact the Spanish ambassador to Canada, wherever he was.

He was assured that condition would be met so, closing the bridge door and walking between the two Mounties, he set off along the platform and down the ladder to the deck below.

Slat watched with interest as El Serpiente, in a stained T-shirt and dirty jeans but with an officer's hat compete with gold braid perched jauntily on his head, slowly descended the ladder, chewing on a thick brown stogie as he went.

With the crew rounded up, the captain in at least temporary custody and the ship under police control, thanks to the shootings, he would soon be able to start searching for the missing Krieghoffs.

Meanwhile Yakabuski and the photographer were working like demons, clicking away at everything in sight, the former at the top of the lock gate, the latter on the lock wall.

At a command from their officer the police rounded up the sullen crew of La Coruna and escorted them down the rope ladder one by one, hustling them into the Seaway Authority control office where they were held under guard, scared and miserable, understanding nothing that was said to them.

Commander Challefour told Slat it was now safe for him to board the ship and, under supervision from two police officers, to start his search.

The commander set off for the office to discuss the situation with El Serpiente, to call the Spanish ambassador and to lay any charges he thought were warranted.

Yakabuski and Pitlik were warned against making any attempt to board the vessel. They were told the ship was Spanish territory and they could be arrested for trespassing if they did not obey the law.

In response to a call placed by an officer in the Seaway building an ambulance came screaming down the narrow road from the highway, siren blaring and lights flashing, to retrieve the bodies and take them to Cornwall General Hospital's morgue until the authorities had completed their investigations, when they could be released and shipped to Spain.

Slat started to drag his unwilling bulk up the rope ladder swinging from the side of the ship.

He had a pathological fear of heights and, after foolishly looking down at the receding dock below, wondering what would happen if the ship swung out into the lock due to the pull of the current and he fell between the thick boiler plates of its hull and the concrete lock wall, being simultaneously crushed and drowned, he found himself clinging to the ropes, unable to climb up or down, sweat pouring from his body.

Taking gulps of cold air to clear his mind, he decided to focus on counting the rivet heads in the hull as he climbed slowly and tortuously up the green side of the ship like a crab in a trench coat.

He was not a man devoted to regular physical exercise and that, coupled with the effect of his penchant for Camel filters, made the climb a nightmare from which he feared he would never awaken.

After what seemed like two weeks his head suddenly popped up over the side and his eyes scanned the decks for signs of life. Two Mounties were waiting for him.

They grasped his shoulders and helped him straddle the railing before pulling him over onto the deck where he sat unceremoniously on the floor to recover his composure and his breath.

After five minutes he rose groggily to his feet, tucked his shirt back inside his trousers, fumbled for and lit a cigarette and was ready to start work.

Searching an ocean freighter, even one as small as La Coruna, seemed like a daunting task for just three men but they soon found it was relatively simple.

The majority of the vessel consisted of grain-filled holds covered by large metal lids..

Slat wondered if it might be possible to open one of those holds if necessary. One of the Mounties spoke on his walkie-talkie to the officers on the dock and within a few minutes the second mate emerged from the office, escorted by another Mountie, and started climbing the rope ladder to the deck. He would operate the derrick at Slat's command.

La Coruna was about five hundred and fifty feet long and sixty feet wide. She was a compact, fast and efficient little ship, designed with a minimum of space for captain and crew, the majority of space being devoted to cargo capacity.

The crew's quarters were cramped and tiny, as was the captain's quarters, the galley and mess room.

Slat decided to start his search below decks towards the stern, leaving the deck free for the ambulance crew who were examining the bodies, searching for signs of life prior to removing them and lowering them over the side on stretchers.

They searched every cubicle in the crew's quarters, even going through personal belongings. The search was easier for Slat since he knew that what he was looking for was fairly large, flat and rectangular and would be wrapped in some form of bags or papers. That saved looking into small corners and squeezing toothpaste tubes as the Mounties were doing since they were searching for drugs and similar evidence which might implicate the captain in the two deaths.

They made their way from aft to fore, opening every door which would be opened, even checking behind and underneath the massive diesel engines and around the bulkheads which supported the hull and the vast holds.

Slat opened one door high in the bow. When he stuck his head out he could see miniature figures on the dock below and a vista of snow-covered fields off in the distance. He slammed it quickly shut, panting from the exertion.

Then they re-crossed the ship to the stern deck, searching every piece of equipment before entering the bridge where they found drawers of maps and charts, likely hiding places for stolen paintings, Slat thought.

They found nothing.

They returned to the engine room for a second look. Its maze of pipes and tubes, the massive engines humming loudly in neutral, provided dozens of nooks and crannies which could disguise and hide any number of packages. Even in this hospital-clean environment the heat and humidity were intense. Soon Slat was sweating profusely.

After an hour and a half of fruitless searching the two Mounties were becoming less enthusiastic despite their hilarity at the efforts of this short, fat man, and were starting to show signs of impatience at his insistence that they keep on looking.

They were midway through the engine room when it dawned on Slat that anyone stealing precious paintings would not be likely to hide them in an environment which could cause them damage from heat and steam.

Leaving the Mounties to complete the engine room search, he climbed laboriously to the deck and sat on one of the grain bin lids, scratching his sweating crotch and puffing on a cigarette.

It had always been his habit when conducting a search to try to put himself in the mind and location of his quarry.

"If I had stolen those paintings and put them on this ship, where would I want to hide them for safekeeping but where they could come to no harm on the voyage?" he asked himself.

Slowly he moved around the grain bins, one by one, examining every corner and side of the huge hatches.

It took half an hour of perambulation before he finally signalled to the second mate to start the crane and lift the hatch from the bin closest to the forecastle.

As the crane swung into life and moved over the hatches he stood in the shadow of the second derrick watching the operation. It was a slow process. The operator suspended a cable and hook over the first hatch, then applied the brake and left his cab to climb down to the deck where he attached the hook to a large steel eyelet atop the hatch.

Once the hook was attached and locked into place, the second mate climbed back up to the crane and slowly hoisted the hatch into the air, holding it suspended about ten feet above the bin, swinging ever so slightly in the cold wind.

He motioned to Slat to begin his search.

Slat was very nervous about walking underneath the swinging slab of metal. One slip by the crane operator, accidental or otherwise, and he would be about the size and shape of a Pontefract cake.

Summoning his courage he walked beneath the hatch and peered down into a large cavern filled with rusty-orange grain. A few grains were falling from the underside of the swinging hatch, striking his head and shoulders as he leaned over the cargo.

At first he could see nothing in the darkness of the hold. He peered and peered, trying to accustom his vision to the darkness and the changing light caused by the swinging hatch above.

He was about to move away and signal to the second mate to lower the hatch when a thin yellow string attached to the inside lip of the grain bin caught his eye.

It hung straight down into the grain, innocent looking, scarcely visible to the casual observer who might have thought it had broken away from the underside of the hatch.

Slat knelt down on the cold steel deck and yanked tentatively on the string, afraid he would lose his balance and fall into the sea of grain which, like quicksand, would have swallowed and drowned him in its shifting orange sea.

With the hatch still swinging overhead, its shadow falling across the bin in the weak sunlight penetrating the scudding leaden clouds, he tugged on the string.

Sweat poured down his face from the combination of exercise, fear and excitement. Cigarette smoke burned his eyes, his teeth were clenched until his gums ached and his trench coat billowed out behind him like the coattails on the statue of J. B. Priestley in Bradford.

After a few tugs the string started to move upwards. Gritting his teeth he pulled again, slowly and deliberately as if in a state of suspended animation.

Slowly the sea of grain parted and a large canvas bag appeared, rising from the rusty mound like a breaching whale off Vancouver Island.

Smiling grimly now, he continued tugging. Soon another bag appeared, slung further down the string which was starting to burn his numbed hands.

The sea of wheat rose slightly, parted and fell back with a rustle as two more bags and the end of the twine came out of the depths with a sudden rush almost upending him on the deck.

He wrestled the bags to the lip of the bin and grabbed the top one with his frozen hands, lifting it down and laying it gently on the deck before repeating the process for its mates.

As he straightened up for a breather and to get out from under the suspended hatch, the two Mounties arrived on deck, shaking their heads in the negative and telling him their search had been fruitless.

"It's all right, men. I have what he came for right here," he said.

A fast check by the officers inside the necks of the bags showed him they contained green plastic garbage bags and that inside those were the missing paintings.

They carried the bags clear of the hatch and signalled to the second mate to lower the hatch.

That done and the mate safely back in the warmth of the Seaway office, they clambered back down the side of La Coruna and Slat headed for the office to call Clement Vanderhoof. The search was over.

The Mounties carried the bags of paintings into the office where they were opened, tagged and listed for evidence.

El Serpiente blanched at the sight of what he had been carrying in his hold.

The officers read him his rights, telling him he was under arrest for smuggling, theft and murder.

CHAPTER TWENTY

As Slat walked into his office very late that afternoon, a cheque for $150,000 of Clement Vanderhoof's wealth in his pocket, the phone was ringing.

"Yes," snarled a tired Slat. "How may I help you?"

It was Andy Hocking, commander of the special forces working on the GO train massacre.

"Mungo, I heard about your work on the Vanderhoof paintings. Congratulations. We have some news for you at this end which might add some icing to your cake. We picked up a young woman in the garden of Vanderhoof's house this morning. It seems he had locked her in the bathroom but she managed to escape through a small window, shinny down a drainpipe and was legging it across the lawns when he grabbed her. She fought like a tigress and called the officers every name in the book and a few they hadn't heard before. Guess what, Mungo. Your hunch about that bracelet was right on the money. We showed it to your Professor Ibanez and he confirmed it was indeed inscribed in Aljamiado. We went to the expert he recommended and had it translated. The words were from the Bible and said "Lo how the mighty are fallen."

"What is even more interesting is that it is stolen property from the Prado Museum in Madrid, taken about two years ago. We had it verified at the Art Gallery of Ontario and the Royal Ontario Museum just to make sure. It is in Arabic writing but is in phonetic Spanish as you discovered. The woman broke down when we showed her the proof of its origins. Apparently it was made in Toledo, Spain in about 1400AD by a Spanish silversmith who was a Jew. It went with his family to Morocco after 1492 and disappeared into the desert sometime during the last five hundred years. Without your efforts it might never have been recovered. The museum described it as priceless and should be insured for no less than five million dollars It seems that out little friend is the daughter of a sheik from some desert tribe in North Africa.

"What is more interesting is that she said she and her brother were involved in the theft of Vanderhoof's paintings along with an Englishman named Tony Royce. They were stealing works of art for a syndicate in Italy. Perhaps you would like to come down here and have a chat with her yourself, Mungo. You might learn something else we, or you, could use."

Slat didn't miss the "we", a reminder that his cooperation with the police would be expected.

"Thanks, Andy. Give me a couple of hours and I'll be there."

As he hung up the phone he grinned. Things were starting to come together at last.

Even though the two men he had seen twice on the GO train were not aboard the La Coruna he felt close enough now to smell them and knew he would soon apprehend them and find out if they had killed Marge McCracken and, more importantly, why.

He sat back in his chair, lit a cigarette and drew on it pensively.

"God, I'm tired. Still, Vanderhoof has his paintings back and Yakabuski has his story and I won my bet with that rich bastard. But Marge McCracken is still dead and so are all those people killed on the GO train. I'd better get down and see that Arab woman in the cells and find out if there is a connection there," he said aloud to nobody in particular, Sebastian still being asleep, snuffling and grunting in his dreams.

He stroked his stubbly chin and rubbed his tired, itching eyes. During the past twenty four hours he had done more physical work than he had since he was a rookie cop and he had to admit that in hindsight he had loved every minute of it. Well, almost every minute.

He thought of the nerve-wracking climb up the hull of La Coruna and agreed with himself that he wouldn't want to repeat that soon.

He thought with satisfaction how he had said his final goodbyes to Clement Vanderhoof, who had quickly written the cheque for the promised amount, thanked him gravely, offered him a cigar and whisked him out of the Rosedale mansion without even a sip of Scotch and soda. Some miserable buggers just run true to form, he thought.

Pulling a small electric razor from the desk drawer he buzzed his tired face sending the sensitive Sebastian into fits of alarm at the noise. Then he pulled the gun from his coat pocket, grateful he hadn't needed it, and replaced it in the top drawer.

He decided to grab a meal at Sam's deli and tell him about the rescue of the paintings since it was his help which had provided an excellent lead.

As he rose to open the door the phone shrilled again.

"Is this Mr Slat? Mr Mungo Slat?" asked a voice with a pronounced New York accent.

"Yes, this is he. How may I help you?"

"Mr Slat, this is Sergeant Nick Nowotny of the New York City police department. I'm afraid I have some bad news for you. Is anyone with you at the moment?"

"What is it, man?" snapped a now impatient Slat, eager to get downtown and interview the woman in the police cells.

"Mr Slat, this morning we found the body of a young woman in an apartment close to Central Park. According to the information in the apartment he name was Sylvia Slat. We found your phone number in her address book. Her landlady called us, worried that she had not seen her for three days. She had entered the apartment to see if she was ill and to take her some hot chicken soup. She found her dead in her bed and we have reason to suspect she was suffocated using her pillow. Would you be able to come to New York and identify her body for us, Mr Slat? Then you can make arrangements to take her back to Canada for burial. Mr Slat? Are you there, Mr Slat?"

With a massive effort of will Slat pulled himself together.

"Yes, I'm still here. Thank you for the call. I'll be there in a couple of days and we can get this sorted out. Do you have the bastard who did this?"

"Nossir. Not yet. We believe it was a young man who came home with her from her trip to Italy a few days ago. The landlady had seen him coming and going a couple of times so we have a description of a kind. He seems to have disappeared but we are hunting him and should have him in custody soon. We are checking with the airline passenger lists to find the name of the person sitting beside your daughter so we can put a name to the suspect. I understand you were a police officer and I have some idea what you must be feeling right now. Don't worry, Mr Slat, we'll catch this perp if it's the last case we ever solve."

Slat gently thanked the man for caring and hung up the receiver in a daze.

He sat down slowly as the impact of the news flooded over his exhausted brain.

His Sylvia was dead. His only daughter was dead. That laughing little redhead he had dandled on his knee, that impish one who had grown into a beautiful and talented young woman planning an arts career was dead. Not only dead, but murdered. What kind of monster would want to squeeze the life out of such a gentle, giving, kind person?

Sorrow mingled with his exhaustion to overwhelm him and he broke down into gulping sobs which gave way to hot tears of grief.

First Clare has been snatched from him in a senseless highway accident. Now his pride and joy, the young artistic Sylvia, had been taken in her prime. Was there no end to the unfairness of life?

After about an hour of rage and tears he fell asleep where he sat, Sebastian gently licking his hand with his huge pink tongue, concerned and knowing in his generous bulldog heart he would never leave this man's side until his problem, whatever it was, had been resolved.

When Slat awoke in a stupor he had momentarily forgotten about the call from New York. Then he looked down at the notepad.

He had jotted down the name of the officer who called, the phone number of the precinct office and the address of the morgue where he was to find and identify his daughter's dead body.

A fresh wave of sorrow swept over him.

He realised he needed to contact his son and tell him the news but didn't want to do so over the telephone.

"I'll call him once I get used to the idea and after I have been downtown to wrap up this other matter," he promised himself, figuring that if he kept busy he might just somehow find a way to cope with this second gut-wrenching loss.

His cheery mood of an hour ago had evaporated into cold, bitter anger.

He reached into the desk drawer and retrieved the revolver, slipping it back into his trench coat pocket before closing the door.

CHAPTER TWENTY ONE

For Abdel Salam the morning had been a dead loss.

After parting from Tony Royce, whose back he was, frankly, glad to see, he caught the bus to the underground railway station, made his connection to the airport express bus and was soon in the departure lounge at Pearson International Airport waiting for his sister.

He had an open first-class ticket to Rome via Alitalia and noticed with displeasure that the next flight was leaving at four that afternoon. That left him with about six hours to kill. He found a chair and curled up but was afraid to close his eyes for long in case he missed Farida or the police walked into the lounge and he had to flee.

By noon he was getting increasingly nervous. He had a small Luger in his jacket pocket since he had not yet gone through the customs control and luggage search. It was left over from the attack on the train and he had three rounds of ammunition left. His temporary plan if the police approached him was to seize a hostage and shoot his way out if he had to.

Two more hours passed during which he drank two cups of coffee and visited the toilets twice.

Still there was no sign of Farida. Why hadn't she arrived or even called the airport and had him paged so she could explain her absence?

He felt in his guts that something had gone awry with the escape plans and that he was now alone and in danger, waiting to see from which quarter the attack would come.

Downtown in the police cells on Dundas Street, Farida bin Salam was as frightened as she had ever been in her young life.

She was in a locked room in the bowels of a huge glass and concrete fortress where she had been taken in a police van after her vain effort to escape from the Vanderhoof mansion by climbing through a bathroom window and sliding down a drainpipe, tearing her blouse in the process.

She remembered bitterly the ashen face of Casey Vanderhoof as she was led past him to the police van, handcuffed, shackled and guarded by two armed officers.

How she hated those rich bastards and their miserable paintings. She spit on them all and on their sons and wives.

At noon a small grate in the wall slid open and a plate of food was pushed through. The grate closed again.

She stared at the hamburger and chips, hungry but afraid to eat the food lest it had been poisoned or else drugged to make her talk. She decided to leave it untouched.

Half an hour later the grate opened, the food was removed and the grate closed again.

She listened to the echo of the officer's heavy boots on the floor as he carried the tray away and she breathed a sigh of relief.

The relief was short, changed when she heard another set of feet, then distinguishable as two sets of feet, approaching the door. She heard the clinking of keys and the sound of one being inserted into the lock.

She decided to come out swinging.

As the door swung open she screamed every Arabic obscenity she knew and flew at the first man she saw, inflicting a long cut on his face with her fingernails. The second man grabbed her, pulled her arms behind her back and grabbed her flying feet as she kicked at him, yanking her bodily into the air away from the first man's face which was bleeding profusely by now.

It was a very undignified exit from her cell for the still screaming Farida bin Salam. She was lugged, squirming and wriggling, into a small room where she was thrown onto a hard wooden chair and told she would be tied to it if she offered further resistance.

Then the questioning began.

Unaccustomed to being questioned about any facet of her life because of her status as the daughter of a sheik, she fell easily into the subtle traps they laid for her.

As time passed the cell became stuffy, the air foul from the cigarette smoke from the two officers. She grew weary and her attention started to wander.

That was when the question was asked which blew away all her resistance.

"Where did you get that bracelet you wore, the one with the script in Aljamiado?"

The fact that the police knew of the existence of the bracelet and had been able to decipher it and knew of the existence of the ancient language of her ancestors stunned her.

"It was a present from my father. It has been in our family for generations and he gave it to me when I left to study at university."

"And which university was that?"

"At Bologna in Italy. I was studying fine arts before I came to Canada."

"And why did you come to Canada?"

"I was invited for a holiday by a friend I met at university. I had never been here before so I accepted his invitation and came to Canada."

"Was that friend named Casey Vanderhoof?"

"Yes. He said his family was interested in art and he wanted me to see his father's collection."

"Did anyone else know you were coming here or did anyone come with you?"

"My brother knew I was coming."

"Where is your brother now?"

"He is at the Toronto airport where he is supposed to be meeting me for the trip back to Bologna."

They had what they wanted.

It was apparent from her answers that Farida bin Salam knew nothing about the massacre on the GO train, the murder of Marge McCracken or the attempt on Mungo Slat's life.

"One more question. Did you ever meet a man called Mungo Slat?"

The question was gentle, almost a last minute throw away.

"I met him once at Mr Vanderhoof"'s house, He came to discuss some business. He asked me about my bracelet, they talked about the missing paintings, then he left.

"Did you ever see the paintings that were later stolen?"

"Yes. Casey Vanderhoof took me to his father's gallery the day before they were stolen."

"Is it true that you wrote down the names of some of the paintings during that visit?"

"Yes. I was interested in them and wanted to learn more about their history and about the places they depicted. I also wanted to know why Mr Vanderhoof liked those particular works."

"Where did you go that afternoon when the chauffeur dropped you off near the Eaton Centre?"

"I went shopping and for a coffee."

"What did you buy?"

"I bought a silk scarf and some writing paper."

"Do you have receipts to prove that is what you bought?"

"No."

"Isn't it true you bought two sports bags?"

"No. That's not true. Why would I need two sports bags? I don't even need one."

"Where did you get the bracelet with the inscription in Aljamiado?"

"It was a gift from my father. I already told you that."

The questioning continued for two more hours. By the end of it she was exhausted, weeping and red-eyed from lack of sleep.

At the end she told them she had met her brother, Abdel Salam, and Tony Royce that afternoon in the Eaton Centre and had given them the list of names and locations of the Krieghoffs.

They led her, broken and weeping, back to her cell where she was given a cup of tea and two sugar biscuits to restore her strength and stave off the pangs of hunger.

The two detectives started typing their report from the tapes of the interview and sent it to Inspector Andy Hocking. That was when he placed the call to Mungo Slat.

About an hour later she was again taken from her cell, this time offering no resistance to the two men who came to escort her.

They were the same two who had come the first time. One wore a gauze bandage on his cheek where her nails had raked his face.

She was taken to a small room, still in handcuffs, seated on a hard chair and left to her own devices for five minutes.

The door swung open and in walked Mungo Slat, still wearing the navy blue trench coat, a cigarette dangling from his lips.

This was a different Slat from the man who had appeared interested in her bracelet when they met in Vanderhoof's library three days earlier.

The cold fury in his eyes, the tight lips and the sneer on his face made her fear for her own safety.

He sat on a chair in front of her and stared at her for a full minute, saying nothing.

"So, Miss Salam, we meet once again. We are going for a ride, you, me and a couple of officers you already know. In this pocket I have a revolver and will not hesitate to use it on the slightest provocation. Do I make myself perfectly clear?"

She nodded, certain now he was going to remove her from the police station and murder her. She would never see her father and brother again.

All she and Abdel had worked for would be in vain if she were gunned down in some frozen back alley in this glittering, heartless city.

"Before we go, Miss Salam, I have a question to ask you and I want you to consider the consequences of lying to me before you answer. Why are you wearing a bracelet in an ancient phonetic language used by the Jews of North Africa and what has that to do with the theft of the paintings from Clement Vanderhoof's gallery?"

There was no room for compromise in his voice and she sensed she had better get the answer right the first time or she could be in real trouble from this troubled and vicious-sounding man.

If Andy Hocking had even guessed at the strain Mungo Slat was under at that moment and that he was speaking to one of the people responsible for his daughter's murder he would never have broken departmental rules and allowed a private detective into the interrogation room.

Only the lack of clues on the GO train case had moved him to use Slat as a weapon in his dwindling arsenal.

"I wear the bracelet because it is a symbol of the revolution we are trying to sponsor in my country. The state of Israel, our promised land, wants to rid the world of dictators like Moammar Ghaddafi. We need money to finance our revolution and to support the large numbers of Ethiopian Jews who have finally been accepted in Israel as real Jews but who cannot finds jobs or homes there. By stealing works of art for a syndicate in Italy we can earn thousands of dollars so we can mobilise our people and achieve our goals."

Her own bitterness spilled over into her voice. Centuries of clandestine living, repressed religion, feeling like a second-class citizen in her own land all welled up inside her and she vented her hatred of a culture which, in its darkest moments of madness, decreed death to all infidels and especially to the Jews.

On another day and under different circumstances Slat might have felt more than a twinge of sympathy for the beautiful young woman weeping in the chair across the table from him.

"Well now, the desert sons of Israel will just have to wait a bit longer for their revolution, won't they, Miss Farida bin Salam?"

Farida was led from the cell block to a walled yard and placed in the back seat of an unmarked police sedan. Soon she was being whisked across the city towards the international airport.

Armed with Abdel Salam's name the police had started a search of the airport where they believed he was waiting for his sister to join him.

They were urgent in their search because if he escaped and went to Libya he would be safe there since that country had no extradition treaty with Canada for the return of suspected criminals.

A strike force of crack professionals was en route to the airport, taking the shortest possible route, while Slat and his companions meandered along the most circuitous route possible to allow the forces time to take up their positions within.

There were two terminals at the bustling airport. The first, fifteen years older than the second, was a multi-storey building with self-contained parking. It was used for international flights while the newer, less user-friendly terminal catered to domestic and charter flights.

It took an hour for the special teams to arrive at Terminal 1, seal off all entrances and exits and surround the building.

Inside the car Farida sat beside a malevolent Slat, silent and preoccupied.

He had managed to persuade Andy Hocking that taking Farida

to the airport could be their best way of finding her brother and capturing him alive to face trial for the theft and, Slat hoped, for the GO train murders and that of Marge McCracken.

Two burly detectives occupied the front seat. This was their arrest, their case and they were not going to let this woman out of their sight, not even for Mungo Slat, no matter how close to Andy Hocking he was.

Farida noticed the cordons of police vehicles around the airport when they arrived. They were waved through and she was hustled inside the building and told to find her brother.

"You have twenty minutes to find your brother and bring him here to us. You will be watched every step of the way. This is the only way you can save both him and yourself," Slat told her grimly.

Shocked and amazed she felt a brief taste of freedom as the handcuffs were removed. She walked calmly and confidently to the Alitalia counter where she was told her brother had checked in for the four thirty flight to Rome.

She started to walk the perimeter of the round building, hoping to find Abdel in the coffee lounge, a bookshop or perhaps sleeping on a bench waiting for her to come.

Slat knew he was taking a major risk allowing her to find her brother alone. She might make a break into the departure lounge with him and try to barge onto some other flight, or even find a way to sneak out of the terminal and back into the city, though that was unlikely given the cordon of heavily armed police officers outside. His cohorts, for their part, were distinctly unimpressed by the tactic but so far they had said nothing.

After her first circumnavigation of the terminal and with no sign of Abdel, Farida hit on an idea.

She knew he must still be in the building, staying out of sight. She also guessed he would be armed and that meant they could still find a way to escape.

Boldly she walked to an information counter where a young man greeted her cheerfully and asked this strikingly beautiful young woman how he could help her.

"Yes, please. I have a problem. I have lost my brother in the terminal and he is, well, a bit slow, you understand?" she asked shyly with a smile which revealed dazzling white teeth. "In addition, he speaks no English. I need to find him because he is due for his next dose of medication and without it he could fall into a coma. Do you speak Arabic, sir?"

"No, Miss I'm afraid that one is a little beyond me at the moment. Italian, French, Spanish and Portuguese are all I can manage."

"Do you suppose it might be possible for me to use your microphone and call him myself in our own language so I can tell him where to meet me? If he hears my voice he will be all right."

Her pleading tone and worried look, complete with furrowed brow and pouting lips, melted the young man's initial resistance and he agreed to allow her to page her brother on his machine.

She picked up the microphone, pressed the button and paged Abdel Salam in Arabic.

"Abdel, this is Farida. I am in the terminal but there are official problems. There is a tunnel leading from this terminal to the other one. Go there now and I will meet you and we can escape to the other terminal together. Do it now, Abdel, or we may never see one another again."

She thanked the man graciously for the machine and walked towards the sign pointing to the tunnel leading to Terminal 2.

Outside the tunnel an Arabic-speaking detective from the Metro Toronto Police heard her voice, called his colleagues on a walkie-talkie, relayed her message and sauntered along the hallway looking for the pair.

Slat had heard Farida's call over the loudspeakers but hadn't recognised her voice when she spoke in Arabic. When word of the planned escape was relayed to him he broke into a run, determined to be in on the capture and arrest of Abdel Salam.

He knew once the pair reached Terminal 2, with its miles of concrete floors covered with drab carpeting and the vast distances between the gates which make travellers feel as if they were walking to their destinations rather than flying there, his chance of keeping up with them would be slim.

As Farida reached the tunnel entrance she became apprehensive.

Few travellers were using the pedestrian walkway and that made her suspicious. In addition, she wasn't absolutely sure Abdel would meet her there. He might suspect a trap and stay in hiding, believing her call was a bait to flush him out.

The tunnel was almost empty because the police had sealed it off at the far end and allowed no passenger access until their trap had been sprung.

Armed officers were in position at the tunnel entrance in Terminal 2 and around a bend inside the tunnel, out of sight from anyone entering it from Terminal 1, three officers armed with assault rifles waited.

Passengers were told the tunnel was closed for essential maintenance and were gently rerouted, assisted by Air Canada supervisors, to minibuses which waited outside to ferry them to Terminal 1. All was now in readiness.

As Farida waited close to the tunnel entrance she could see a man in a beige raincoat reading a newspaper beside a phone booth. He was wearing dark-tinted spectacles.

At her glance he lowered the newspaper, moved to the phone, inserted a coin and dialled a number. Inside the tunnel the tactical squad leader received the relayed message and alerted his men.

After an agonising five minutes Farida finally saw the slight frame of her brother moving towards her, hugging the wall as he walked. He had one hand in his pocket and she knew he was armed.

Pretending they were lovers reunited after a flight, she ran to meet him throwing her arms around his neck and holding him tight.

"I'm so glad to see you, Abdel. For a moment I thought you wouldn't come," she sobbed into his neck from relief and fear.

"Well, little one, I am here. Now we have to find our way out of this mess. Your idea of paging me was brilliant. I hope it fooled the police and we can get away from here."

As they stayed in their lingering embrace he told her he had no escape plan in mind when he arrived other than to trade in their tickets and buy new ones for a flight to some place such as Vancouver from where they could make their way home, possibly on a freighter.

She didn't tell him she had been brought to the airport by Mungo Slat and that she had been set free to find her brother for the police.

They started walking casually into the tunnel as if transferring from one terminal to the other.

As they entered Farida looked over her shoulder just in time to see the man in the raincoat leave his position beside the phone booth and stroll towards the tunnel about fifty yards behind them. She also saw Mungo Slat huffing and puffing his way towards the mouth of the tunnel and knew in that instant she had been deceived and had led her brother into a trap.

"Abdel!" she screamed. "It's a trap. The police are right behind us."

Her brother hissed in disbelief, swung around to see for himself and found himself staring straight at Mungo Slat. He recoiled in recognition and disbelief. That man was supposed to be dead. He had shot him himself on the GO train. What was he doing here now? Was his mind playing tricks on him due to lack of sleep?

He grabbed Farida's arm and started dragging her into the tunnel at a run.

She started out, stumbled over her high heels, then paused to kick off the shoes. As she straightened up she saw that Slat and the other man were already in the tunnel.

Abdel Salam drew the Luger out of his jacket pocket. He was prepared to use against Slat or anyone else who threatened him or his sister.

So far the pursuers were maintaining a safe distance and he didn't want to waste his ammunition unless he had a clear target.

The pair tore along the carpeted tunnel towards the sharp curve where it veered towards Terminal 2.

As they rounded the bend they saw a phalanx of police officers blocking their way a hundred yards ahead. They halted, trapped and desperate. Farida leaned against the wall, tears trickling down her face as she realised the hopelessness of their situation.

Abdel calculated the odds and decided to tackle Slat and the lone officer with him. He raised the Luger and fired once. The man in the raincoat spun against the wall, clutching his arm as his weapon clattered to the floor.

Abdel raised the gun again and Slat ducked to the side. As he watched, the terrified Abdel, his face bathed in sweat, started to aim the gun directly at him. He raised his own revolver and fired once. The bullet smashed into Abdel's chest, dropping him in his tracks.

Blood stained the front of his shirt and his body twitched with pain. He tried to crawl towards Farida who was huddled against the wall, recoiling in horror from the blood. He called her name twice then rolled onto his side, arms outstretched, and died at her feet.

In seconds it was all over.

Too shaken to move Farida stared down at her brother's body. His shirt was a mass of blood, his eyes were rolled back in agony and his fingers still clutched the handle of the revolver.

She didn't see or hear Mungo Slat approaching until a firm hand encircled her waist and she heard his voice telling her to accompany the police officers straight away.

She stumbled away, looking over her shoulder at Abdel, knowing she would never see his face again and that she would always bear the shame of knowing she had betrayed him and led him to his death.

An hour later the body was in an ambulance on its way to the morgue and traffic was returning to normal at the two airport terminals.

Mungo Slat went downtown to the police station to file his witness report and to describe the events in the tunnel.

The wounded officer was taken to St. Michael's Hospital where he would undergo surgery to remove the bullet from his broken arm and to reset the bone.

Once the report was filed, Slat planned to catch a flight to New York City to take care of the most terrifying task of all, identifying and claiming the dead body of his only daughter.

CHAPTER TWENTY TWO

After Tony Royce left Abdel Salam he set out alone to find his way back to the border and onwards to New York City.

On the bus ride to the Humber Loop he saw a trucking terminal where articulated lorries brought in fresh fruit and vegetables from as far away as Florida, California and Mexico. There was a steady stream of trucks moving into and out of the yards.

He figured he could probably hitch a ride with one of the drivers, even as far as the border where the trucker would have to pass through a United States Customs checkpoint. From there he could cross into New York State and catch a bus back to the city. Failing all else, he thought, he would hijack the truck and drive to New York with or without the driver.

As he set off at a steady lope towards the truck terminal he wondered if Farida had met her brother and they had managed to catch their flight and escape. In reality he didn't care much. They had used him, toyed with his emotions to get him into this, and now he was a fugitive in a foreign country, his only consolation being that its residents spoke the Queen's English, or at least a close approximation to it.

He walked into the terminal and found a short, squat trucker checking the tyre pressure on his eighteen-wheeler prior to setting out for another long haul. The tractor was shining iridescent blue and was hooked to a Dixie Bee refrigerated fruit trailer.

Ian McMurchy was a Scot. He had been in Canada for twenty years, a trucker for most of them. He was in his early forties and bore the signs of a hard life in his face and body.

He had grown up tough on the mean streets of Glasgow. By eleven he had been in court, charged with beating up the leader of a rival street gang, breaking his nose and jaw. His victim had been fifteen at the time.

His prowess with his fists had come to the attention of a police officer who ran a club for underprivileged boys on his patch and who had started a boxing programme to teach them a healthy way to release their anger and aggression. He offered McMurchy a place in the club and was pleased when he accepted and actually showed up.

It took seven long years of hard training but by the time he was eighteen McMurchy was the Scottish lightweight champion and in training for the Commonwealth Games in Perth, Western Australia.

That was where he met Tamara Biggins.

Rich, widowed at twenty three and a boxing groupie, she followed the fights and the fighters. Before long she developed an insatiable passion for the spunky young Scotsman who thrilled her when he donned his gloves and legally beat the bejeezus out of his opponents in the square ring.

Tamara was an American from Nebraska, daughter of a rancher and widow of an oilman's wealthy only son who was killed in a car crash after carousing with his buddies one late summer night.

Within a year of meeting her McMurchy was out of boxing, out of condition and out of his mind on the drugs to which she had introduced him.

They married and moved to Nebraska where he bought a truck and hauled cattle for four years until the marriage soured and a bored Tamara turned her attention to the new generation of fighters and threw him out.

He headed for Florida and found work hauling loads of citrus fruit up to Canada. There he met and married a woman in the trucking business and settled down to domestic life with three children and a dog. He still made his runs from Orlando to Toronto but was getting tired of being away from home and had decided to sell his rig and find another line of work.

He was preparing for his final run, planning to drop off the rig at its new owner's yard in North Carolina, when Tony Royce walked into his life.

McMurchy was in good spirits as he checked the tyres for what he hoped would be the last time, so when the young man, a fellow Britisher, asked for a lift to New York State he cheerfully agreed. It would be a chance to have some company for a while and to find out a bit of news from his homeland.

They set off along the Queen Elizabeth Way towards Fort Erie where they would cross the Peace Bridge and take the interstate highway through Buffalo.

They chatted about England and Scotland, McMurchy reminiscing about his youth, the boxing, his successes and his failed marriage.

Royce invented a long, convoluted story about an upbringing in India where he attended a private school and played cricket with boys who now played international matches for India.

He said he was on his way to New York to meet an old school chum and had hit on the idea of hitching a lift so he could save his fare money for the good time he expected to have there.

They chatted away like magpies, smoking occasionally, until they crossed the bridge at the border where McMurchy said he would have to take the truck into the customs compound for inspection which would take about two hours depending on how many vehicles were ahead of him.

Royce thought he might have trouble at customs if there was a search warrant out for him because of the murder of Sylvia Slat. He decided to take action.

He waited until the truck was slowing as it climbed to the crest of the Peace Bridge then pulled out his revolver, jamming it into the side of McMurchy's head behind his left ear.

"Now you listen to me, old man. This truck is not going to customs today. You will do exactly what I say or I will blow your brains out. Understand?"

As the frightened McMurchy nodded his assent, Royce gave him instructions on the next move.

When a startled United States Customs officer looked out of his booth window a minute later he saw a giant truck careening down the road towards him at high speed, air horn blaring and lights flashing.

He dived to the floor and heard the truck barrelling straight through the barricades. He caught a glimpse of a small red-haired driver with a young man with blond hair holding a gun to his head as the truck raced through the clearance zone and own the ramp to the New York State Thruway, heading towards Buffalo.

He grabbed the phone and called the border patrol. In less than a minute a yellow and khaki cruiser filled with armed state troopers, blue lights flashing and siren screaming, dashed down the ramp in pursuit of the rogue truck.

"Good work, old man," Royce shouted over the sound of the straining engine. "Now get me to Depew. Do you know the way?"

McMurchy nodded angrily. He knew the way to Depew all right but he'd be damned if he as going to take this bastard anywhere near where he wanted to go.

Without moving his head he glanced in the rear-view mirror and was satisfied to see the flashing lights of a police cruiser gaining rapidly on his truck.

This would be the end of the idiot with the gun, he thought, so long as he himself could come out of this alive. He decided a little surprise of his own might be in order to repay this ingrate for his surprise on the Peace Bridge.

So far as he could tell, Royce hadn't yet seen the pursuing police car.

Once he noticed the cruiser, McMurchy figured, he might just become distracted enough for the canny ex-fighter to fend for himself.

His plan was doomed from the start.

It was the wailing of the police siren which alerted Royce to its presence. He stayed calm, waiting until the cruiser drew alongside the truck, then slammed McMurchy over the head with the gun butt and wrenched the steering wheel to the left.

The huge truck with its fifty-foot trailer swung across the dividing line and smacked the cruiser's front fender, shoving it over the steel guard rails into three lanes of northbound traffic where a semi-trailer rig, unable to stop, ploughed into it, killing all six occupants.

As the dazed McMurchy fought to prevent his rig from jack-knifing and rolling over, Royce shoved the gun into his ribs and snarled at him to stay on course for Depew or he was dead.

As the truck shuddered and shimmied its way back into its own lane, McMurchy knew he needed a better plan of attack if he was going to survive this journey.

He decided to head for Depew while he thought his way out of the dilemma. The Englishman might not know the way but he could read highway signs and would know if he was being deceived.

Sweating profusely, McMurchy handled the big rig through the traffic and headed east towards Depew.

When they were off the thruway and safely on a street in the suburb of the steel city beside Lake Erie, Royce ordered McMurchy to find a quiet parking place behind a large building and to stop the truck.

That's when McMurchy really saw red. He figured this lunatic was going to kill him and steal the truck. It was already damaged from the collision with the police car and would have to be repaired before he could deliver it to its new owner

He cruised a major street, through one intersection, then another, the gun still in his ribs.

In the middle of the second block he saw a gas station. Quickly he cranked the wheel over, sending Royce off balance so that he slid across the seat into the far door. Slamming the gearshift into neutral he allowed the rig to coast towards the service station where helpless gas pump attendants and mechanics fled in terror. As it rolled he kicked Royce in the stomach as hard as he could.

The blow knocked the wind out of Royce but he recovered sufficiently to fire a single shot which smashed into the middle of McMurchy's forehead, killing him instantly.

As the truck rolled towards the gas station, Royce yanked the door open and jumped clear, rolling underneath a parked trailer.

The unsteered rig, its driver dead in the cab, slammed into the gas pumps and burst into flames.

As the flaming truck fuel ignited the pumps their underground storage tanks, filled during the night, erupted into an inferno.

Royce rolled clear of the back of the trailer and scaled a wooden fence behind the station, knocking over an elderly black woman hanging out her washing. As she staggered to her feet she saw a giant fireball ascend into the sky and saw flames burning her fence and melting the shingles on her roof. She dropped to her knees to pray to her god but was unable to escape the intense heat which sucked all the air from her lungs, choking her to death while incinerating her body to a cinder.

By then Royce was half a block away, running pell-mell to whither he knew not, hidden amongst the horde of people running away from the fire.

He turned a corner and halted to catch his breath and recover from the blow to his solar plexus scored by McMurchy's boot. He could see dozens of people running, some away from and some towards the fire, and he could hear sirens as fire engines and state troopers converged on the remains of the gas station.

He trotted down another block and flagged down a passing taxi.

"Where to?" the driver asked as Royce threw himself, panting, onto the back seat.

"Take me to the helicopter plant, please. The large one on the edge of town."

The driver, delighted at finally getting a real fare after a morning of nickel and dime rides with correspondingly small tips, set out for the five-mile journey, his mind on the fare and the tip he hoped to collect.

CHAPTER TWENTY THREE

As Mungo Slat completed his report for the Toronto police and was calling for a taxi to take him to the airport he heard the police radio telling about an incident at the Peace Bridge where a runaway tractor trailer had crashed through the customs barrier and fled down the state thruway towards Buffalo, killing a car filled with state troopers as they attempted to apprehend it.

The bulletin gave a description of the driver and passenger of the truck as furnished by the customs officer.

Hearing the description of the man with the dirty blond shoulder-length hair who was holding a gun to the trucker's head, Slat was sure it must have been Tony Royce and that he was headed to New York City.

An earlier report from the New York police about his daughter's murder said they found in her purse the stub from a return flight to Rome. Slat wondered if she had somehow met Royce on that flight, invited him to her apartment and been murdered for her trouble.

He was now sure Royce had killed his daughter as surely as he had killed Marge McCracken and the passengers on the GO train and that he was now the sole living perpetrator of the theft of the Krieghoffs.

"So, you bastard, we are to meet in New York City," he threatened out loud.

The truck crash meant Royce could be headed back to New York for his return flight to Italy. Farida bin Salam had said he was an Englishman studying at Bologna. Slat wondered if he might fly elsewhere, perhaps to London, now that the paintings were, as he would believe, on the La Coruna and his business with Abdel and

Farida was finished. He would need to move quickly to escape the New York State troopers who would be on the trail of the stolen truck within hours.

If Royce was headed to England, Slat guessed he would take the supersonic Concorde as the fastest way to his destination.

He called the airport and asked about Concorde flights from New York that evening. A man with a plummy accent, not unlike Clement Vanderhoof's, told him the next flight would be leaving Kennedy Airport in Jamaica, New York, in about four hours.

He doubted that Royce would be able to drive to that airport from Buffalo in that time but called Sergeant Nowotny in New York, gave him Royce's description, the time of the Concorde flight and asked that he be arrested, preferably alive, at Kennedy International Airport and held until Slat arrived with a warrant for his extradition to Canada.

He then called the police dispatcher, told him he was working for Inspector Andy Hocking on the GO train murder, and asked him to call the airport and reserve a seat on the earliest possible flight to Kennedy airport in New York, the ticket to be left at the special services desk for him to collect at Terminal 2.

The call came back before he was out of the room. Fog and freezing drizzle were setting in over the area and the airlines were cancelling all flights until further notice.

That set him back on his heels for a moment. He picked up the phone and called Andy Hocking and asked if there was an available police aircraft which could fly him to New York to pick up Tony Royce.

Thankful for his help with the Krieghoffs, Hocking told him to stand by while he called the police aircraft traffic controller to make the arrangements.

It took ten minutes, during which Slat paced the room like a crazed animal, smoking cigarettes one after the other, interspersed with cups of strong black coffee provided by a bright young cadet policewoman.

"Mungo, this is Andy Hocking. I have made the arrangements for you and contacted the NYPD, asking them to offer you any assistance you need. The pilot is a police officer and he will escort the prisoner back to Canada when they have finished with him there. By the way, you will be flying in a helicopter because fixed wing aircraft are forbidden to fly during this weather.

Forty five minutes later a large BK117 Helicopter built by MBB Helicopters Canada Ltd at their Fort Erie plant lifted off from the roof of police headquarters with Mungo Slat strapped in beside the police sergeant, a former Yukon bush pilot.

The chopper had been built for the ministry of natural resources for fighting bush fires in northern Ontario. It was undergoing final testing in Toronto and was on loan to the police prior to departing for the north where it would be based in Sault Ste Marie for the summer, patrolling for forest fires, hydro line problems and other situations.

Its large cargo bay and seating for eight meant it could carry a heavy payload of men and materiel to any site in an emergency.

The machine would also serve as a first rescue effort in case of marine hazards on the Great Lakes and across the thousands of smaller lakes which dotted the northern reaches of the vast province, many times larger than the British Isles.

As soon as they received clearance from the control tower at Toronto Island Airport the giant helicopter, looking like a bumblebee in its black and yellow livery, lifted off and swung over the city and around the CN Tower on its way towards the border a hundred miles away.

The pilot, aware of deteriorating weather conditions, told Slat he would be flying above the Queen Elizabeth Way to Fort Erie before heading due east to New York City.

As they left, dispatchers contacted border patrols and the United States Air Force, telling them of the flight and its plans, receiving clearance for an uninterrupted journey to Kennedy International Airport.

Slat didn't want to end his days as the victim of a missile fired by some triangular supersonic fighter because nobody warned the Americans about the flight and they hadn't taken kindly to a stray foreign helicopter straying into their air space.

Below the chopper cars crawled like ants on the ice-slicked highways of Toronto.

With the heater on at full blast, the windshield was staying clear. Giant wiper blades slapped rhythmically against the glass cowling.

The pilot said the flight would take close to three hours if the weather didn't worsen or other atmospheric conditions didn't interfere.

Mungo Slat was not a good flier.

He wasn't built for sitting scrunched up in a single seat for long periods of time, constrained by a tight seatbelt and safety harness as the machine bucked and kicked in the strong wind which threatened to pluck it from the sky and dash it to the ground.

Unable to stretch out, unable to smoke, with nothing to read and no real desire to do so, he stared out into the darkness, unhappy, uneasy and completely at the mercy of the pilot, the helicopter and the elements.

As they flew pilot Burton Cutler explained the safety features of the aircraft, one of a new breed of whirlybirds produced by the former Messerschmidt company of Germany for the American market.

"This is the safest helicopter in the world, built in Canada by a German manufacturer with the aid of federal government loans repayable over twenty years. One of the new features of interest is a device on the nose cone which prevents it be coming entangled in electrical wires. A running blade and cutter actually shears the wires so the helicopter can fly away. The wire runs down a pulley to cutters under the belly of the machine where they are snipped off, just like that. This is a boon in urban rescues where overhead cables and wires often prevent helicopters from being used to remove injured people and to lift obstacles from the top of people and vehicles."

Slat was impressed. As the flight progressed he warmed to the features of the giant machine and soon was sipping hot coffee from the pilot's thermos bottle and chatting amiably with the aviator who had learned his skills flying across the frozen tundra of the nation's northern fastness, taking off and landing in some of the worst weather conditions on the planet.

Slat still carried the revolver in his pocket, something he hated doing but which had proved providential at the airport earlier in the day. He promised himself that once this case was over he would sell the gun. Killing was not his style.

As Slat was flying towards the border ahead of the worst ice storm of the young winter, Tony Royce was leaving the taxi in front of the gates of the Italcottero plant in Depew. This was the building he had spied from the bus on his way to Canada from New York City.

He was tired, dishevelled and desperately hungry.

Despite his hunger and the biting cold, he thought of nothing but getting to Kennedy Airport and onto a flight to Italy. Once inside the terminal he could clean himself up, buy clothes if he needed to and relax with a hot meal during the flight home.

Already the darkness was closing in. It was drawing closer to the winter solstice and night came early.

In his imagination Royce saw himself working on copying the paintings with Dottore Ferragami, creating flawless fakes which would see for hundreds of thousands of dollars on the international art market while the priceless originals were carefully stored in climate-controlled isolation in the catacombs beneath a Franciscan convent in Sorrento.

Despite the mistakes he had made such as killing Sylvia Slat in New York, Marge McCracken in Port Credit and Ian McMurchy in Depew, he felt no regrets, seeing such events as part of the job. Human beings who got in the way of the project simply had to be removed.

Besides, he told himself, their deaths, necessary for him to escape without witnesses to testify against him later, were both swift and merciful.

What bothered him was that at times he found himself actually enjoying the danger and power he felt when he pressed the cold metal of a gun against his victim's head, watching as the face filled with terror and apprehension in the seconds before he squeezed the trigger, It was that look in the eyes which excited him, a fleeting moment of pure recognition that the person was face to face with death and could do nothing to avoid it.

As he approached the main gate the helicopter plant appeared closed for the day.

There were a few lights burning in office windows as executives completed their tasks before the coming weekend but for the most part the huge complex was in total darkness, isolated by its location on the fringe of the community where the noise of chopper engines would provide the least interruption to neighbours, many of whom had initially opposed the plant's existence in their town, but most of whom had friends or relatives now working there.

Just inside the main gate there was a small cabin housing a security guard.

Royce saw that the perimeter of the entire property was surrounded by a ten-foot high chain link fence with three strands of barbed wire atop it.

To avoid being noticed by the guard he walked slowly away from the gate and along the side fence. A cold wind was biting his cheeks and it was starting to rain.

He needed to find a way over that fence and across to the lee of the building behind which he could see the flashing lights on two helicopters being tested by crews rushing to meet late delivery schedules.

As the wind velocity increased he huddled down into his jacket, cold and weary. The rain was starting to freeze, stinging his cheek with tiny slivers of flying ice.

He needed to move quickly. That freezing rain could place his whole plan in jeopardy unless he got into the air and away from the storm in a hurry.

He sauntered along the perimeter fence, hoping it was not alarmed and that he was not being watched on a closed circuit television set in the guard hut.

At the very rear of the property he found a spot where the fence ran away from the street towards a heavily wooded area which was near the end of a runway from the converted airport which now housed the factory.

Just outside the fence stood a tall, wide maple tree with one long branch which would take him, if he could climb the trunk and crawl carefully along it, to within a couple of feet of the top of the fence.

The tree was already wet from the rain and some of its upper branches were beginning to glisten from the ice forming on them as the freezing rain settled in for the night.

Carefully, slowly, he crawled towards the tree, staying close to the ground to avoid detection.

He shinnied up the trunk, using the notches and bumps in its bole for hand and foot holds, and wriggled his way onto the branch, removing his jacket at the juncture of the branch and the trunk. He could feel the icy rain stinging his skin through his shirt, raising goose bumps and adding to his misery.

He needed the jacket to protect his hands when he reached for the strands of barbed wire across the fence top. He planned to bend the wires inwards and somersault over them into the factory grounds.

He crawled along the slippery branch like a giant sloth in the darkness.

Now he could see over the fence and across the street below. A patrolling police car passed, its driver unable to see Royce because of the deepening gloom, its driver preoccupied with clearing the slush and ice from the windshield while his partner wrestled the lids from two paper coffee cups.

He stopped in his tracks, motionless until the cruiser passed slowly beneath, breathing deeply, the frigid air hurting his throat and lungs.

The cruiser's red tail lights disappeared around a corner and he set off again along the branch like a stalking leopard.

Through the thickening mist he could make out the outline of the giant hangar behind the production plant, its flagpole carrying the stars and stripes of the United States and below that the green, white and red Italian tricolore.

There was no sign of activity in the area. Two small helicopters stood on the tarmac of the testing range. One had its red navigation light flashing and he could hear its motor idling.

The other, plugged into a yellow mobile electrical power unit, was in silent darkness.

He guessed that the technicians were inside the hangar, either malingering because of the freezing weather, or enjoying a coffee break, chatting animatedly in Italian, playing one of those perennial card games where cards are slapped onto the table to the accompaniment of loud shouts.

He inched forward, feeling his legs slipping around the branch, his trousers becoming sodden and heavy from the icy rain which pelted him.

At the edge of the fence he paused, checked fore and aft to make sure he was still unobserved, then wrapped the jacket around his hands and reached for the barbed wire strands above the fence.

He grasped the wire with one hand and stopped, silent and waiting. No alarm sounded, there was no electrical current in the wire, and he could see no renewed activity in the hangar area. He breathed a sigh of relief. The fence was not equipped with monitoring devices.

Apparently the plant owners felt secure because they were close to the perimeter of a United States Air Force base and were within the confines of city limits and subject to frequent police patrols.

Drops of water were striking his forehead and trickling into his eyes, stinging them, but he was unable to reach up and wipe them away. Any sudden motion could upset his delicate balance on the branch and he would fall either into the barbed wire or to the ground outside the fence from where he would have to start the entire operation again, if he was not injured by the fall.

He licked his dry lips, shook his head to remove the offending droplets, and depressed the barbed wire with both hands. It gave slightly so he applied more weight to it until the strands bowed inwards to an arc three feet wide and two feet deep across which he could hurl his body before the wires sprang back.

He had no solid footing to help him propel himself over the fence, thanks to the ice accumulating on the branch.

Slowly he crawled forward until his head and chest were across the barbed wire and inside the fence, then wriggled further forward until the full weight of his upper body was over his wrists which still held the wire down beneath his hands which were bleeding by now despite the protection afforded by his jacket.

In a sudden motion he somersaulted over the fence, using the taut wires as a fulcrum but letting go of them a split second too soon. As the wire snapped back to position it caught his right foot, throwing him sideways do that he landed on his right shoulder, crying out in pain as the shoulder hit the ground and was dislocated from its socket.

Despite the intense pain he scurried crabwise to the base of the fence closest to the tree trunk and sat hunched in the gloom, wondering if his cry had been heard. All was silent. The sound of the pelting rain and the thickness of the fog would muffle any sound from the ears of the security guard.

Inside the hangar, two hundred yards from where Royce crouched, two old friends were sipping coffee and relaxing, glad to be inside out of the foul weather.

Paolo Tomassini and Ettore Lomascolo had come to Depew from Italy as part of Italcottero's expansion plans to set up new assembly lines, train American technicians in the fine points of quality control and waste management, and to learn all they could about the conditions facing North American pilots where the climate was much more changeable and treacherous than that of their sunny homeland.

Alone in a strange land, speaking only minimal English, they had clung together for companionship, living in adjacent rooms at a motel close to the factory which was to be the centre of their lives for the next two years.

They were working late this evening. They preferred evening work since they had no social lives and were content to see their American colleagues going home to their families or out to the bowling alleys where so much community life seemed to take part.

As they drank their coffee and warmed their extremities, they were unaware that out of the thickening gloom a hunched figure was creeping towards the helicopter they were testing for General Electric, a machine which would be employed in monitoring electrical power lines in northern Michigan, using a special infra red sensor.

Royce crawled on his belly across the side of the hangar wall which loomed above him, topless in the fog. He gently backed up to the wall, sitting on his backside in the wetness, pain racking his arm and shoulder.

He found a small piece of wood on the ground and picked it up in his left hand, moving slowly because of the pain.

He lifted the wood, placed it between his teeth, bit down on it and, bunching his left hand into a fist, smacked his right shoulder, slamming the joint back into its socket.

When he regained consciousness ten minutes later he realised he had fainted from the pain of the operation. His arm still throbbed but, gently testing it, he found he had some restored motion.

As his head cleared and the churning in his stomach subsided, he began to crawl towards the small silver and blue helicopter on whose tail fin he could see a round emblem and the words General Electric. Its red light was still flashing and there was still nobody in sight.

A small wedge of yellow light shone through a crack between the hangar doors and he envied the technicians, safe and warm inside on such a night. Only a fool or a desperate man would be out in this filthy weather, he told himself, adding quickly that he was no fool.

At the end of the wall he rose quietly to his feet and sprinted across the open space to the helicopter, wrenching open the door and flinging himself into the cockpit, hurting his tender shoulder in the process.

Once the door was quietly closed he started scanning the controls in the gloom, trying to become as instantly familiar with them as he could.

He strapped himself into the seat belt and harness and slowly started to rev the engine until the small bird lifted about six feet from the ground where he hovered for a full minute as he checked and double checked the controls.

Inside the hangar the sudden sound of the revving helicopter engine drew a simultaneous shout of alarm from the two technicians. Tossing the coffee cups to the floor they ran towards the hangar doors, Paolo Tomassini in the lead.

As he slid the door open they could see the small craft hovering above its pad, the silhouette of a pilot in the cockpit.

"Gesucristo! Hanno preso l'elicottero!" Tomassini shouted.

The two mechanics in their blue overalls sprinted towards the suspended machine in the pelting ice and rain.

The sudden beam of light caused by the opening of the hangar doors surprised Tony Royce and he watched the two men running towards him through the gloom.

He slid open the slide window at his left side, pulled out and aimed the revolver and fired a shot towards the two. As the bullet spanged into the tarmac beside his feet, Tomassini instinctively flung himself to the ground and lay still.

Ettore Lomascolo, seeing his friend lying on the ground, turned and dashed back inside the hangar where he grabbed the phone and called the security shack.

"allo! 'elp! They have killed Paolo and stolen the helicopter," he shouted.

Seeing one man down on the ground and the other running back inside the hangar, Royce yanked the joystick and the helicopter rose high above the factory. He turned it in a semicircle before setting off towards the southeast, heading for New York City about four hundred miles away.

About thirty miles north of Depew, Slat and the BK117 pilot were approaching the international border confident that they could outfly the ice storm and reach Kennedy International Airport in time to catch Tony Royce.

Both were wearing headsets and Slat was listening to a new world of radio communications, hearing about flights being cancelled and delayed from Toronto and Buffalo airports and about delays to incoming flights due to the build up of ice on their wings which added to their weight and reduced fuel efficiency.

Suddenly a new, urgent message crossed the air waves. A helicopter had been stolen from an Italian factory in Depew N.Y. and was being flown southeast across the state. The machine was registered to General Electric and the pilot was unknown.

Slat felt in his waters that Tony Royce was flying that helicopter, making a desperate bid to escape to Kennedy Airport for his connecting flight out of the country.

Speaking into the unfamiliar mouthpiece he informed the dispatcher of their presence in the area and gave what information he could about the fleeing pilot. He and Burton Cutler agreed they would pursue the stolen chopper, keeping it in sight but not interfering with its progress until it landed.

"If you guys start sending up pursuit aircraft in this messy weather you'll just create problems for yourselves and for us up here. You could cause him to panic and crash the machine, possibly into a subdivision or a busy street where innocent people would be killed. He has already killed dozens of innocent people and we want him alive to face justice in Canada."

There was a long silence on the other end of the line. Then the speaker crackled to life and he received word that the commanders of the State Highway Patrol, United States Air Force base and police agencies agreed that he should continue the pursuit but that once the helicopter landed, its pilot was theirs. He would be charged with larceny and tried in the United States before being extradited to Canada to face the music for whatever crimes he had committed up there.

Slat had no choice but to agree to those terms and nodded to the pilot, who commanded a few knots more airspeed from their chopper and set out after Tony Royce in the darkness and rain.

After about five minutes the radio crackled into life again. This time it was the Highway Patrol from Depew advising them that their quarry was armed and dangerous. The officer outlined what had happened at the Peace Bridge and about the explosion at the gas station in Depew. He gave a description of the fugitive taken from the customs officer and from the taxi driver who had taken him to the helicopter plant.

Slat smiled thinly at the news. It was Tony Royce all right.

All along the stolen helicopter's flight path spotters monitored its progress by radar and by sound and relayed the information to air traffic control at Buffalo Airport. Soon a pattern was established which showed that Royce was flying diagonally across the state towards New York City like a bee flying back to the hive with a load of pollen.

The same information was relayed to Slat and Burton and they adjusted their course to stay behind the fleeing Royce rather than trying to intercept him at some point during the flight. In foul weather and with decreasing visibility they would rely on their greater speed and power to catch up to the fugitive and force him to make a mistake or land where they directed him to land.

Ahead of them Royce, concentrating on flying the little machine which was bucking in the gusts of wind, was unaware of the chatter on the airwaves or of the fact that he was being pursued and all flights cleared from his path. He had neglected to put on the headset.

They flew for half an hour into the gloom.

Then Slat saw it. Directly in front of them, flying about five hundred feet above ground, was a tiny, flickering red light, zigzagging slightly as Royce struggled to maintain a straight course from Depew to Jamaica because of his hurting right shoulder.

Slat opened the charts for the pilot, showing that soon they would arrive over the Hudson River, which he figured Royce would use as a navigation aid.

They were already over Ithaca, home of the famed Cornell University, when they first sighted their prey. Its flight path would take it north of Binghampton and down between the Catskill Mountains and the Pennsylvania state line.

As he flew on in the rain, which was becoming less icy now and diminishing, Royce allowed himself a few minutes to relax. He was flying on instruments now, marking his path from a map he found in the cockpit. He calculated that at his present speed he would be over New York City in about four hours. A glance at the fuel gauge told him he had no worries on that score. The Italians had filled the tanks just before he stole the machine.

He breathed deeply, rubbed the sore shoulder and settled in for the flight, looking for a sight of the Hudson River, which he would follow into the city.

A mile behind him and slightly higher, his pursuers, grim and determined, maintained the same speed.

Slat cleaned and reloaded the revolver and placed it beside him on the seat.

As he flew over the towns below Royce checked them against his map: Liberty, Ellenville, Walden, then Newburgh and his first sight of the mighty river.

Wide, masculine, roistering and boisterous, the Hudson River flowed majestically towards its destined cohabitation with the Atlantic Ocean, carrying on its broad back the trade and commerce of a nation in the barges and freighters which plied its channels. The river originated in the watershed of the Adirondack Mountains in the Lake Champlain area near Burlington, Vermont and ran unchecked a thousand miles down the eastern seaboard of the United States to its final salty destination.

As Royce reached the river he swung the little helicopter around in a wide circle, wanting to be on the east bank of the river as he flew, looking for Long Island Sound, his next major landmark, where he would search for the airport at Jamaica.

That was when he saw another helicopter flying behind him about a hundred feet above him. It was black and yellow and larger than his machine. It was definitely in pursuit since it also swung in a wide arc and took up a position directly behind him.

"Bloody hell! I wonder how long they have been there," he muttered.

Cursing his stupidity he grabbed the headset, jammed it on his head and fiddled with the tuner to find the channel his pursuers might be using.

Most channels were silent other than occasional chatter from the pilots of incoming aircraft talking to control towers and local and international airports.

Realising the pursuing chopper as making no move to intercept him, Royce decided that gave him time to think and continued on his course, every mile taking him closer to freedom. He made no effort to elude the pursuers, guessing that would be futile, given the size, power and range of their helicopter.

He flew over a massive military complex, not knowing it was the West Point Academy where some of America's finest soldiers and officers are trained.

He was over Croton-on-Hudson when he saw a tiny Amtrack train standing in the station. It was the express from Niagara Falls to New York's Grand Central Station. Its next stop, at tiny Croton Harmon, was its last before it entered the huge city on Manhattan Island.

From his position above and behind Royce, Slat also saw the train and, further downriver, a string of large bridges allowing passage across the river from New Jersey into New York.

The bridges gave him an idea.

"If we can divert his attention, maybe we can get him hung up under one of those bridges and catch him in the river," he thought. He floated the idea to his pilot.

"That should be easy to do. All I have to do is turn on this baby's searchlights and fly close behind him. The lights will blind him and might temporarily panic him so he starts twisting and turning to get out of their beam. He will forget all about the bridges below, if he sees them at all."

The BK117 slowed and dropped into position directly behind Royce's helicopter and the searchlights were turned on, illuminating the sky and bringing the blue and silver helicopter into sharp focus at its flew southward.

The sudden flooding of light into the cockpit took Royce completely by surprise. He knew his pursuers were now closing in for the kill. To make matters worse he had now lost sight of the outside world in the glare of the powerful beams.

Tightening his grip on the controls, he put the chopper into a series of swoops, dives and darts designed to get him out of that light and away from his pursuers.

He was at best a mediocre pilot and no match for the expert flying behind him. The lights kept coming at him from behind, seeming brighter and brighter.

Slat's strategy was working almost too well. He could see Royce diving and soaring to avoid the lights, every move predictable from their viewpoint and easily followed by the greater speed and agility of their helicopter.

The designers of the BK117 were the same company which had specialised in building fighter aircraft which regularly strafed Lancaster bombers and outran the Spitfires in the Second World War.

The agility and control of the machine were amazing to the untutored Slat and the pilot, who had not expected such a workout on his first flight in the new machine, was enchanted.

"Wow! Look at this baby go!" he yelled as they soared, dropped and finally circled around the tiny Italian helicopter which looked like a helpless beetle trying to escape the voracious jaws of a praying mantis.

Then it happened.

Royce flung the small chopper into a violent upwards climb, banking sharply to his right in an effort to shake off his pursuers. Only at the last second did he see the massive iron bridge with yard-wide girders staring him straight in the face.

Panic stricken he yanked the controls to the left as hard as he could then listened dry mouthed and terrified as the rotor blades shattered against the bridge deck, dropping his machine like a stone into the icy Hudson River.

Slat watched horrified as the little helicopter hit the water, sending a vast spray into the air, then started to sink immediately. They hovered over the spot, fixing their spotlight on the craft as it began to settle in the water.

They watched as the cockpit door opened and the figure of Tony Royce clambered out to the top of the aircraft which was already being dragged downstream by the powerful current.

He still had his gun and they saw him aim and fire three times at their helicopter, the bullets whistling past, wide of the mark.

The chopper in the river suddenly flipped over onto its side, tossing the tow-headed Royce into the swirling water underneath the bridge.

Carefully, slowly, the pilot lowered the helicopter until it was level with the bottom of the bridge deck. Their searchlight soon spotted Royce's head bobbing in the water, being carried downstream and away from the shore.

They rose up and across the bridge, causing drivers to brake sharply as the giant bird arose from the side of the bridge and flew low over their heads, to disappear down the other side.

Once there they flew back and forth across the river looking for Royce.

Slat finally saw him about a hundred yards downstream, his arms flailing, his head being dragged underwater by the current.

They hovered above the drowning man and Slat tossed down a lifejacket and a rope.

As the jacket hit the water Royce disappeared from sight and they saw him no more.

They hovered over the river for another hour waiting for signs of life. The pilot called local search and rescue units and the fire department, promising to stay on station until they arrived and to provide light and any other assistance they might need.

In twenty minutes another helicopter arrived. Its pilot, a U. S. Coastguard officer, said he would take over the lighting of the river and that they should land on the shoreline.

For two hours the rescue teams and helicopter searched the river for signs of Tony Royce. They found nothing.

Slat and the pilot were advised by radio that the search was unsuccessful and was being called off. They were advised to fly on to Kennedy International Airport where they could refuel, have a quick meal and return to Canada. They would be contacted when Royce's body was found.

Slat parted company with the pilot at the airport. The latter would have to file a flight plan and meet local and state police officials about the reason for and culmination of the flight.

Slat had to make a statement for the record then he waited for a connecting commuter helicopter shuttle to the roof of the Pan Am building in downtown Manhattan.

Three hours later, exhausted and angry, he was in the hospital morgue looking down at the dead face of his beloved daughter Sylvia.

The identification completed, he followed Sergeant Nowotny, who had contacted him in Toronto, to a downtown police precinct office where he made the necessary statement and filled out interminable forms authorising him to have Sylvia's body returned to Canada since there would be no trial, the chief suspect having drowned in the Hudson River.

He went to breakfast with Nowotny and after a hearty meal, endless cups of coffee and his first cigarette in hours, told him what had happened in Toronto, about the theft of the Krieghoffs, the GO train massacre and the incidents at the Peace Bridge and in Depew.

"I'm real sorry we didn't catch that bastard alive for you. It would have been interesting to get the two of you face to face for a few minutes, unofficially, of course. I might have been tempted to have a go at him myself after what he did. The best deal for him would have been about ten years on Riker's Island before sending him back to Canada for you guys to deal with after that, if he survived," Nowotny said.

Slat thanked him for his concern and set out for a nearby hotel to catch some long overdue sleep to regain some of the sanity he was sure he had lost during the past three days.

CHAPTER TWENTY FOUR

That evening's television news was filled with reports of the action at Pearson International Airport and the shooting of what the reporter called "a Libyan terrorist who had been attempting to enter the United States from Canada to assassinate President Ronald Reagan after killing hundreds of passengers on an early morning commuter train".

Commentators were lamenting the fact that justice had been denied the families of the murdered commuters and the people of Toronto. At the same time a stalwart Inspector Andy Hocking was stoutly denying any unjustified use of force by his officers.

No mention was made anywhere of the murder of Marge McCracken. Other than Mungo Slat nobody seemed the least bit upset at the savage killing of an anonymous old woman in her Port Credit home.

In the rosewood library at the Vanderhoof mansion the television set was on but nobody was paying any attention to it. The murder of the commuters and the subsequent apprehension of Farida bin Laden and her brother aroused little interest in the newspaper tycoon. He had his paintings back and that was all that mattered to him.

Cigars were lighted, brandy glasses charged, and Clement and his miserable son Casey, along with a select group of friends, were toasting Mungo Slat in absentia for recovering the paintings and for winning his bet against what seemed like impossible odds.

"Mind you," pontificated Clement Vanderhoof in his plummy pseudo-English accent," he wouldn't have been able to pull it off in the end without my influence and intervention. The riches he pretends to despise are precisely what helped him solve the case. I hope he will be bright enough to realize that now and change his attitude. I also hope he uses some of my money to replace that terrible navy blue trench coat he insists on wearing all the time."

He laughed at his little joke and the rest joined in to a man, though not one of them other than the unsmiling Casey had ever set eyes on Mungo Slat.

At the offices of The Tribune editors and reporters were toasting Regis Yakabuski while he basked in the fleeting glory of another major scoop, all the sweeter because this one involved Clement Vanderhoof himself.

The story would be trumpeted on the front page of the tycoon's largest rival newspaper while his own editors would face disgrace and banishment for not reporting the story. Vanderhoof had a convenient memory and would, in time, forget he had ordered a complete news blackout until his paintings were recovered and that by doing so he had shut his own staffers out of the news story of the year.

Within a week he would summon the publisher and managing editor into his office and tear strips from them for an hour or more, revelling in his power but angry that the upstart Yakabuski, a perennial thorn in his side, had done it to him again.

What was galling was that he knew in his heart that it had been done with the aid and abetment of Mungo Slat but he knew he could never prove it.

As Slat slept in New York City the Tribune's presses were being webbed and inked for their edition of the story which would garner a major award for its writer and would definitely spoil Clement Vanderhoof's day.

Regis Yakabuski knew Mungo Slat would not be satisfied until he had spoken again with Farida bin Salam, locked up for now in the Vanier Correctional Centre for Women in suburban Brampton, awaiting her deportation hearing. In deference to his son's misery and guilt, Clement Vanderhoof had uncharacteristically decided not to press charges against her.

As the party at the Rosedale mansion wound down, Vanderhoof summoned the young butler and handed him a box of expensive rapier cigars.

"Take these personally to Mr Mungo Slat's office right away and leave them for him with my compliments," he ordered.

The next morning Mungo Slat was back in Toronto and at the funeral home where the rosary was being said for the soul of Marge McCracken, being buried that day by her sorrowing family in a small cemetery north of the city.

Flanked by his son and daughter-in-law, Slat gave thanks for his own delivery and prayed for the soul of his lovely young daughter and, after a long struggle with his conscience, for that of her murderer.

He allowed his mind to drift back to the capture of the La Coruna in the Iroquois locks, the violent death of Abdel Salam in the airport terminal and the slow death of Tony Royce in the Hudson River. He realised his work was not yet fully completed.

He had seen the captain of the Spanish freighter manacled and led into a police cruiser on his way to prison where he would be later visited by a representative of the Spanish ambassador to Canada. The remainder of the crew had been taken to the Coastguard station in Prescott.

Coastguard officers piloted and navigated the ship to Cornwall where she was moored to a dock off Montreal Road in Le Village, the French quarter, in quarantine until its release was negotiated by the Canadian and Spanish governments.

Slat snapped his mind back to attention as the rosary ended and made the sign of the cross mechanically as the priest rose from his knees to bless the body in the casket and the congregation.

He picked up his trench coat from the back of the chair and, rooting in an inside pocket, retrieved the cheque he had received from Clement Vanderhoof.

Walking to the front of the small chapel he thanked the priest for his kindness in conducting the prayers and handed him the cheque for $150,000.

"Father, this is for the poor of your parish, in the name of Marge McCracken and my daughter," he said simply before turning and walking out into the winter night.

He turned the corner to his tiny Renault 5, unlocking the door with one hand, brushing aside the snow which was starting to stick to his windshield with the other.

Under the snow he found a ten dollar parking ticket which he stuffed into his coat pocket.

He poured his bulk behind the steering wheel, lit a cigarette and, laughing at the ludicrousness of the situation, headed for his empty apartment.

CHAPTER TWENTY FIVE

At noon the following day Slat received a call from Inspector Andy Hocking of the Metro Toronto Police asking if he would like to speak with Farida bin Salam, now formally charged as an accessory to murder and theft.

He set out on the GO train, finding the passengers this time relaxed although still unfriendly and avoiding eye contact in typical urban fashion. The apprehension of a week ago seemed to have evaporated with the news that the killers had been found and dealt with.

In a police interview room he sat across a small table from Farida, subdued in prison attire, still beautiful even without makeup and hair care.

He asked her what she knew about the deaths of Marge McCracken and Sylvia Slat. She could tell him little other than that she knew her brother and Tony Royce had planned to kill Mungo Slat from the moment they heard he had been hired by Clement Vanderhoof to protect his paintings.

"But why was my daughter killed in New York?" Slat asked softly, tired and grieving.

"She was an accident. Tony Royce met her on the way from Italy to Canada and spent a night at her apartment. He wanted to kill you and thought perhaps that he could hurt you by killing your daughter. I think she was killed because she had the same name as you and she was Canadian. I am truly sorry for that. All I ever wanted to do was help with the theft of the paintings. I had no idea there would be murders as well. I know the killings on the train were because they had failed to kill you in your apartment. The old woman was killed because they thought she was you coming home. They needed to kill you and when they saw you on the train that morning they set out to finish you once and for all. I believe they thought they had succeeded until you showed up at the airport when Abdel was shot."

"Tell me, Miss bin Salam, what was the destination of the stolen paintings," Slat insisted, tears welling up in his eyes at the thought that so many people had been killed when he was the intended victim.

"I have nothing to lose now so I might as well tell you all I know. The paintings were to be taken to Barcelona on a Spanish ship. There they would be offloaded to a smaller vessel and transported to Sorrento in Italy and taken to caves beneath a Franciscan convent where they would be meticulously copied and the copies sold for millions on the black market while the originals would be stored in climate controlled quarantine."

She lowered her head onto her arms and began to weep softly, her betrayal of the Franciscan friar who had sent them on this fatal mission the last straw in her resistance.

"Who was it that sent you to Canada to steal the paintings?" Slat asked, more gently now.

He could see no point in wasting his seething anger on this woman who, while a conspirator in the theft, had been unaware that her brother and Tony Royce were committing murders as well.

She was suffering now, mourning the loss of her relationship with Casey Vanderhoof with whom she had been slowly falling in love and whose anger and rejection hurt more than any punishment the legal system could devise.

"The man who sent is was Dottore Pasquale Ferragami, a teacher of fine art at the University of Bologna. He hired Abdel and me and we contacted Tony Royce, who was to work on the copying when the paintings were safely in Sorrento. The professor was in charge of the operation. He paid the ship's captain to carry the paintings but the captain didn't know what he was carrying, only that he was paid a huge sum of money to delay the ship in some port for bogus repairs until the goods were taken aboard, then set sail for Barcelona."

Slat thanked her for her assistance and asked that coffee be taken to her as he left the room.

She would be appearing in court the following day for a preliminary hearing. Eventually she would likely be sentenced to a long term in prison for her involvement in the most heinous crime in modern Canadian history. The sentence would be long because she was the sole surviving member of the gang and would bear the brunt of society's anger at their offences

The last Slat saw of her were her heaving shoulders covered in long black hair as she sobbed convulsively, her head flat on the table top.

He walked slowly upstairs, the weight of his losses heavy in his body. In a staff smoking room he lit a cigarette, sitting in a battered armchair, the wind completely knocked out of his sails by Farida's revelation about the motive for the GO train massacre.

He sat deep in solitude for half an hour before a cadet officer asked if he would step into Inspector Hocking's office for a chat before he left.

As he walked in he saw Hocking pouring two shots of Scotch into small glasses. He handed one to Slat and, wordless, they sipped the biting fluid, each thinking about the events of recent days, neither finding the right words to say.

Finally, with a huge effort, Hocking broke the heavy silence.

"Mungo, I had no idea your daughter has been murdered in New York City by that bastard you chased down the Hudson River. If I had known, I would have refused permission for you to go. As it was, you handled the situation in an extremely professional manner. My boys could learn a great deal from what you did. I hope you are going to take some time off and get your head straight after all this. I know I am taking a short leave myself and I haven't been nearly as involved at a personal level. Even so, this has been the worst case I have ever dealt with and I owe my family some time with them. Maybe you should consider going somewhere warmer, perhaps Florida or Mexico."

"I need to tell you that I have the name of the bastard who masterminded the heft of the Krieghoff paintings from Vanderhoof's gallery," Slat said, ignoring the kind comments.

He gave the name of Fra Pasquale Ferragami to Hocking.

"I think I'll take that holiday you suggested in sunny Sorrento. I want to meet this guy in person. I have a few scores to settle with him, friar or not. He needs to be made aware of the effect his greed has had on so many people here."

Hocking smiled grimly.

"There's no need for that, Mungo. We got the name from Farida bin Salam yesterday and he is already under arrest in Italy. The Carabinieri picked him up in his rooms in the middle of the night and he is safely under lock and key, awaiting the arrival of the RCMP to help the local police with their investigations. Your meeting him would only aggravate the situation and if you got close enough to attack him might give him grounds for freedom. I understand how you feel. I'd like to wring his bloody neck myself for what he has done to you and yours and to hundreds of other innocent people in this country. The only winner in all this seems to be Clement Vanderhoof. He got his paintings back and no doubt they will have increased in value after all the publicity surrounding their removal and recovery. Now he refuses to press charges against the girl because of his son's involvement with her and to avoid any more publicity. In any case, the murder charges will overshadow any theft charges we might bring against her. She may be able to mitigate the sentence by pleading guilty as an accessory to the thefts but she won't see freedom for many a long day. She'll be well past her sell-by date when she gets out of prison."

Slat nodded his agreement.

"Perhaps you're right, Andy. Maybe I will take some time off and get some sunshine. Right now there seems little point in going back to divorce cases and such matters."

He rose and shook hands with his old friend and walked out to the parking lot.

A stiff wind was blowing off Lake Ontario, bringing with it the first flakes of an impending blizzard.

He pulled the collar of his trench coat around his ears, lit another cigarette and started walking to Union Station for the journey home.

Tears rolled down his cheeks as he walked, unaware of the uneasy glances of passers-by ashamed at the sight of an old man weeping openly on the streets of Toronto.

"It's time to quit this racket once and for all," he told himself. "I think I'll go back to my native Yorkshire and start all over again. My son is married and doesn't need me here. Besides, anything has to better than this perpetually freezing climate."

He walked onto the platform as the green and white diesel engine of the GO train rumbled into the station, bell clanging, ready for yet another Lakeshore run.